"Do you ever wish on the moon?"

Laura stepped away from Mitch, into the moon's full light.

"I thought people wished on stars."

"The moon's bigger, closer, more touchable." She glanced at him, her smile mysterious. "Wishes are like pictures you draw in your mind. They're always there, whether you know it or not, just waiting to come to life. You can make it happen."

Mitch regarded her, captivated. "So, what are you wishing tonight, or can't you tell me?"

"Sure I can. Then you can wish it, too. Two wishes are more powerful than one." Laura stared up at the moon with enough intensity to brand her wish there permanently. "I wish Dad back on his feet."

"I'll second that."

She faced Mitch with a mischievous grin. "See how easy it is? Even for skeptics."

"I have reason to be skeptical."

"Maybe you just stopped wishing."

Dear Reader,

Welcome to Silhouette **Special Edition** . . . welcome to romance. Each month, Silhouette **Special Edition** publishes six novels with you in mind—stories of love and life, tales that you can identify with—romance with that little "something special" added in.

May has some wonderful stories blossoming for you. Don't miss Debbie Macomber's continuing series, THOSE MANNING MEN. This month, we're pleased to present *Stand-in Wife,* Paul and Leah's story. And starting this month is Myrna Temte's new series, COWBOY COUNTRY. *For Pete's Sake* is set in Wyoming and should delight anyone who enjoys the classic ranch story.

Rounding out this month are more stories by some of your favorite authors: Lisa Jackson, Ruth Wind, Andrea Edwards. And say hello to Kari Sutherland. Her debut book, *Wish on the Moon,* is also coming your way this month.

In each Silhouette **Special Edition** novel, we're dedicated to bringing you the romances that you dream about—stories that will delight as well as bring a tear to the eye. And that's what Silhouette **Special Edition** is all about—special books by special authors for special readers!

I hope you enjoy this book and all of the stories to come!

Sincerely,

Tara Gavin
Senior Editor
Silhouette Books

KARI SUTHERLAND
Wish on the Moon

Silhouette Special Edition

Published by Silhouette Books New York

America's Publisher of Contemporary Romance

To my husband, Steve,
for his giving nature and unconditional love.
And to my son, Kenny,
for his acceptance and friendship.

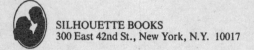

SILHOUETTE BOOKS
300 East 42nd St., New York, N.Y. 10017

WISH ON THE MOON

ISBN: 0-373-09741-7

First Silhouette Books printing May 1992

Printed in the U.S.A.

KARI SUTHERLAND,

a former English teacher and home decorator, likes to mix and match colors as well as words. She says redecorating a room is almost as satisfying as writing a book. *Almost.* A reader of romances since she was a teenager, she found that writing romances became her escape, work and emotional outlet when back surgery interrupted her life-style. Kari, who resides in Pennsylvania with her husband of twenty-one years and their twenty-year-old son, loves kittens, romantic movies that make her cry, and peaceful surroundings.

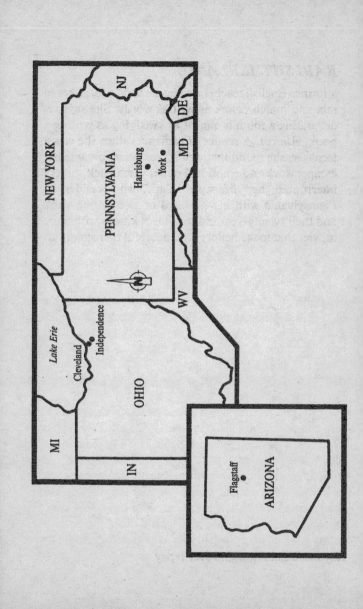

Chapter One

Mitchell Riley stabbed at the doorbell, wondering what he'd find behind the door. Hopefully, Laura Marie Applegate Sanders. He'd seen her high school graduation picture. He'd heard enough about her to know she'd been a hellion as a teenager. Six years ago, she'd broken her father's heart. Now, if Mitch could convince her, she was going to help mend it.

He jabbed the bell again and impatiently thrust his hands into the pockets of his gray leather jacket. Ray Applegate had filled a yawning hole in Mitch's life. The older man gave him encouragement, trust and belief in himself. Mitch smiled, remembering hours spent with Ray as they worked at the jeweler's bench. If not for Ray Applegate, Mitch's designs would still be stacked in a pile collecting dust. He would do anything for the man who'd taken the place of the father who'd pushed Mitch away again and again. He owed Ray more than he could ever repay.

The door to the two-story Colonial finally opened. Mitch stared. Laura's high school picture taken eight years ago hadn't begun to prepare him for the woman standing before him. Her wavy, layered, shoulder-length hair drew his eyes first. It was the color of the late October leaves scattering the sidewalk—burnished gold with the radiance of the sun and a bit of glow from the moon.

She had a piquant face, a small nose, a delicately pointed chin. And eyes. Gray eyes so big and wide he could almost fall into them. She couldn't be more than five foot three. So this was the irrepressible, irresponsible Laura. Her tie-dyed sweatshirt and ragged well-washed jeans seemed in character with the girl Ray had described.

Her tone was friendly, her smile welcoming. "Can I help you?"

Her eyes had gone from the scar on his face, down the breadth of his chest, then back up to his eyes and stayed there. Most people stared longer at the line down his cheek. He was used to it. Once, the scar had been a source of torment because it had made him different. Now it was simply part of him.

Just then a whirlwind came barreling out the door and wrapped around Laura's legs. "Is it the pizza man?"

Laura ruffled the child's dark brown pageboy. "No, poppet. Not yet."

"But I'm hungry! I want to eat now." She looked up at Mitch. "Who are you? What's that mark on your face."

"Mandy!" Laura gave him an apologetic smile. "I'm sorry. She's so curious about everything—"

"It's all right." Mitch's sense of purpose shifted as he peered down at the little girl. Children laid life flat on the table, and he respected her curiosity. "I had an accident when I was a boy, and my name's Mitch Riley. What's yours?"

She seemed satisfied by his brief explanation. "Mandy Sanders." She pushed away from Laura.

Mitch's eyes swerved to Laura. For some reason he'd never expected her to have a child, not with her penchant for following her own whims. The way Ray had talked about her, Mitch had expected to find Laura living in a loft with her artist husband, leaving responsibility outside the door. Of course, maybe the child wasn't hers.

"She's your daughter?"

Laura laughed. "Yep. Since before she was born."

Her laugh reminded him of the tinkling silver bells his mother always hung on the door at Christmas. *What a notion, Riley! Remember who this woman is. Remember how she hurt her father.*

"Mommy sang to me when I was in her tummy. She told me."

Apparently Mandy had learned spontaneity from her mother. From what he'd heard, Laura was a master at it. He grinned at the little girl to encourage her. A few minutes of uninhibited honesty from a child could go a lot further than a two-hour conversation with an adult. "What else did she tell you?"

"That Daddy used to rub her tummy and talk to me. I don't have a daddy anymore. He's in heaven. But I have George and Anne. And Puffball."

Laura didn't seem embarrassed. "Why don't you help Anne and George fix the salad while I find out how I can help Mr. Riley."

"He can come in and sit down."

Laura gave her daughter a little nudge. "He probably doesn't want to. Go on. I'll be in soon."

With a last glance at Mitch, Mandy took off.

Mitch paused to absorb the information he'd just garnered. Doug Sanders was dead. Laura's father didn't know. Who were George and Anne? And why in God's name was he wondering what it would be like to run his hand over Laura's stomach?

Mitch stared straight into Laura's eyes, angry with himself because she distracted him. He was here to give Ray the best possible chance for recovery. His wayward thoughts made him brisk. "It's not a good idea for her to be so friendly with strangers."

"She's only four and a half and has an idea that everyone wants to be a friend. I hate to disillusion her."

"You might have to for her own protection."

Laura's eyes asked why he cared. "Independence isn't a major crime center. But don't worry. I keep a close eye on my daughter, Mr. Riley." Her gaze traveled over his navy cashmere turtleneck and wool slacks as if looking for some reason for his visit. "How can I help you?"

He didn't want to tell her his news while she was standing at the door. "Maybe I *should* come in."

"I'm not as naive as my daughter. *I* don't let strangers in the house."

"I need to talk to you about your father."

Laura's face paled. "Who are you?"

Get ready, Riley. This is going to be a bumpy ride. "I've been Ray's partner for four years."

"I ... see. What is it you have to tell me?"

Mitch looked over her shoulder but she made no move to invite him inside. He plunged in, knowing there was no easy way to say it, no way to soften the words. "Ray's in the hospital in critical care. He had a heart attack Wednesday."

Her mouth rounded to an O and she turned white. Mitch clasped her shoulder gently, hoping her reaction meant she still cared. "Are you okay?"

One of his fingers trapped a lock of hair. It was silky. Her shoulder felt ... fragile. His body responded, startling him.

He had to remind himself he was here for one reason and one reason only. He dropped his hand.

Laura pulled in a bolstering breath. Her voice was a soft whisper. "Maybe you'd better come in."

Mitch followed her into the living room. Laura chose a platform rocker covered by a colorful patchwork quilt. His gaze swept the room. It was a hodgepodge of furniture. Nothing matched or coordinated. He parked on the black vinyl sofa. It reminded him of an escapee from a bachelor pad. A huge gray cat that looked as if it had mohair for fur was curled on a needlepoint hassock in front of the window. The animal lifted its head, yawned, then turned its nose sideways on its paws to go back to sleep. Was this Puffball?

Voices and laughter from the kitchen wafted into the living room while Mitch waited for Laura to speak.

Laura stared at her hands in her lap, thinking about the night her father had disowned her. She couldn't forgive him, but she didn't wish him harm. The shock of learning her father was in the hospital rocked her in a way she hadn't expected. It brought home the fact her dad was mortal and still her father, although he didn't consider her his daughter.

Exactly what had happened to him? Guilt grabbed her and along with fear made her tremble. Why hadn't she tried to contact him after Doug's death?

Because her father's rejection could still hurt her.

"Has my father been ill long?" she asked, unable to keep the tremor from her voice.

Mitch unzipped his jacket and his voice gentled, as if to protect her from further upset. "No. The doctor gave him a clean bill of health six months ago. The heart attack came on suddenly. I'm thankful it happened at the store so someone was with him."

"You were there?"

He shook his head. "I was at the Harrisburg store. Ray's assistant manager called 911."

"The Harrisburg store? Is that new?"

"Two years. Ray stays in York. I handle Harrisburg."

She took another shaky breath. She had grown up thinking *she'd* be her dad's partner. This Mitch person had taken her place. Raising her head, she studied him. Tall, broad-shouldered, superbly fit. The long scar from his temple to jawline added to his rugged appeal. She wondered how he'd gotten it as she noted the quality clothes he wore and the blue lapis ring on his finger. She couldn't tell his age. His jet black hair sprinkled with strands of gray gave her no aid. Thirty-five?

How close was he to Ray Applegate? Had he taken her place in her father's affection, along with her dream of working beside him?

"How did you find me?" Her father didn't even have her current address.

"I found your social security number on some old records. A private investigator found you from there."

She felt violated at the idea of a stranger tampering with her privacy. "I can't believe you dug into my life—"

"It wasn't intended to be intrusive, Mrs. Sanders. We did no digging—we didn't have time. I had to find you fast. I didn't know your husband had died or that you have a daughter."

Mitch's eyes were the color of an icy blue lake, the specks of silver like spokes of a wheel. Did they lose the sharpness when he was happy? Did the silver ever twinkle with fun? She pushed the questions away because she'd never know.

"Why didn't you telephone instead of coming here personally?" she asked.

"Because I want you to go back with me. Ray is having a double bypass Monday morning. If you fly back to York with me tomorrow, he can go into the operation with peace of mind.''

Leave tomorrow? What if she lost her job? What if she lost her father?

"Is there a problem?" he pressed.

"I manage a jewelry store. I don't know how much time—''

"Do you understand this might be your last chance to see your father alive?''

Seeing her father. What would it be like facing him again after all these years? Would she see the same frustration, the same disapproval, the same coldness on his face? He'd thought raising a child meant laying down rules without discussing them. He hadn't realized Laura needed hugs and kisses and a father she could talk to, especially after her mother died. Rules and expectations had been his way of dealing with her. She'd rebelled.

Mitch's trip to Ohio to fetch her didn't seem to jibe. She couldn't imagine her father admitting he needed or wanted anything—certainly not a reconciliation with her.

"Did my father send you?" she asked abruptly. When Mitch didn't answer immediately, she had her answer. "He didn't, did he? You came on your own. My father could care less if he sees me.''

Mitch shook his head. "That's not true. He's too proud to admit he needs you there.''

"You're assuming too much. He kicked me out of his life. Are you saying he's ready to apologize for that?''

Mitch's voice took on an unexpectedly hard edge. "What does he have to apologize for? He gave you everything. And you—'' He stopped and sighed. "None of that matters now. What matters is giving Ray whatever support he needs to survive surgery and recover.''

Laura recognized Mitch Riley's reserve was disapproval disguised. It was evident he had deep feelings for her dad.

She could only imagine what her father had told him. But as he'd said, the past wasn't important now.

George came around the corner and perched on the arm of her chair. "Everything all right?"

Her red-haired, lanky housemate was as protective of her and Mandy as an older brother. He and Anne had been close friends before Doug died, her family since. The three of them now shared expenses, responsibilities and good times.

"I'm fine," she answered, then introduced George to Mitch and watched the two men size each other up.

"Mr. Riley is my father's partner. He wants me to fly home. My dad's having bypass surgery on Monday."

George emitted a low whistle. "Are you going?"

Her father didn't want to see her. That made a difference; her presence could upset him as much as help him. Could she trust Mitch Riley's judgment? "I don't know."

Her friend's voice was gentle. "You make your own decision, babe. But think about how you're going to feel if you don't go and something happens to him."

She leaned her head against the back of the chair. "I know. But there's Mandy."

"Anne and I will take care of her."

"I won't leave her for more than a few days."

Mitch sat forward and interrupted, his posture conveying his urgency to clear any obstacle in her path. "There's no reason you can't bring her along. There's plenty of room at the house."

"I'm not concerned about the amount of room. I'm concerned about Mandy's sense of security."

"Certainly, a week or so—"

She shook her head vehemently, suspecting he hadn't had much experience with children. "When Mandy's father died, she withdrew. I won't take the chance that anything like that will happen again." Laura looked at George. "I'm going to ask her."

"You're going to consult a four-year-old on a decision like this?" Mitch's expression said he thought Laura belonged on another planet.

"I'm going to find out how she feels before I make any decisions." She called, "Mandy? Come here please."

Her daughter came running, using a step between a hop and a skip. "He came in!"

Laura turned her daughter away from Mitch and pulled her up onto her lap. "Your grandfather's sick."

"You mean the man in the picture upstairs?"

"Uh-huh. I'm thinking about taking an airplane to go see him."

"Does he have a cold?"

"It's worse than a cold."

"Is he gonna die like Daddy?"

"I hope not. But I want to know how you feel about going with me."

"George and Anne can't come?"

"Not this time. If you don't want to go, you can stay with them."

Mandy played with the hem of her Superwoman T-shirt. "An airplane flies in the clouds."

George said, "You can tell everybody at preschool what they look like up close." He added, "If you go with your mom, she won't have to rush back because she won't be lonely with you there."

Laura gave him a dirty look. She didn't want Mandy to know guilt.

Mitch spoke up in a gentle voice and smiled at her daughter. "Mandy, you and your mom will stay in a big house with lots of rooms to explore. There's a great big yard with a pond and a stream."

Laura drew her eyes away from Mitch, remembering every inch of the backyard—the birdbath where she'd

watched blue jays play, her tree house, the bench where she
and her mom had had long talks.

"What's 'explore' mean?" Mandy asked.

Mitch was at a loss for a moment. "It means to...look
at, walk through, touch things."

"Do you live there?"

"I stay sometimes."

Mandy looked up at her mom. "Can I take Puffball?"

Laura exchanged a look with George. When he shrugged,
she responded, "I don't see why not."

The doorbell rang. Mandy said, "I'll get it."

George took her hand as she hopped off Laura's lap.
"We'll both get it. It's probably the pizza."

Laura said to Mitch, "I hope the cat's not a problem.
She's declawed and doesn't go out."

He stood. "If that's what it takes, you can bring a zoo."

She stood, too, and tipped up her face, feeling at a defi-
nite disadvantage. Tall men usually gave her the feeling of
protection and well-being. Doug had been a tall man,
though he'd never been protective. After Mandy was born,
Laura had often wished—

She cut off the thought. Maybe Mitch Riley's height was
intimidating because she sensed there was so much restraint keeping him reasonable, cool and polite. He was the
kind of man she'd never been attracted to. She supposed it
was because those qualities belonged to her father, too.

Trying to bridge the gap between them, she explained,
"Mandy latched on to Puffball after Doug died. The cat's
her security blanket." The cool look left Mitch's eyes. Im-
pulsively Laura took advantage of the softening. She was
grateful for Mitch's concern for her dad and wanted to express her thanks. "Would you like to stay for supper? Pizza,
salad and butter pecan ice cream."

"No, thank you. I have some arrangements to make. If I can get a ticket for Mandy, we'll be leaving on the two o'clock flight. I'll call you in the morning to confirm it."

He was distancing himself again, making sure she knew this wasn't a social occasion but a favor he was doing for Ray Applegate. Fine. That was okay by her. They could remain strangers if that's what he wanted. She could be as polite as he could. "Do you think Mandy's ticket will be a problem?"

"I'll get it if I have to trade ours in for first class."

"I can't afford—"

"I'm paying. This is my idea. I'll take care of it."

Laura responded quickly and firmly. "No. I don't take handouts. We pay our own way."

Mitch took a few steps closer until they were toe-to-toe. She smelled leather intertwined with spicy cologne and a heady, more masculine scent that made her want to step even closer, despite her conclusion he wasn't her type. Then he spoke.

"Being a rebellious teenager might have worked when you were sixteen, but the stakes are higher now. Think about that."

He stepped away as quickly as he'd approached. "I'll call you in the morning."

Without a backward glance, he walked to the door, said goodbye to George and Mandy, and left.

When Mitch saw Laura and her entourage at the passenger loading station, his body tensed. The one-piece turquoise jumpsuit fit her curves like it had been sewn on. It wasn't tight, but it clung to all her dips and bends. And that hair—loose, fluffy, damnably sexy. What would a handful feel like? Smell like? It hid her face as she bent to talk to Mandy.

Guilt stabbed Mitch. He'd been unreasonably sharp with Laura yesterday. He hadn't slept well since Wednesday because he'd been so damned worried about Ray. But that was no excuse. He had no right to condemn Laura, despite his reservations about her character.

Glancing at the group again, he supposed the dark-haired woman with George was Anne. What was their connection to Laura? Were they a couple? Or were George and Laura involved?

Mitch strode toward them, not liking George's proprietary air with Laura but not taking time to analyze why. He sighed. Laura. She was going to be difficult all the way. He should have expected it. When he phoned her this morning to tell her he'd pick her up, she coolly informed him she'd meet him at the airport. It would have been more practical for them to drive into Cleveland together, but at this point he didn't care.

Her history reminded him so much of his brother Carey's. Listening to the stories Ray had told, Mitch had assumed Carey and Laura were two of a kind. If she was as unreliable and headstrong, he just wanted to get her to York for Ray's sake, then send her back to Independence before she caused trouble.

Ray had said she'd been spoiled and wild. Mitch couldn't understand the idea of any child throwing away a father's love, wealth and a stable future. Laura had been foolish and irrational. Mitch hoped she cared about Ray enough to put him first this time.

Mitch reached the group and Laura introduced Anne.

Mitch nodded. "I'm glad you're on time."

Laura took her poncho, in multi-shades of rose, from George's arm. "Punctuality's one of my virtues."

Mitch stifled the urge to ask if she had any others and directed his attention to Mandy. A streak on her cheek looked like the path of tears. His insides tightened. He hated the thought of a child feeling sad or hurt.

He crouched down to meet her at eye level. "Are you ready to fly?"

"Puffball's lonely. She can't ride with me. We had to give her to a lady."

He addressed Laura. "Do you want me to see what I can do? It's a short flight. Maybe they'd let her—"

With a warning look, Laura shook her head. "I showed Mandy the hands on my watch and she understands when she'll see Puffball again."

"Mommy says people ride with people and cats ride with cats."

Evidently Laura had settled the matter with Mandy. Mitch didn't want to upset the balance. He stood.

Anne said to Mandy, "Let's visit the ladies' room one last time." She took the child's hand and led her away.

George mumbled, "I'll get her a candy bar to take along," and headed toward the machines.

Laura smiled. "I guess they thought we might want to talk. I hope I prepared Mandy for everything on the drive here. She asks so many questions. Is there anything I should know that she shouldn't hear?"

He wondered if the reason Laura hadn't wanted to ride with him was really to allow her to answer her daughter's questions in private. "It's hard to believe she was ever withdrawn. She's such a bubbly child."

"When Doug died, she cried constantly. She stopped talking. She wouldn't eat. I'd lost him. I was afraid I'd lose her."

Mitch tried to hold himself aloof from the pain in Laura's eyes. But he couldn't. It touched an empty part of him, a part his father had damaged long ago. "What did you do?"

"I held her, talked to her about Doug, took her for walks. George bought Puffball and after that she perked up."

"You knew George then?"

"He worked with Doug."

Had she been involved with many men since her husband died? According to her father, in her teens she had gone through boyfriends like milkshakes. It didn't matter. It wasn't his business.

Laura touched his arm. "So is there anything I should know before we arrive in York?"

Her fingers seemed to scorch him through his suit coat. "Just that I don't want Ray to get upset. You're there to reassure him, not to make his blood pressure soar," Mitch said more tersely than he'd intended.

She looked horrified and snatched her hand back. "I would never do that."

He could still feel the imprint of her fingers. "I'm just concerned for Ray's health."

Her chin tilted up mutinously. "Look. I don't know what kind of person you think I am, but I wouldn't do anything to hurt my father. I'm making this trip to see him through his surgery. You and I don't have to be friends, but at least we can try to have an . . . amiable relationship."

He'd get along with Laura for Ray's sake. "Amiability's not a problem."

"I guess you'll have to prove that, won't you, Mr. Riley? Your amiability hasn't been excessive since you barged into my life yesterday."

He glanced at her speculatively and wondered exactly what would happen if they became . . . amiable. Since yesterday, erotic thoughts were becoming a habit. He'd just have to wipe them out of his head.

Mandy jumped up and down with excitement, tugged on Laura's arm, and pointed while they boarded the plane, found their seats and fastened their seat belts. She was fascinated by every detail of the airplane and asked innumerable questions, some of which Laura couldn't answer but Mitch could. He seemed to delight in Mandy's enthusiasm and that surprised Laura.

During his visit to their house, she'd classified him as cultured, aggressive but reserved. He held on to his opinions and emotions with tight control. She recognized those qualities because she was so different—the opposite, really. She said what she thought, she played with the moment, she let her feelings show much too easily.

She could understand why her father had chosen Mitch as a partner. They were very much alike. Except . . . Besides Mitch's outward attractiveness, something inside him called out to her. Was her woman's intuition working overtime? Probably more like her imagination, she thought with chagrin. Whatever it was, she shoved it aside. Mitch was simply someone she had to contend with while she was in York.

York. Where her mother had died, where her father had shut her out, where love had become an ultimatum. Her feelings for her father were confused. Part of her still loved him. But part of her still hurt, too, even after six years.

When Mitch shifted in his seat to find an easier position for his long legs, his shoulder bumped hers. She was entirely too aware of the bulk of him, the cut of his expensive suit, the aura of pure masculinity that surrounded him.

"Being short has its advantages," she quipped as he finally settled his right foot across his left knee.

He grimaced. "Instead of smoking and nonsmoking, they should have short and tall compartments."

She laughed. He smiled back. Aha. He *could* be friendly. She gestured toward the science fiction novel he was reading. "Is that any good?"

"It's intriguing." He nodded to Mandy looking out the window rather than using the crayons and coloring book on the tray in front of her. "But sometimes I'm more fascinated by the view. It stirs my imagination."

What did he do with his imagination after it was stirred? "When I was a little girl, I saw pink castles behind every cloud."

"You lived in a house large enough to be a castle."

She stared at his long black lashes rather than into his probing eyes. She knew nothing about him. He seemed to know a lot about her. "Oh, but it didn't have turrets or moats. And in my castles, only happy things happened."

"We learn too soon life isn't like that. Maybe reading kids fairy tales is a bad idea. It sets them up for disappointment."

There it was again. The sad note that drew her, made her want to touch him to give him solace. She tapped his book. "Adults need escape. Children need it more."

His blue eyes were penetrating. "But I know the difference between fantasy and reality. They don't."

"That's a parent's job—to kindly teach the difference."

Mitch thought about her reply, then glanced at Mandy. "Are you going to take her to see Ray? We can probably get special permission."

"No."

Mitch's jaw tensed into a stiff line. "Why not?"

She'd met fire with fire before, but with Mitch it seemed she was doing it every other sentence. "If he's in critical care, he's hooked up to monitors, an IV. Right?"

"Yes. Oxygen, too."

"I won't scare her like that. She gets nightmares from watching monster cartoons."

Mitch twisted in his seat to face her more directly. "He's her grandfather. He needs to see her. It might make a difference."

He couldn't make her squirm or back down. "After surgery will be soon enough."

"And what if he doesn't make it?"

"I won't think that way."

He grunted. "Isn't that a Pollyanna attitude?"

"It's an optimistic attitude. The last time I saw my father, he wasn't overweight, he didn't smoke, and he drank on a few social occasions. Has any of that changed?"

"He's not careful about what he eats. He fired his cook last year so he eats out a lot."

Mitch's reply was quick. He knew her father's habits well. How much time did he spend with him? Why did it matter? Was she jealous? No. Simply curious. "Does he have a housekeeper?"

"A cleaning lady comes twice a week."

"I'll have to hire someone. He'll need help when he comes home."

"We could take care of him."

She wondered if Mitch had seriously considered that option. If he cared about her father enough to take care of him, he must love him. "Dad doesn't even know I'm coming. He might want me to turn right around and go back if our last encounter is any indication. Besides, if you took care of him, the business would suffer, wouldn't it?"

Mitch hooked onto the first part of her response. "And if he doesn't want you to turn around?"

"I have two weeks. After that, I go back to my life in Independence."

"And George?"

The look in Mitch's eyes said he thought she was a callous, ungrateful child. But she couldn't expect her father to be any different today than he was six years ago. Now her independence not only directed her life, but Mandy's, too.

Her head bobbed up. "Yes. And Anne." Laura suddenly thought of a glitch. "Are you going to stay with Mandy while I see Dad?"

He shook his head vigorously. "You can't walk in there unannounced. You'll shock the sheets off of him. I need to prepare him."

"But I can't take Mandy—"

"My mother will stay with her."

Mitch's unilateral decision reminded her of her father's rules and regulations, curfews and standards. "I don't want to leave her with a stranger."

"We can only see Ray for twenty minutes. You won't be away from her that long."

Laura had always been so careful to consider Mandy's needs first, but Mitch made sense. She remembered the last time she'd put her daughter's needs before her husband's wants. They'd argued; he'd gone sailing . . .

A flight attendant asked if they'd like anything to drink. Mandy asked for a soda, her eyes wide and pleading.

Laura responded automatically, "You should have milk."

"Please?"

Mitch chuckled. "Who can say 'no' to that face?"

Laura sighed. "Okay, honey. This time."

After the attendant served them, Mitch touched Laura's hand. "Don't worry about Mandy staying with Mom. She loves kids."

His fingers on the top of her hand sent heat up her arm. Her eyes met his in surprise, and she witnessed his own flash of sexual awareness. He jerked his hand away and picked up his drink.

"Mr. Riley's drinking cola, too," Mandy piped up, easing the sudden tension.

"I'm surprised you didn't order something stronger," Laura remarked, wondering out loud. He seemed like a Scotch man to her, like her dad.

"A glass of wine with dinner is as strong as it gets."

"Why?" She peered at him over the rim of her glass.

His eyes darkened with a deep emotion. "I have my reasons."

Did his reasons have something to do with the sadness in him? "I'm sorry. I didn't mean to pry."

Mitch said quietly, "Alcohol killed my father."

She wanted to stroke his cheek, the one with the scar, and comfort him. But she wasn't that foolish. She glanced at Mandy as her daughter picked up a crayon and colored an elephant blue.

Laura's mother had died when she was eleven. "I know how it feels to lose a parent."

"But I don't know how it feels to walk out on one."

Laura took a sip of her soda to stall her temper. "Maybe you don't know the whole story."

"I know Ray Applegate is a good man. He didn't deserve the kick in the teeth you delivered. I met him five years ago and he was the saddest man I've ever seen. Even though you created chaos when you were around, you were his life. You walked away and left him with nothing."

Over and over again, she'd analyzed what she could have done differently. She regretted her wild behavior as a teenager. That had changed when she'd gone to school at eighteen; she'd found her purpose and her niche. At twenty she'd known exactly what she wanted. But her father couldn't accept her independence or her making her own decisions and choices. He'd erased her from his life and wouldn't answer her letters.

Laura angrily tapped the ice cube in her glass, making it spin. "My father is a traditional, strict, inflexible man."

Mitch lowered his voice. "That doesn't mean you had to cut him out of your life. Do you know the joy Mandy could give him?"

She met his gaze boldly. "I don't have to defend myself to you or anyone. I stopped doing that when I grew up."

"I'm not sure you're there yet," he muttered.

"Do you have a patent on maturity? You know how it's done right?"

"I know by your age it should be done."

"You don't know me, Mr. Riley."

He raised his glass to her in a toast. "Maybe we'll have to rectify that."

The gleam in his eye said he didn't want to know her at all, but he'd play with the pretense so he could keep her under his thumb.

Chapter Two

The lump in Laura's throat wouldn't disappear with any amount of swallowing. Mandy clutched her mother's hand as they walked up the brick path to the front door and Puffball meowed from her carrier. Laura paused in front of the double cherry door that was only one of many entrances into the Old English-style estate home. She'd always loved the Tudor house with its multicolored stone, gables, and chocolate-brown shutters. Her grandfather had built it for her grandmother.

Memories flooded through her mind faster than she could count them. She'd spent twenty years in this house. So why did she feel like such a stranger to it now? The answer was simple. She'd left this life behind six years ago.

Mandy must have sensed something. "What's wrong, Mommy?"

Laura shrugged off her melancholy. "Nothing, poppet. This is where I grew up. I'm wondering if you'll like the house as much as I did."

Mitch came up behind them with their suitcases. He set them down and unlocked the door.

"How long have you had a key?" Her father had never given a key to anyone not in the family. She'd brought hers along for that reason.

Mitch picked up the suitcases and looked at her intently. "Since Ray and I became partners and we opened the second store in Harrisburg. I have an apartment there, but I stay here when I'm in town."

Her father and Mitch were definitely more than business partners. "You don't stay with your mother?"

Mitch crossed the threshold into the foyer and waited until Laura and Mandy stepped inside before answering. "She lives in a one-bedroom apartment. It's easier and more convenient for me to stay here." As if he felt he should explain further, he added, "I'm a night owl. When I stay with her and work late, she waits up or hovers. She loses sleep. I don't get the work done. Your father goes his way, I go mine, and we don't interfere with each other."

Laura set the cat carrier on the floor. At one point in her life she'd desperately wanted her father to interfere, to show her he loved her. But when she'd asserted her freedom to become an adult, he'd interfered in the wrong way—not out of love, but because he'd wanted her to fulfill his dreams for her. He'd tried to manipulate her.

A bit wistfully, she said, "It sounds as if you and Dad get along well together."

Mitch studied her carefully. "We do."

His tone carried a warning that she'd better not try to meddle. Impatient with his "I'm in control" attitude, she walked into the living room. The marble fireplace, the rose Queen Anne chairs, and the Stiffel lamps were arranged exactly as she remembered them...as if no time had passed at all. Through the living room's French doors, she could see the dining room with its crystal chandelier and mahogany table. Mirroring light from the adjacent sun-room's stately paned windows, the gloss on the table was still unmarred and perfect.

Whenever they ate at that table, Laura feared she'd spill her milk or hurt the finish in some way. Her mother had always acted as a buffer between her and her dad, convincing him to treat Laura as a child rather than a small adult.

Mandy let go of Laura's hand and released Puffball from her carrier. The cat sniffed the new atmosphere, then regally strolled toward the sun-room with its rattan furniture and bright yellow striped cushions. Mandy ran after her.

Mitch said, "I'll take your suitcases up to your rooms later. I'd better go get Puffball a litter box and food and pick Mom up so we can get to the hospital."

Mitch had called his mother from the airport and she'd agreed to stay with Mandy. He'd also called the hospital to find that Ray was still stable.

Laura unbuttoned her poncho and threw it over a wing chair. "I'll give Mandy a tour and try and get her settled."

Mitch watched Mandy scramble after Puffball as the feline jumped from the settee to the back of a chair so she could look out the window. "There's milk in the refrigerator and a package of Oreo cookies in the cabinet over the microwave."

Laura felt like smiling for the first time since she entered the house. "You have a passion for them, too? Mandy and I are addicted. We eat a package a week."

When Mitch grinned, the angles of his face gentled, his eyes twinkled. "Maybe I'd better pick up another one. Unfortunately, I eat more than my share."

Her eyes skimmed his lean physique. There wasn't an ounce of fat anywhere. She'd like to see what he looked like in jeans—relaxed, happy, having fun. "Oreos must agree with you." She couldn't hide the appreciation in her voice.

His grin evaporated and he appraised her for a long moment. "You'll only be here two weeks, Laura. Don't count me among your trophies."

Her mouth dropped open. She quickly closed it. "That wasn't a come-on, it was an observation. I'd think you'd be experienced enough to know the difference."

In two steps, he was standing in front of her, his blue eyes dark with annoyance and a fire he was attempting to quell. "I'm experienced enough to know trouble can be wrapped in an attractive package."

She wished she were five inches taller so he couldn't physically intimidate her. "Nothing I say will change your mind about me. But I'm not going to watch every word while I'm here. That might be your style. It's not mine."

"Cautious versus reckless?" he taunted.

"No, cold versus warm." She turned toward the sunroom.

Mitch's words stopped her as efficiently as his hand could have. "Just because the prodigal daughter has returned doesn't mean all is forgiven."

Heat suffused her cheeks. "You won't be the one to decide."

"No, Ray will." Mitch strode to the foyer and out the door.

Tears pricked Laura's eyes. What a homecoming!

When Mitch parked his Buick in Ray Applegate's driveway an hour later and switched off the ignition, his mother made no move to get out. "Carey called while you were gone. He's coming home for a few weeks."

Mitch sighed heavily. Just what he needed right now—Laura's male counterpart. "Is he in trouble again?"

Nora Riley averted her eyes. "I don't think so. He wants to talk to you about something."

"He wants money again." Mitch's tone was as resigned as he was to his brother's escapades.

Nora grew defensive. "He didn't say that."

They had traveled this route many times before. "Mom, why else would he come? We go for months without hearing from him. He comes home when he's in trouble or needs something."

Her head tilted. Mitch could see his own stubbornness and determination came from this woman, not his father. "Carey is my firstborn. He's done many deeds I'm not proud of, but I'll always love him. Just as I'll always love you."

Unconditional love. Thank God for mothers. But he had to be realistic for her sake as well as his. "Answer me one question, Mom. If we were as poor as we were ten years ago, do you think he'd be coming home?"

"I hope so."

Mitch fell silent. His mother had always been naive where Carey was concerned. She consistently made excuses for him just as she had for her irresponsible, gambling, drinking husband. Carey had been his father's favorite. And unfortunately he had picked up many of their dad's bad habits. Mitch had inherited *his* goals, industry and ambition, from his mother. During all those years, she'd kept food on the table and a roof over their heads by working in a sewing factory and taking in private work at night. She deserved love and admiration from Carey, not heartache.

Mitch finally asked, "Did he say when he's coming?"

"Next week, maybe. He wasn't sure." Nora tenderly touched the scar on Mitch's cheek. "You still blame him, don't you?"

"No. But I do blame him for the worry he caused you."

"He was hurting, Mitch. He missed your father—"

Mitch's hand swished through the air in frustration. "What he wanted always came first and it still does. Another paycheck would have helped us make ends meet. Instead he ran with his buddies and left town at the first opportunity."

She assessed him cautiously. "We're all a little selfish."

Mitch closed his eyes. He supposed so. But some were a lot more selfish than others. Carey and Laura were prime examples.

Laura. Lord, that woman rubbed him the wrong way. Her eyes never stopped studying him, questioning. Maybe she had an innate curiosity like her daughter. What did he care? Because he was trying to figure her out...and suddenly, himself too. Just when he thought he had his reactions to her under control, something went haywire. The best thing to do was keep his distance.

He opened his eyes and unlatched the car door.

"Laura! Mandy!"

Laura would know that deep baritone anywhere. It not only echoed up the spiral staircase to the library-loft, but resonated through her body, vibrating a hidden part. "We're up here," she called.

Mandy ran to the top of the staircase and started to climb down. Laura's "Be careful, honey," was lost as her daughter found Mitch at the bottom. Her excitement spilled out. "We were explorin'. Mommy let me go into all the rooms. We sat on the bed she slept in when she was little. It's pink and white." She waved to the loft. "And there's bunches of books up there."

Mitch had discarded his suit coat and tie and rolled his sleeves above his forearms. Laura noted the black wavy hair and wondered if his chest was covered with it, too.

He lifted Mandy into his arms as if she were as light as a bag of Oreos. "You've been busy. There's someone downstairs I want you to meet."

Laura was thankful Mitch's cool reserve didn't extend to her daughter. She descended the stairs, careful of her footing.

As she neared the bottom, Mitch blocked her path. "Re-familiarizing yourself?"

She could smell his cologne, stronger this morning, now faded into a nuance she could hardly distinguish. She wondered how he smelled without it. Did he always look so sexy?

She ignored her increased pulse rate. "Mandy was fascinated by all the rooms. She's never seen so many doors. I think the most fun for her was opening and closing them."

"Are you going to put her in your old room?"

On the second step, Laura was as tall as Mitch and could look straight into his incredibly blue eyes. "Yes."

"I found a dog and a teddy bear and pretty dolls in the closet. Wanna see?" Mandy interrupted.

Mitch straightened an overall strap that had slipped down her shoulder. "Maybe later."

He stepped away so Laura could come down the remaining curved steps. After she did, they moved down the hall at the same time. Her breast brushed his elbow. The contact electrified her. She saw the startled look in his eyes. When he quickly averted his gaze, Laura walked ahead of him.

A woman was sitting on the edge of the living room sofa, waiting. She stood when she saw Laura and smoothed her hands down her navy skirt. Her hair, once black, was streaked with gray and framed her face with soft, tight curls. Her eyes were the same blue as Mitch's. Laura liked the way the older woman's smile disappeared into full rosy cheeks.

Wondering what Mitch had told his mother about her return, Laura extended her hand and introduced herself. "I'm

Laura Sanders and you must be Mrs. Riley. It's a pleasure to meet you."

Nora's pudgy fingers enveloped hers. "You, too, dear. Please call me Nora. I'm glad I can help out. I admire your father and wish him all the best. He's been good to Mitch."

Mitch set Mandy on the floor. "And this is Ray's beautiful granddaughter. Mandy, this is my mother."

Mandy looked at Laura, then stood in front of Nora. "Hi."

Nora sat on the sofa to be at Mandy's eye level. "Hi there, honey. Mitch told me you drew pretty pictures when you were coming here in the airplane. Do you think you can draw me a few?"

Mandy's head bobbed up and down, swinging her hair across her cheeks. "Sure. But I'm hungry. Can we eat first?"

Laura glanced at the grandfather clock. "We were so busy exploring, we forgot about the cookies. What time can we see Dad?"

"Whenever we get there. I'll go get us fast food hamburgers."

"Nonsense," Nora protested. "I'm sure there's something in the refrigerator. Let me go look."

Laura objected immediately. "Mrs. Riley, I can't let you do that! You're here to keep Mandy company."

"Child, I love it most when I'm cooking or taking care of others. Now, if you want to help, that's fine. But I'm not letting you put all that fat and those preservatives into your bodies when I'm around."

Laura didn't need more of Mitch's disapproval. She looked at him for his opinion.

He lifted his shoulders. "When Mom gets an idea in her head, there's no stopping her. C'mon, Mandy. Let's go find Puffball and show her her new litter box."

As Mandy scampered beside Mitch, his mother reminded Laura, "You can call me Nora, dear."

Laura liked Mitch's mother. She'd feel good about Mandy staying with her. She wondered if Mitch had decided they'd have supper now so she could spend more time with Nora and be comfortable leaving her daughter. He definitely had a caring side. She'd like to see more of it. The thought stuck. Why did she want to see more of it? Because that would make life easier. She reminded herself again, men like Mitch didn't interest her. She preferred men who were outgoing, friendly, accepting. Mitch was none of those, at least not with her. But there was something elemental about him, powerful . . .

Cut it out!

Laura was silent on the ride to the hospital. Mitch glanced at her a few times but didn't force conversation. She was aware of each look, each movement, the heat from his body, the line of his jaw. She wanted him to smile at her, not because he forgot his disapproval for a moment, but because he meant it.

What did it matter what he thought of her anyway? It didn't. Concentrating on Mitch was simply easier than dealing with her feelings about her father. A cacophony of emotions assaulted her every time she thought about him lying in a hospital bed. She felt sadness, guilt, disappointment, remnants of anger, worry and hope. Hope for what? That they could again establish a relationship? How? If so, what kind? Stranger to stranger? Friend to friend? Father to daughter? Then again, how much could happen in two weeks?

As they took the elevator to the coronary care unit, other visitors pressed Laura and Mitch toward the back. Laura felt awkward as Mitch's arm pressed against her shoulder and his hip nudged hers. When the elevator came to an abrupt halt, she swayed against him. His arm went around her to steady her.

When his eyes met hers, his arm dropped. But the heat remained where his arm had supported her back. They left the elevator and followed the winding corridor.

Mitch stopped in front of the doorway to the waiting room. "You can stay here while I tell him you've come."

When he would have turned away, she grabbed his elbow. "If he doesn't want to see me, I can go back to Independence tomorrow."

"Is that what you want?" Mitch's voice was as hard as his eyes.

"I want what's best for him."

He canvassed her face thoroughly, as if attempting to see into her soul. He must have decided she was telling the truth because he nodded. She released his arm and watched him walk away.

Laura paced the empty room, picking up a magazine, tossing it onto the chair where she found it. She felt six years old, as if she'd again taken one of her dad's golf clubs and chopped up the manicured lawn, attempting to hit the ball. He'd been furious and sent her to work with the gardener for a morning so she'd realize how much work she'd made for him.

When her mother was alive, her father had been stern but fair. Sometimes almost tender. Laura fingered the gold chain around her neck and tugged out the miniature gold rose. She'd always loved the rose garden. She used to go there and sit on the bench when she wanted to think, or wait for deer, or reread one of the classics in her father's library.

He'd given her the necklace on her eleventh birthday. She'd worn it almost every day since then, not only to remind her of the garden but to remind her her father had been thoughtful enough to know how much it meant to her. Where had all the tender feelings gone? Had he been so devastated by her mother's death that nothing had mattered but his work? She'd been a duty and a responsibility he had to keep in line. At least that's the way it had seemed to her.

When Doug died, she hadn't felt like going on either, in spite of the problems that had surfaced after Mandy was born. He'd been her first lover, her first serious relationship, the only person since her mother who'd accepted her as she was. Having Mandy had grounded her in reality and given her a sense of responsibility she'd never experienced or expected.

Doug had loved Mandy, there were no doubts about that. He loved to hold her and cuddle her and play with her as a child plays with a child. But he'd treated her like a doll and when he stopped playing, he hadn't wanted the responsibility of twenty-four hour care. When Laura remembered their last argument...

She sighed. Mandy had given her the impetus to create a good future for both of them. There was no way Laura could ever disown *her* daughter, no matter what she did.

Laura had always felt as if she'd failed her father after her mother died. What could she have done to make him less sad? What could she have done to establish a good relationship between them? Why couldn't he take her in his arms and share his grief with her? Wasn't she good enough? Wasn't she pretty enough? Didn't he love her anymore?

She'd tried to be good, quiet, studious, perfect, following all the rules. But when that hadn't worked, she'd tried the opposite. That hadn't worked either.

Now... What would her father say, what would he do, what did he feel?

When Mitch reappeared, his tall, broad-shouldered frame filled the doorway. She was afraid she wouldn't have the opportunity to find out what her father felt or thought.

Mitch looked so troubled she wondered if she'd even need to unpack her bags.

Before she could ask, Mitch said, "He'll see you now."

So many questions popped into her head. Did he really want to see her? Was he glad she was here? Had the news upset him? None of the questions came out because she was afraid of the answers. She had to see for herself.

She followed Mitch to the room. He said, "Ray wants me to wait out here. Call if he needs me."

Need. She was curious as to just how much her dad *did* need Mitch. With her heart pounding, she stepped into her father's room. His brown hair had receded and thinned. There were many lines radiating from his eyes and mouth. He looked pale. The IV and oxygen tube seemed out of place attached to a man she'd always known as vigorous and energetic. He looked worse than she'd imagined, and she was determined not to say or do anything to upset him.

Crossing on wobbly legs to the bed, she stood at his side. She wanted to kiss his cheek or stroke his hand, but didn't know if either gesture would be welcome. So she said, "Hello, Dad."

His eyes held hers. "Your hair's longer, but you look the same," he said gruffly. He motioned to the chair next to the bed. "Sit."

She lowered herself onto the blue vinyl, her hands tight on her purse. A hug would mean so much... But her father had never been the hugging kind. "How do you feel?"

He scowled, his brows pulling together. "Like someone turned off my power. I've never been so damned tired in all my life."

"Mitch said—"

"What do you think of him?"

That was a loaded question. "I haven't spent much time with him."

"I hope you will." He paused without explaining, then continued. "He said you manage a jewelry store?"

"It's what I know best." She loved working with jewelry and selling it to customers who appreciated it as much as she did.

"Mitch isn't too enamored with the business side. He'd rather design and work with the gold and gems."

That surprised her. She suspected the still waters ran deep, but Mitch's giving his imagination the freedom to design seemed out of character. She kept quiet, letting her father direct their conversation.

"I'd like to ask you a favor. Call Mitch in here, will you?"

So much for a father-daughter reconciliation. Weren't they going to talk about what had happened? Why they hadn't seen each other for six years? Or was Mitch to be included in every little thing? She stuffed her resentment. She couldn't take the chance of exciting her father. She had to do what he asked.

She went to the door. "Mitch, he wants you to come in."

When they were both standing by the bed, Ray Applegate said, "I know I'm going to make it through this surgery tomorrow. So we're not going to start spouting words we might regret. But it is going to be a while until I'm back on my feet and up to full speed again."

"You don't have to worry about anything," Mitch assured him. "We have good people at both stores."

"I know we do, but they're not us. You have your exhibit coming up and I know you're busy with that." He gazed at his daughter. "Laura, Mitch told me you plan to stay two weeks. I'd like you to change your plans and stay six weeks, take over managing the York store until I can go in at least part-time. What do you say?"

One glance at Mitch told her this was a surprise and an unwelcome one. Either he didn't like the idea of her staying or he hated the idea of her being involved in the business. Maybe he thought of it as his domain.

"I don't know if I can be away for six weeks," she said quietly.

Her father growled. "Won't your husband let you help your father?"

Mitch shot her a be-careful look.

"I'm a widow, Dad. I'm self-supporting and I need a job when I go back."

He appeared shocked. "When did that happen?"

"Two years ago."

"I'm sorry." She doubted his sincerity when he asked, "Was he doing something crazy like racing his motorcycle?"

She held on to her anger, trying to remember that her father was a sick, though still infuriating, man. "He was sailing and got caught in a storm."

Her father grunted.

He'd never understand how happy she and Doug had been, once—without his money and without his approval. She sighed. Six weeks. Lord, that was a long time to be gone. Would her supervisor let the assistant manager take over for that long?

"Dad, I'll think about it and give you my answer after your surgery."

His eyes closed for a moment and he sighed. "I guess I shouldn't have expected an immediate 'yes.'"

She wanted to reach out to him somehow, tell him not to worry, that she'd help if she could. But the past inhibited her. She could only offer one thing. "You'll have to recover quickly so you can meet your granddaughter."

His eyes flew open. "What's her name?"

"Mandy."

"How old is she?"

"She's four."

"Where is she now?"

Mitch answered. "She's at your house with my mother. They took to each other right away."

"Nora's a nice lady." Ray focused his attention on Laura. "Maybe she'll help you with Mandy while you're here."

She didn't need anyone's help with her daughter. Didn't her father think she was capable of doing anything right? Instead of expressing her thoughts, she said, "We'll see."

A nurse bustled in, nodded to Mitch and Laura, stuck a thermometer in Ray's mouth and wrapped the blood pressure cuff around his arm. When she finished, she said, "The doctor prescribed a sleeping pill. I'll be back with it shortly."

When the nurse had gone, Mitch moved closer to the bed. "We'd better be going. You need your rest. I'll be here during surgery tomorrow."

Laura patted her father's hand. "I'll be here, too. We'll be in to see you as soon as they'll let us."

"Surgery's at seven-thirty in the morning. You could wait for the results at the house."

Mitch shook his head. "We'll be here."

Ray refolded the hem of the sheet over his chest. "Nora's welcome to stay overnight. That way you won't have to get the child out of bed in the morning."

"Don't worry about anything. We'll work out the details." Mitch extended his hand and Ray took it.

Laura saw understanding pass between the two men and was suddenly jealous she didn't have that rapport with her father. When Mitch crossed to the door, she followed. Feeling awkward, she turned and said, "Try to get a good night's sleep." There didn't seem to be anything else to say.

Walking down the corridor to the elevator, Mitch finally spoke. "You could have told him you'd do more than think about staying."

Her chin lifted. "Was I supposed to lie to him?"

"I guess to you a job would be more important than your father."

All her frustration from the moment she'd opened her door to Mitch spurted out. "I don't know how important my father is. This is the first I've seen him in six years, through his fault as much as mine, and I'm trying to assimilate that. I do know one thing though. Mandy comes first. I have to have a decent job to go back to if we're going to survive. So don't give me that holier-than-thou attitude when you know nothing about my life!"

He didn't back down. "How can you say Mandy comes first when you live like you do?"

She stopped in the middle of the hall. "And just how do I live?"

"Practically in a commune!"

Somehow, she held onto her fuse though it was getting mighty short. "Right. Just like the flower children I've read about."

A couple passed them in the hall. Laura waited until they were out of hearing distance before she finished. "The sixties are gone, Mitch. Anne and George are good friends. I live with them for practical reasons."

"I saw the way George looked at you. Is that your practical reason?"

If they weren't standing in a hospital hallway, she might have slapped him. Instead, she stiffened her arms at her sides. "What you saw was good old-fashioned affection," she said through clenched teeth. She took a few steps closer to him and knew she was courting danger but didn't care. "Maybe you think you saw something because of the awareness between *us*."

He appeared shocked, as if she shouldn't know about it, think about it or voice its existence. "There's awareness all right. The awareness any man feels when he's in the same room with a pretty woman."

One thing she'd always been was honest. She wasn't going to start hiding the truth now. "You can reduce it to that if it's easier for you to digest. I only know I haven't felt this 'aware' for a very long time. I don't think it's an everyday occurrence for you either. We don't have to like it, but it's ridiculous not to admit it's there."

His nose was a few inches above hers, his head close enough for her to feel his warm breath on her cheek. "I suppose you've been celibate since your husband died?" The question was as mocking as it was bold.

She met it with the same boldness. "Yes, I have."

He looked as if she'd told him Christmas was occurring in July this year. "Give me a break, Laura. A woman like you—"

"You might have heard many tales about me from my father, but the one thing you never heard was that I'm a liar. I tell the truth. Always. I learned that from my *mother*."

For the first moment since she met Mitch, she saw respect in his eyes. But she didn't know if it was there because she'd been celibate or because she'd told the truth.

As they rode the elevator to the lobby and walked to the parking garage, Mitch tried to sort his thoughts. Ray's face had registered shock that Mitch had brought Laura to York. But there was no censure. Mitch had worried about that on the flight home, unsure he'd done the right thing. His doubts had vanished when he'd seen the spark of hope in Ray's eyes when he asked Mitch to bring Laura to his room.

Laura sure as hell confused Mitch. He'd had a picture in his head of the woman Ray had described—an irresponsible, uncaring hoyden who thought of herself first, last and always. She hadn't dispelled that image but she wasn't that one-dimensional, either. Maybe that's why she made his head spin. But that made her all the more dangerous.

What if she saw Ray's invitation to stay as an opportunity to take over the business? He and Ray had a simple partnership agreement, if any contract could be called simple. But it could be terminated by either of them and the option was there for either to buy out the other if they both agreed. Mitch could never afford to buy Ray's share. But Ray Applegate could buy out Mitch easily.

What if he wanted to do that? After all Ray had done for Mitch, how could Mitch stand in his way? What if Laura put pressure on her father and pushed her way back in? Would Ray allow that? Would he rather have his daughter as a partner?

When they opened the store in Harrisburg, Ray had told Mitch it was his to make a success. Mitch had put most of his savings into the inventory. He had that back now, plus. He'd made the Harrisburg store the success it was today. Ray wouldn't cut Mitch out, would he? Of course not. Ray was not like Mitch's father. And they were more than business partners.

But neither of them had considered Ray's health would fail. If something happened to Ray...if Laura took over control...Mitch wouldn't let her. He'd keep his eye on her and not let her make a move without his knowledge.

The only problem was she was too damn sexy for his peace of mind. The fluffy blond-brown hair, enticing lips temptingly pink, a smile that could dazzle Edison when she switched it on high. For such a small person, she had long legs. He thought of sliding his hand up her thigh and his body responded. Damn! His hands clenched into fists. What in God's name was he thinking of?

Lust. Deprivation. It had been a long time since he'd made love to a woman. That's all it was. She awakened basic male urges.

If he had to stick close to her, he'd have to keep his urges under control. That had never been a problem. Not even with Denise, though he'd considered marrying her. There was no earthly reason why he couldn't be in the same room as Laura and ignore the "awareness." Unless she was a witch.

He smiled. He was too old and too wise to believe in witches or love potions. He was dealing with a mortal woman. A woman he was going to watch closely.

Chapter Three

When Laura saw her daughter fast asleep on the sofa, she wanted to curl up beside her. Instead, she crossed to her little girl and gazed at her innocent face, letting her love for Mandy well up and wash over her.

Nora set her crocheting on the end table. "She fell asleep about fifteen minutes ago. Poor thing couldn't keep her eyes open."

"She had a long day." Mitch strode to the sofa and looked down at the child in the pink gown. He lifted his head and his gaze met Laura's. "Would you like me to carry her upstairs?"

She nodded. "I'd appreciate it. Maybe if you do it, she won't wake up. I jostle her too much."

Mitch scooped Mandy into his arms. "Mom, can you stay the night so we don't have to get Mandy up in the morning?"

"Here? Does Ray know—"

"He suggested it," Mitch replied casually, as if the whole matter was no big deal.

She pursed her lips. "I suppose I can stay. It would look better since you're staying here, too. Not that you and Laura need a chaperon. But people do talk."

Mitch rolled his eyes toward the ceiling. "We know about that, don't we? Dad and Carey..." He stopped, as if suddenly remembering he and his mother weren't alone. "I don't think rumors are a concern now."

"They might be for Ray. He's very proper."

Laura wondered if Nora knew her father well. She seemed to have him pegged.

Nora continued, "I'll need a change of clothes."

"After I take Mandy up, I'll go get what you need."

"It's times like these, I wish I could drive," Nora said.

He sent her a slanted grin. "You can still learn."

Her cheeks pinkened and she became flustered. "Goodness, no. I'm much too old."

Mitch nudged her with his elbow as he passed her. "You're only as old as you think you are."

Pain twisted in Laura's chest. She'd never get over losing her mother. Seeing Mitch interacting with Nora made her realize how much she'd missed her. Her mother would have loved Mandy, probably spoiled her.

As Mitch carried Mandy up the stairs, Laura said, "I didn't want to impose on your mother."

He didn't stop climbing. "I did it for you."

The tone of his voice should have warned her, but she never did take warnings seriously. "Why?"

"Because I didn't want you to have an excuse not to be at the hospital."

What could she say? Thank you, but stop taking potshots at me? What if she stayed six weeks? He wasn't hostile, but he was so suspicious. So unlike Doug. The man she'd married had had a live-and-let-live attitude. Doug had taught her she didn't need anyone else's approval. As long as she was true to her heart, no one else's two cents mattered. Until Laura's sense of responsibility for Mandy had put a damper on spontaneity and Laura couldn't run off at the drop of a hat to go sailing or whatever the latest adventure was he wanted to share with her.

When they were first married, they thought alike, they dreamed alike, they believed alike. Make the most of the moment. Live for today; love for today. If passion was sometimes lacking, it didn't matter because they were such good friends. Falling in love with Doug had introduced her to the world of adult emotion...and adult heartache. When he died, she'd had to grapple with grief, fear and the stark knowledge he had taken one too many risks. That might have been her fault. She'd never know. Anne and George had helped her rid herself of the blame.

After the sense of loss subsided enough for her to think about the future, she'd planned her future and Mandy's without looking for a man to share it with them. Did all men resent the time and care children took? Her father seemed to. Doug had. George loved Mandy like a brother loved a little sister and Laura could trust him to care for her, but George had never been more than a friend and never would be. That was just the way things were. So Laura had directed all her energy into raising her daughter to appreciate life, squeeze every moment of happiness out of it, and be nurtured with the freedom to think for herself and become the person she wanted to be.

Mitch waited for Laura to come into the bedroom and fold down the covers. Gently, he laid Mandy down and covered her.

Laura leaned over and kissed Mandy's cheek. As she smoothed the spread under her daughter's chin, she said, "I think I'll sleep in here with her tonight so if she wakes up and doesn't remember where she is, she won't be scared. The rooms here are so far apart. She's used to me being in the same room."

"You sleep together?"

"We have twin beds."

His blue eyes darkened. "What about Anne and George?"

She almost smiled in exasperation. He was determined to examine her life under his microscope. "They have separate bedrooms. As I told you, we're all just friends."

He walked toward the doorway, his movements athletically smooth. "How did you come to live together?"

Apparently he believed her. He wasn't still questioning her life-style; that was progress. "Doug didn't have any life insurance. When he died, I couldn't keep up with the bills and mortgage payments. Anne wanted to go to grad school, but couldn't afford it. By sharing expenses with me and baby-sitting for Mandy she could. George is trying to save for a house of his own and staying with us he can save money."

"So it's not permanent."

She shrugged and tossed her hair over her shoulder. "Nothing's permanent. I learned a long time ago to grab the moment for what it's worth."

Mitch frowned, the brackets around his mouth deepening. "What about building for the future, planting roots, saving enough to cover the proverbial rainy day?"

With a last look at Mandy, Laura crossed to him at the door. "Are you familiar with Shakespeare?"

"Somewhat."

"There's a line in *Othello,* 'Who steals my purse steals trash.' That's the way I look at money. It's necessary, but it's discardable. Memories, feelings and people are the real treasures."

Mitch leaned against the doorjamb, preventing her from leaving. "It's funny how people who've had money most of their lives decry its value. Have you ever wanted for anything?"

She thought about it. When she'd left her dad's house, she'd left with nothing. She had postponed the second term of her apprenticeship to work while Doug finished his schooling. But as soon as he'd finished, he'd found a job and she'd completed her training. Money wasn't abundant, but she'd always managed to pay the bills on time. It was good training for after he died. Even then, by budgeting carefully and sharing expenses with Anne and George, she and Mandy had never been in need.

"I've never been hungry or cold, if that's what you mean."

"That's exactly what I mean." His blue eyes bored into her.

He'd known poverty, and he'd known need. Sometimes he was easy to read. Laura wondered if he knew that. Compassion for him made her voice husky. "Were you cold and hungry often?"

He was quiet, as if thinking about not answering. Finally, he admitted, "Not if Mom could help it. But we ate boiled potatoes more than once a week."

He meant for a main course. "How long did that last?"

"My father never worked steadily so it happened on and off."

She didn't mean to interrogate him but she wanted to know more about him. "How old were you when your dad died?"

"Fourteen."

"You were the only one?"

"No. I have a brother who's a year older."

Was that the Carey he spoke of? "Does he live here in York?"

"No."

From his detached answer, she knew she'd better stop. But her curiosity got the best of her. "How did you get interested in designing jewelry?"

A faraway look came into his eyes. "My mom had a ring that her mother had given her. It was beautiful, a cluster of rubies and pearls. When my father gambled it away, she cried and cried. I swore some day I'd replace it. I used to stop in front of jewelry stores and stare at the gems, the combinations and arrangements. After a while, I started drawing my own ideas. I imagined the colored stones in my hand and the countless pictures I could create with them."

The passion radiating from him startled her. This was a side she guessed few people saw. He loved brilliance, color, clarity and form. "I'd like to see your work."

He cocked his head and smiled as if pleased by her interest. "I can arrange that. Do you design?"

His smile could make anyone feel special. "I've never had the money for the materials."

"Your store doesn't repair jewelry?"

"No. Repairs are sent out. We don't even have gold solder."

Mandy turned over in bed and Laura was instantly alert. Her daughter didn't wake up but hugged her pillow.

"I have to get her doll. If she wakes up, she'll want it. It's probably downstairs."

He straightened and moved into the hall. "And I have to make another trip across town."

The bit of friendly conversation gave her hope that they could find common ground. "Mitch?"

He stopped. "What?"

"I do care about my father. I want him to get well."

He aimed a soul-searching look at her. "Then we want the same thing."

As Mitch walked in front of her down the hall, she suspected he didn't believe it.

* * *

Nora was looking through the kitchen cupboards when Mitch returned with her overnight case. "I thought you and Laura would be watching television."

"Laura tried to keep me company but I could see how tired she was and concerned about Mandy waking without her there. I told her to go to bed."

He set the case on the beige counter. "Do you think it's an act?"

Nora stared at him as if she didn't know what he was talking about. "What?"

He took off his suit coat and hung it on the back of one of the four plank-bottom chairs at the smaller table in the kitchen. "Her motherly concern."

Nora's hands fluttered in the air. "It's no act! She loves that little girl. You can see it in her eyes and hear it in her voice. Why would she put on an act?"

His mother had confirmed his gut feeling. Laura and Mandy seemed as close as any mother and daughter could be, and he was ashamed of his suspicion. But his concern for Ray led him to play devil's advocate. "Maybe she's trying to win us over and make us sympathetic toward her."

"I know you love Ray like a father. Even more because you didn't have a proper father and Ray fills up that space in your life." Her voice held regret and pain, but she continued, "Laura may have hurt her father once, but six years is a long time. She's not a teenager now. She probably wishes those six years were different as much as he does."

Mitch had the feeling Laura didn't regret walking away from her father one iota, let alone living however she wanted the last six years. She was a free spirit, all right, with her grab-the-moment philosophy. He knew from experience that free spirits resisted shackles at someone else's expense. Enough about Laura. He was thinking about her too often as it was.

When Nora opened another cupboard, Mitch asked, "Can I help you find something?"

She pushed a peanut butter jar aside. "I'm looking for the pancake mix. Thought I'd get ingredients ready for breakfast."

"Mom, you're not here to cook and take care of everybody—"

She stopped searching. "Can't you let me do what makes me happy?"

He felt guilty. Laura had touched a nerve earlier. His mother would like nothing better than him staying with her when he was in town. She liked taking care of people. She was happiest when she performed some service for someone. But she didn't need to do that now. She didn't have to sew for anyone; she didn't have to provide for and worry about him and Carey. So what did she do? She volunteered at a day-care center.

He angled around the counter and opened a cupboard. When he couldn't find the mix there, he peered into the cabinet she had last opened. The back of the box faced him. "Here it is. I'm surprised you didn't see it."

She looked at the front of the box. "This is different from what we use. I guess that's why I missed it."

"I wish you'd see the optometrist again. I can make an appointment for you—"

"No. I'll do it myself."

"Soon?"

"Yes." At his scolding glance, she said, "I promise." She opened the freezer, found a package of bacon, and transferred it to the refrigerator.

"I'm going to work for a while, but if you want to go to bed, feel free. Do you remember when Ray gave you a tour of the house? You can sleep in the room with the yellow curtains."

"I remember. But I was going to sleep in the housekeeper's quarters down here."

A sitting room, bedroom and bathroom stretched behind the kitchen. Mitch supposed the cleaning lady kept it clean and aired out, but his mother wasn't sleeping there. "You're not the housekeeper. There's no reason you shouldn't sleep upstairs with the rest of us."

"If you think that's what Ray would want..."

Mitch was firm. "That's what he'd want."

"Okay. But I'm not going to bed yet. I'll get the coffee ready and set the table for breakfast, maybe watch TV and keep you company."

He'd thought he'd work in Ray's den, but he supposed he could sketch on the couch just as easily. "I'm going to change into something more comfortable. I'll be down in a few minutes."

As he climbed the steps, he knew he wouldn't get much work done. His mother would interrupt a hundred times, commenting on the TV program or asking to see what he was designing. He smiled. They'd spent many Sunday afternoons like that. They hadn't done it lately.

On the way to his bedroom, Mitch passed the open bathroom door. A billow of steam and a flowery scent surrounded him. Gardenias?

Laura was hanging her bath towel over the wooden rack next to the sink. She wore a short flannel robe with bright violet, vivid yellow, and emerald stripes. Didn't the woman believe in muted colors? Her bare feet invited his eyes to skim her legs. Did she wear a sedate gown like her daughter or was satin more her speed?

When she went to the sink and picked up a brush, she saw him. "Did you want to get a shower? I thought you'd use the bath off of Dad's room."

Her hair was a combination of gold and tiger's eye, fluffy and wild around her face. His fingers itched to glide through it, smooth it, stroke it. He cleared his throat. "No. I came up to change. I thought...uh...we should leave at seven-thirty tomorrow morning. Mom said she'll make breakfast."

"She doesn't have to."

"I know. But don't argue with her. She wants to."

Laura came toward him. The scent of gardenias was even stronger. Was it shampoo, perfume, lotion? Lord, this woman oozed sensuality. The colors she chose, the style of her hair, the large gray eyes, the way she walked. He was hypnotized by her and felt like a fool, but he couldn't move away.

"Awareness" she'd called it. Whatever it was, it was potent. If he touched her, would sparks fly? If he touched her, would he want to stop? He couldn't touch her. She was Ray's daughter. Her values contradicted his. Her view of life hurt the ones she loved. His mind told him, *Stay away, keep clear, don't get involved.* But another source seized him and made his insides riot, urging him to act on feelings he'd suppressed for a long time.

Laura's blood pounded at her temples. She hadn't realized sharing her father's huge house with Mitch would seem this intimate. His top three shirt buttons were unfastened as if he'd begun unbuttoning his shirt while climbing the stairs. Tendrils of black hair swirled underneath. Her stomach lurched. She knew chemistry when she felt it. Maybe because it rarely gripped her like this. She could usually brush it off and go about her business.

Sleeping under the same roof with him shouldn't bother her. The house was certainly big enough. She slept under the same roof as George every night. But that was different. He was a friend. Mitch was a...disturbance.

Was the allure the mystery behind Mitch? The undercurrent between them? The bond of being concerned about her father? His reserved attitude with her but his gentleness with Mandy?

Laura's fingers went to the chain around her neck. Mitch's eyes followed them. She hastily stuffed her hands in her robes pockets. "Uh . . . are you going to bed?"

"No, I'm too wound up."

The deep huskiness of his voice made her start chattering. "I know what you mean. My body's exhausted, but my mind's clicking away. Maybe if I crawl in with Mandy, I'll relax. It's going to be a long day tomorrow—" *Shut up, Laura. You're acting like a besotted teenager who's never felt hormones stirred up before.*

His eyes traveled over her as if imagining her taking off her robe and sliding into bed. She shivered. Sweeping her hair away from her cheek, she turned off the light. Mitch stepped back so she could enter the hall. He walked with her to the doorway of Mandy's room.

When she stepped over the threshold, he stayed in the hall but peeked inside. Laura's pink bra and teddy lay on the bed, her panty hose and jumpsuit sprawled across the chair, her shoes stood next to the dresser. A neat bedroom wasn't one of her virtues. She expected Mitch to comment.

"Mandy has a visitor."

Laura didn't understand for a moment until her gaze followed his. Puffball was curled on the spread next to Mandy's knees. "She sleeps with Mandy at home."

Mitch rested his hand high on the door frame just above her head. "I always thought cats were independent."

He was long all over. Long fingers, long arms, long legs, long waist. Catching herself before she could dwell on a picture of him naked, she responded, "They're like people. They project an aloof image but they crave affection and attention, too."

"Not everyone craves affection and attention."

"That's a macho attitude that causes more problems than it's worth." She knew she should watch her tongue but she'd never done that very well.

No longer looking casual, he took his hand from the polished wood. "It has nothing to do with macho. It concerns priorities."

"What priority tops your list?" she challenged, wondering why he had the power to rouse her.

"The business. Creating beautiful pieces of jewelry."

"You don't need someone to hold you and hug you and tell you you're wonderful?"

His body language became defensive as he crossed his arms over his chest. "Pop psychology doesn't interest me."

She blew out a breath. He sounded just like her father, who denied his feelings at all costs. "Psychology has nothing to do with it. Feelings do. Human beings need warmth and each other." She looked Mitch up and down. "But then maybe you and my father are the exceptions. Steel hearts. Nothing can penetrate them." She thought she'd outgrown the bitterness, but she could hear it in her voice.

Mitch didn't defend himself. "You don't know your father if you can say that."

How she wanted to. Her throat constricted and she knew tears weren't far behind. "If I don't know him, it's because he never let me in." Reaching for the doorknob, she said, "Good night, Mitch. I'll see you in the morning."

When she shut the door, she leaned against it and took several deep breaths. After a few moments, she heard Mitch's footfalls grow faint as he walked down the hall.

Sipping coffee from a paper cup, Mitch covertly watched Laura. Her canary yellow slacks and orange sweater with yellow flowers made her the center of focus in the drab waiting room. A middle-aged man across the room glanced at her every few minutes and looked as if he'd like to start a conversation. She seemed oblivious to him and her surroundings, her chin tucked down as she read the novel she'd begun on the plane.

Mitch drained his cup and stood. "Laura, I'm going for more coffee. Would you like a cup?"

She put her book on the chair and rose. "No, but I'll walk with you. I can't get my insides to settle down."

So she *was* worried. He studied her face. Little if no makeup. A hint of copper shadow over her eyes. A touch of lipstick. She looked pale.

His elbow grazed her arm as they walked down the corridor; he wondered if he'd get used to the jolt of electricity he felt each time they touched, however innocuously. "I wonder how it's going."

"I wish they'd give us half-hour reports or something."

Mitch hooked his thumb in the pocket of his khaki trousers, considering the best way to approach a subject they needed to discuss. "I talked to Ray's cardiologist when he decided to have the surgery."

She looked at him, her gray eyes wide with interest. "What did he say?"

Mitch had expected her to be defensive. "The operation briefly stops the heart. That's quite a blow to absorb. Ray's outlook when he comes home is vitally important. If he sees himself as an invalid rather than a recovering patient, it will take him longer to get back on his feet. Psychological recovery is as important as physical recovery."

"I can't see my dad acting as an invalid," she said wryly.

"It depends on how he looks at his life—if he focuses on what he can't do rather than what he can do. Heart bypass patients often spend the time reevaluating their lives and sometimes get depressed because their life hasn't been what they wanted or planned."

"Did the doctor tell you this?" She appeared surprised he knew as much as he did.

He had pored over medical literature, learning what he could about Ray's chances of surviving surgery, complications, aftereffects. "I've done some reading. Family support and involvement in recovery is as important as medication and post-op care. And he needs plenty of time for recovery. If he pushes it because he thinks he has to get back to work, the stress can be damaging."

She didn't slow her step. "I'll be staying the six weeks. I called the district manager this morning before we left. But six weeks is all I can manage. He made it clear if I stay longer, I won't have a job when I go back."

Mitch was relieved. If Ray wanted her here, she was important to his recovery. Trying to reassure her, he said, "I'm sure Ray will give you money if you need it—"

She stopped, her eyes flashing silver. "I don't want his money. I'm not staying to get paid."

Mitch didn't understand either the sadness or anger reflected in her glare. Did she feel she'd managed the last six years without him well enough that she didn't need to accept anything Ray had to give now? If that was her attitude, Ray would suffer. He was a generous man who liked to share his affluence.

"Did you know Ray gives a good bit of money to local charities?"

"You think I fall into that category?"

Damn! He hadn't meant for it to sound like that. "Of course not. I just meant if you give him the chance, maybe he'll forget the past and help with Mandy. Education is expensive."

Laura's color heightened, putting swaths of pink on her cheeks. "Mandy needs love and affection and quality time spent with her. We'll manage her education when the time comes."

Mitch didn't understand the vehemence of her words or her frustration. Of course Ray would spend time with his grandchild, given the chance. Laura's live-for-today attitude would hurt Mandy more than anyone. "Damn stubborn, aren't you?"

She looked as if she was going to explain, then changed her mind. "As stubborn as my father. If we come to an...understanding, it will have nothing to do with money."

He wondered what it did have to do with.

At the coffee machine, Mitch dropped in change. "Sure you don't want a cup?"

"What's in my stomach now doesn't want to stay down." She waited until Mitch was holding the coffee in his hand to ask, "You don't want me to have anything to do with the business, do you?"

Why lie? "No."

"Why?"

She didn't pull any punches. He could be just as blunt. "Because Ray and I have an agreement—we have our own method of doing business, keeping records, et cetera. You're going to be here six weeks. If you reorganize, it will take that much time after you leave to put everything back in order."

Instead of getting prickly or irate as he expected, she said simply, "I know how to run a jewelry store, Mitch."

Careful not to burn his tongue, he took a sip of coffee, then lowered the cup. "You know how you run the store you oversee. We don't work like a chain store."

"So you feel my input would be unnecessary and uncalled for."

Part of him wanted to let her down easy, but the other part that felt a pull toward her directed his answer. "You can oversee the employees and sell as much merchandise as you can, but it would be better if you stayed out of the business."

"How do you know that's what my father wants?" she countered, with a threatening look that indicated she'd do what she damn well pleased if *she* had anything to say about it. "When he asked me to stay and help out, you were as surprised as I was."

"He wants you near him, Laura. That's all. Why can't you see that?"

She pursed her lips and shook her head. "You don't know what you're talking about."

Her attitude confused him. Sometimes she acted hurt, other times angry. What did she have to be hurt and angry about? *She* was the one who ran away with the love of her life. Ray hadn't deserted her; she had deserted him.

Mitch ran his hand over his jaw, noticing a patch that wasn't as cleanly shaven as the rest. He'd been distracted this morning, distracted by thoughts of Ray's surgery, and he had to admit, distracted by thoughts of Laura dressing in the room down the hall.

"We'd better get back to the waiting room," he said.

She nodded and he noted her fingers went to the gold chain around her neck. She did that often. Had her husband given it to her? Was it a talisman? Did it give her strength? He fought the growing need to know more about her as they walked back down the hall. But the more he learned about her, the more disturbed he felt. Was it her complexity?

They were sitting in the waiting room, pretending to be interested in a TV talk show when the cardiologist entered the room dressed in his green scrubs. Mitch and Laura rose at the same time and crossed to him.

After Mitch introduced Laura to Dr. Carlson, the doctor said, "The operation was successful. Only the double bypass was necessary."

"When can we see him?" Mitch asked.

"I don't know if you'll want to see him today. He's attached to tubes and machines and his appearance might be a shock. It might be better to wait until tomorrow."

Mitch stared at him levelly. "Better for him or us?"

"For you. You could only see him for fifteen minutes tonight around seven anyway. Tomorrow you'll be less anxious, he'll be—"

"I want to see him tonight," Laura said softly.

The physician looked at Mitch.

"I agree. I don't want to wait until tomorrow either."

"That's your prerogative. Leave your number at the desk so I can reach you if there's a negative change."

"Is that likely?" Laura's voice shook.

"I don't expect anything. But I can't give you a guarantee. If you don't hear from me, come in at seven."

The cardiologist left and Mitch turned to Laura. She had wrapped her arms around herself and her lower lip quivered. He wanted to pull her close and push her away at the same time. It was damned unsettling. "He'll be fine, Laura."

The tears that trickled down her cheek were almost Mitch's undoing. She wasn't trying to hide them and he wished he could let his emotions flow as easily. The past few hours had tied him in knots but a jog or a game of racquetball would have to be his release.

A tear rolled down her nose. Compromising with himself, he dropped his arm across her shoulders. But when she turned into his chest, his other arm enclosed her naturally. Too naturally. She was warm and small against him. *Comfort her,* a small voice said. But a ripple of need percolated from his head to his toes. The sexual tightening told him to drop his arms and step back, but she was leaning against him. Her hair smelled like the gardenias that had scented the bathroom last night. Contrary to his resolve to withdraw, he couldn't help slipping his hand under it to finally feel its texture. Soft and thick. Seductive. Just like the rest of her.

He smoothed his hand down her back. The ribbed knit of the sweater emphasized the straightness of her spine. His thumb slipped and he felt her bra strap. Only one hook. It must be another wisp of a thing like the one on her bed last night. When his fingers reached her waist, he realized his hands could almost span it.

Her heart beat fast. As her breast pushed against his chest, he imagined holding it in his palm. Blazes! Why couldn't he control his thoughts? He sucked in a breath and stood perfectly still, his arms around her stiffly.

She raised her head and stared into his eyes. There were questions there. It didn't matter. He dropped his arms and stepped back. She wiped her tears with the back of her hand. The gesture reminded him of a child's.

"Thank you." She drew in a steadying breath and bit her lower lip. "I was more strung out than I thought."

Sun flew in the window and rested on her upturned face. There were no marks, no flaws. The symmetry was perfect. One half of a heart meeting the other in a delicate point. Her honey brows were perfectly arched; her skin looked as pinkly healthy as a baby's.

He fought the inclination to open his arms to her again. He couldn't let her know how she affected him. Show someone your vulnerability and they'd use it against you. "It's been a rough couple of days."

"Rougher for you than me. You've known about his condition longer."

The teariness still hung on her words. "Laura, you might want to reconsider seeing him tonight. It might be pretty grim."

She straightened her spine. "I won't fall apart."

He touched her arm, his fingers lingering on her skin despite himself. "Look, if just the tension from this morning caused—"

"Nausea? A few tears? I don't hold in my feelings. If they need to come out, I let them. Are you going to hold that against me?"

He dropped his hand and it clenched into a fist. "I'm only thinking of you."

"Really? Or do you want your face to be the first one Dad sees?"

"Don't be ridiculous!"

"Then don't worry about my well-being. Seeing him will be better than what my imagination cooks up." She went to the chair, shrugged into her poncho and picked up her book.

For a moment he'd felt protective of her. But it was clear she didn't want his protection although she had accepted his comfort. Until it wasn't comfortable. They didn't mix. She was as unpredictable as a shooting star. He was as predictable as a light bulb. She believed feelings should be expressed and shared. He'd found denying his feelings or keeping them to himself was safer.

Six weeks and she'd be gone. That would be best for everybody. Wouldn't it?

Chapter Four

Mitch stared at Laura as they stood by her father's bedside that evening. He was sure she was going to crumble in front of his eyes. She was as white as chalk, her gray eyes huge as she stroked her father's hand. Mitch could read the love and fear in her eyes. No matter what had happened in the past, at this moment she obviously cared about Ray a great deal. His heart went out to her because he felt the same helplessness she did.

He cupped her elbow and murmured, "Our time's up. He'll look better in the morning."

When she looked at Mitch, her eyes were blank, as if she hadn't understood.

"Let's go," he said gently.

She leaned over her father, kissed his cheek, then let Mitch lead her out. He guided her toward two chairs in the hall as he concentrated on the practical rather than the compassion for her creeping around his heart. "Do you need to sit down?"

She nodded. "My knees are a little wobbly." As she sank onto the orange vinyl chair, her gold triangle earrings swung. "He was so pale. And all the tubes... I guess it shocked me. I thought I'd be able to handle it."

She was so damned up-front with what she felt. No excuses. No apologies. How did she do it? Before he reconsidered, he took her hand. "That's why the doctor suggested we wait until tomorrow."

She looked at his hand. She looked into his eyes. "You're not going to say 'I told you so'?"

He couldn't prevent a smile. "Not this time."

"You think there will be others?"

"Absolutely," he replied with mock seriousness.

Instead of matching his attempt at levity, she asked, "You're not looking forward to the next six weeks, are you?"

No, he wasn't. She disturbed his world too much. Just the twist of her smile could make his pulse leap. It was crazy! He was feeling crazy because he wanted to hold her in his arms again like this morning. Ridiculous thought.

Evasiveness was his best bet. "The next six weeks will be difficult for Ray. We talked about rehabilitation before his surgery. He doesn't want to use the hospital's program. When he's ready, a nurse will come to the house three times a week. He wants to get a treadmill, bicycle and weights and use the basement as an exercise room."

"Exercise? After heart surgery?" She shoved her hair behind her ear as she thought about it.

Mitch believed Ray's recuperation depended on Laura's involvement and her understanding of what heart surgery entailed. "It's necessary. He can be in better shape than he ever was. I have some literature if you want to read it."

"I'd better." She bit her lower lip. "This is new to me. There's so much more involved than just the surgery. It's good you already talked about this with him."

"You know your father. He doesn't like surprises. He wanted everything planned out." That sad look was on her face again. But a moment later, it was gone and he thought he'd imagined it.

Laura stood. "I need fresh air. Let's go for a walk." She grabbed Mitch's hand and pulled him along the hall toward the waiting room and their coats.

He resisted. "Here?"

She slowed but didn't let go. "Afraid someone will mug you?"

The hospital was on the outskirts of the city, but York wasn't as safe as it used to be. He warned, "I don't take unnecessary chances."

"As long as we stay in well-lit areas, we'll be fine." She ran her eyes up and down his figure. "Besides, a mugger wouldn't touch you."

Her gaze on his body made him feel...hot. "What about you?"

She hurried him along. "I can run fast."

As they stepped outside, Mitch decided Laura was as much of a whirlwind as her daughter.

The hospital was spread out, the main section flanked by the outpatient clinic and office buildings. The fall-fragrant breeze wove around them as leaves crackled under their feet. Mitch inhaled, taking in the scent of wood smoke emanating from the circle of houses across from the hospital. They walked briskly in the lighted areas, up and down hills, along sidewalks, down macadam paths.

Suddenly Laura stopped and looked up at the stars. She took in a deep breath and let it out on a sigh. "Isn't this wonderful?"

"What?"

She waved at the stars and the moon. "The sky. I don't get a chance to do this often."

"Walk at night?"

"Um hmm. After Mandy goes to bed, I usually have a million things to do."

The moonlight turned Laura's hair into a golden halo as the nipping breeze tousled it. Her gray eyes sparkled with silver lights showing her enthusiasm and joy in life. Any minute he expected her to twirl in a circle like a little girl and let her poncho fly out around her. How long had it been since he'd known joy rather than responsibility? Responsibility for a father who couldn't care less about his younger son, responsibility for his mother so she didn't have to work so hard, responsibility for Carey who thought trouble was something to embrace rather than avoid.

When he'd met Denise, Mitch thought it was time for a stable relationship. And that's just what it had been—stable. Until Denise decided she wanted to get her doctorate. Their breakup hadn't been painless, but it hadn't been... heart-wrenching, either. Had they both been too removed, adult, practical? Had there been joy?

Laura stepped away from Mitch, away from the shadows of a tall maple into the moon's full light. "Do you ever wish on the moon?"

Her profile was perfect. It tugged at him as much as the fancy of her question. "I thought people wished on stars."

"The moon's bigger, closer, more touchable."

"That's not very scientific."

"Neither is wishing. But it works."

"You've studied this phenomenon, of course."

She glanced at him, her smile small and mysterious. "Of course. Wishes are like pictures you draw in your mind. They're always there whether you know it or not, just waiting to come to life. When you picture something, you can make it happen."

He regarded her, captivated by her philosophy and the little girl in her that often appeared. "So what are you wishing tonight, or can't you tell me?"

"Sure, I can tell you. Then you can wish it, too. Two wishes are more powerful than one." She stared up at the moon with enough intensity to brand her wish there permanently. "I wish Dad back on his feet, healthier than before."

"I'll second that."

She faced him with a mischievous grin. "See how easy it is? Even for skeptics."

"My life hasn't been what I wished. I have reason to be skeptical." He remembered the night when reality had taken over. He'd been five. If he hadn't overheard the argument, if he could have gone on pretending his father loved him . . .

"Maybe you just stopped wishing."

Sometimes she was damn clairvoyant. "Maybe." Unbidden, a vivid wish came to mind—his arms surrounding Laura, her legs entangled with his. If Laura's theory was right . . . "We'd better start back or Mandy will fall asleep again before we get home."

Laura gave him a measured look, then rubbed her arms under the wide poncho sleeves as she resumed walking. "Winter's trying to break through. I told George and Anne I'd call tonight. I'll have to ask them to send warmer clothes for us."

Mitch matched his pace to hers. "By the time you leave, there will probably be snow on the ground. You'd better tell them to send boots."

She stuffed her hands in her pockets. "And gloves. Lord, they'll have to go through all my drawers to find them," she muttered.

"That doesn't bother you?" Privacy was all-important to him.

"No. They're my family. They accept who and what I am and would never invade my space to hurt me. I thought you understood that they're like a brother and sister to me."

"I understand that. It's just . . ."

She tilted her face up. "What?"

"Carey went through my belongings without regard to my privacy when we were growing up. He knew it bothered me, so he did it as often as possible." He had never shared that with anyone.

"Kids are like that."

"He was older and should have known better. But he never did care much what others thought."

"You sound bitter."

If she had been judgmental or critical, he would have shut up. But her acceptance led him to ask, "Do I? I thought I'd left my childhood behind. It pops up when I least expect it."

"You and your brother don't get along?"

"It's not a matter of getting along." He knew he was being curt, but to keep the past in the past he had to dismiss it rather than think or talk about it.

After a short silence, Laura asked, "What do you do to relax?"

"Relax?"

"Yeah. You know, when you wear jeans and do something that makes you forget everything else. You *do* own a pair of jeans, don't you?" The question definitely held criticism if he didn't.

"Of course, I do. More than one." The defensiveness in his voice irritated him.

"And what do you do when you have them on?" she probed with a sideways glance.

"Wash the car, run errands, sketch."

"That sounds like work to me," she scolded. "What about roller-skating, tobogganing, dancing, tag?"

"Tag?" He zippered his leather jacket and wondered if he was trying to insulate himself from the weather or her interest.

"Mandy loves when I chase her around the yard, roll in the grass, jump in the leaves."

He could see her and her daughter doing just that. Uninhibited, playful, laughing. God! Had he ever felt like that? Was this the part of Laura that called to him like the Sirens' ancient song? "Having a child around helps you relax."

"I'd make time for it even if I didn't have Mandy." She spared him another quick look. "You should try it."

"I don't have time—"

"Hogwash." She waved her hands and said vehemently, "That's what my dad always said. And look where it got him. You're still young enough to learn."

Relaxing wasn't on his priority list. Designing brought him pleasure, the business a sense of achievement. He told himself he didn't need anything else. "You can't teach an old dog new tricks."

"Maybe not. But you can teach an old dog different tricks. Besides, you're nowhere near being old."

"Thirty-six isn't young."

"Like you told your mother, you're only as old as you think you are," she repeated smugly.

He felt like he was trying to beat off a lion with a toothpick. "Don't you miss anything?"

Her smile was pure deviltry. "Not much. C'mon. I'll race you to the front of the building."

She sprinted off and left him standing. He stared after her and moments later overtook her, his legs pumping easily, his arms swinging in cadence with his stride. When she arrived at the portico, panting, he casually crossed one ankle over the other, propped against the brick wall, and suppressed a grin. "You fell a little behind."

She leaned against the wall only a few inches from him. "My poncho kept tangling in my legs."

He clicked his tongue and shook his head. "Excuses, excuses."

She wrinkled her nose at him and jabbed him in the ribs with her elbow. "We did it for fun. Not to see who'd win."

She was so close, her hair mussed, her face flushed. He was sure she'd look like this after making love—glowing, vibrant, her hair jumbled from his fingers, her skin pink and damp from kissing and arousal. Her breaths were still coming fast. Her scent mingled with the night air and radiated from her with the heat of their run. He turned toward her and propped his hand on the wall above her shoulder. "Was it fun?"

Her eyes dropped to his lips and her voice was low. "Sure. The wind in my face, the release of energy, the moon streaking through the leaves..."

If he leaned any closer, their bodies would touch. Desire stirred and pulsed its demand. When her tongue sneaked out and wet her bottom lip, he almost groaned. Her pupils were dark, almost overtaking the gray. If he merely touched her cheek...

Laura was afraid to move when Mitch's fingers brushed her cheek. Every nerve vibrated and hot feelings blazed through her. She forgot Mitch wasn't her type. She wanted him to kiss her more than she wanted to breathe. She wanted to teach him how to enjoy everyday pleasures, to look for excitement. She was excited now. And scared. If a relationship developed between them, it would be complicated by her father, Mitch's perceptions about her, her six-week stay. But it felt so good to be attracted to Mitch, to experience the thrill of arousal, to want to touch a man again and have him touch her.

The sliding glass doors to the visitors' entrance whirred open. Mitch stepped back and away. Laura's disappointment plunged deep, shaking her. She was feeling too much, too fast. She wasn't a teenager any longer, she was a rational adult.

So was Mitch. The problem was he acted like it, she thought, as he pulled himself up straight and tall, his eyes denying the closeness they'd just experienced.

Nora and Mandy were building a bridge with wooden blocks when Mitch and Laura returned to the house. As soon as they walked into the kitchen, Nora asked, "How is he?"

Her worry for Ray touched Laura. It seemed to be more than concern for a stranger and she wondered again how well Nora knew her father. "He's doing as well as can be expected." The lump in her throat threatened to bring tears to her eyes. Before it could, she hugged her daughter and tickled her.

Mandy giggled. "Don't, Mommy. My bridge will fall down."

Mitch came around to Mandy's other side, turned the chair beside her around and straddled the seat, his arms crossed on the top rung. He studied every angle of the structure. "It's a sturdy bridge. You and Mom do good work. Maybe when you grow up, you can build real bridges."

So…something else learned about Mitch, Laura thought. He wasn't a chauvinist and didn't believe in prescribed roles for men and women. Interesting.

Mandy shook her head. "I want to be a ballerina."

"This week," Laura mumbled. "Last week she wanted to be an animal doctor."

Nora rose and stepped away from the table. "Mitch, why don't you help Mandy build a tower while I talk to Laura."

His brows lifted but he didn't comment.

Curiously, Laura followed Nora to the living room. She asked immediately, "Is something wrong? I'm sorry we weren't back sooner. If you want to go home now—"

Nora's fingers moved nervously. She sat on the edge of the sofa, looking hesitant to speak her mind. "I don't want to go home. I...I mean...today and yesterday I felt...useful again. The kids at the day-care center are always glad to see me but that's just a few hours two days a week. Since I stopped working, I have a lot of time on my hands. Mitch doesn't want me to work but he doesn't understand."

From the little Mitch had said, Laura guessed Nora had had a hard life and he wanted to make it as easy for her as he could now. She admired him for that, but she also realized he wasn't tuned in to his mother's feelings.

Laura parked next to Nora. "You want to feel like you make a difference."

Nora's blue eyes found Laura's. "Exactly."

Laura was puzzled. "But why did you want to talk to me about this?"

"Because I like taking care of Mandy and I think she's already fond of me. What are you going to do with her when you're helping at the store?"

Laura finally understood Nora's earnestness and what she had in mind. "Truthfully, I haven't thought about it. I don't want to put her in day care." To find out exactly what Nora was thinking, she added, "I guess I could take her with me."

"The poor little tyke will get so bored," Nora blurted out. "Let me stay here and take care of her. I can cook the meals and take care of details so you can keep your mind on your dad and the store and have time for Mandy when you get home." She rushed on. "Have you thought about what you're going to do when Ray comes home? Someone will have to stay with him for a while. If I'm here with Mandy, I can look after both of them."

Laura leaned against the sofa back. "Do you know what you're thinking about? Taking care of a four-year-old is hard enough, but Dad could be very demanding."

"He just needs some tender loving care." Quickly, she added, "Not that you can't give it to him, of course."

Nora's cheeks were pink, her eyes bright. Laura smiled. Did Nora have an interest in Ray? If so, did Mitch know? "So you'd like to stay here and take on the monumental job of taking care of all of us?"

"Yes, I'd like to do that."

"Does Mitch know about this?" He could be one very tall obstacle, though she didn't believe Mitch could refuse his mother anything.

"No. I wanted to talk to you first."

How would Mitch feel about his mother working for Ray Applegate? "When Dad's feeling better, I'll have to ask him what he's willing to pay."

Nora held up her hand like a stop sign. "No, I don't want money. I've offered—"

"If we can't pay you, we can't accept your help." Laura was sure her father would feel the same way.

Nora looked indecisive, but only for a moment. "All right. But whatever you and Ray decide will be fine."

Laura patted the older woman's hand. "It's a deal. But I'm going to disappear while you tell Mitch. Mandy and I will go upstairs to call our friends in Ohio, then I'll read to her for a while."

Nora rose with a broad smile. "What time would you like breakfast tomorrow?"

Laura chuckled. "This is going to take getting used to. I'll help you as much as I can."

"If I'm getting paid, there's no need."

Laura felt drawn to Nora. She'd always missed the influence of an older woman in her life. "We'll work together. You're not simply hired help. Okay?"

Nora seemed pleased. "If that's what you want."

Mitch was waiting for Laura as she descended the steps. Her eyes landed on the stern line of his jaw. It was so firm, masculine, unyielding. His strong neck and broad shoulders formed similar uncompromising lines.

He spoke before she reached the bottom step. "You didn't have to agree to let her work here. I suggested she sit with Mandy, not take on the care of everyone."

Laura had guessed Nora's decision would meet with Mitch's disapproval; his brooding eyes and tone proved it. "No, I didn't have to agree, but your mother is the answer to a prayer. Mandy likes her, so I won't feel so guilty when I'm at the store. Besides, I think Nora needs to be needed."

He rested his long-fingered hand on the finial-styled newel post and propped one loafer on the first step. "Maybe you're rationalizing to get what you want."

She stopped to confront the issue straight on. "And maybe you can't see the forest for the trees. Retirement doesn't agree with everyone."

He aligned his gaze to hers. "I want my mother to finally have the opportunity to rest and do what she wants to do."

"Right now, she wants to take care of us. I won't let her overdo, Mitch." She gave him a sly smile and came down another step. "And I'm sure you won't, either. We'll both be under your close scrutiny."

He seemed surprised his intentions were so obvious. His foot dropped to the foyer floor. "I protect the people I care about."

For a moment she wanted to be one of those people. She wanted to feel his protection, know she didn't have to carry life's burdens alone, and could count on his strength to support her. He had strength, not only physical strength but strength of character. That was one of the qualities that attracted her to him.

"They have nothing to fear from me," she assured him.

"Time will tell." He mowed his hand through his hair. "I don't know what Ray's going to say about my mother being here."

Laura was disappointed he was still suspicious of her. "He'll be thankful it's Nora rather than a stranger invading his house."

Mitch thought about it. "You're probably right."

The doorbell rang and Mitch said automatically, "I'll get it."

When he opened the door, she saw his back stiffen and heard, "Carey. We didn't expect you until next week."

Mitch's brother stepped inside and appraised the foyer with obvious interest. His hair was dark brown, thick and shaggy. It hung over his ears and across his collar. His brown eyes gleamed with mischief and his smile had the ability to charm. His jeans sported holes in the knees, the hightop sneakers were loosely tied, his red-and-navy striped shirt was long and stuck out from underneath his black leather jacket trimmed with silver buckles. Laura knew Mitch would never be caught dead in an outfit like that, let alone with the earring dangling from Carey's right ear.

She descended the remaining steps. Carey eyed her thoroughly. Mitch's mouth drew into a taut line. There was something uncomfortable between the two brothers. She could feel it.

Carey said to Mitch. "Introduce me to your pretty lady friend."

Laura crossed to Carey and extended her hand. "No introductions are necessary. I'm Laura Sanders and you're Mitch's brother Carey."

"Damned straight. I've been Mitch's brother for a long stretch." He grinned. "Along with a few other things."

Mitch said offhandedly, "Mom said you weren't coming until next week."

Carey unzipped his jacket, shook it off and threw it over his arm. "I tied up loose ends before I thought I could."

"How did you know we were here?" Mitch asked, watching his brother carefully.

"I didn't know *you* were here. Mom's neighbor told me she came here to take care of a little girl."

"My daughter, Mandy," Laura intervened. "Nora's helping us out of a tight spot."

"Why did you come to York?" Mitch asked briskly, as if he wanted to get bad news settled quickly.

"I was concerned about Mom."

"Sure you were. That's why we haven't heard from you in seven months. It was a postcard from Virginia Beach if I remember correctly."

"I don't live my life like you do. Checking in isn't my style. You should know that by now."

"Checking in would make life easier for Mom. Have you considered that?"

Instead of waiting for the thunder to clap and the lightning to strike, Laura cleared her throat to defuse the tension. "I'll bet Nora can't wait to see you, Carey. Go on into the living room. Would you like something to drink? Coffee, tea, hot chocolate?"

His brown eyes twinkled and his lips formed an engaging grin. "Hot chocolate with a dash of brandy or bourbon would be great if you have it."

"You're pushing it, Carey." Mitch didn't follow his brother as Carey moved toward the room to which Laura had pointed.

"Just stating what I like. But if it's too much trouble, hot chocolate's fine."

Laura wondered what was behind Mitch's anger and why Carey felt the need to goad him. She'd always wanted a brother or sister to feel close to. "It's no trouble. Dad used to keep a stocked bar. I'll check. You go make yourself comfortable."

Laura walked slowly down the hall to the den. She stopped in the doorway, remembering the last time the oak-paneled walls had surrounded her. That night she'd gone from the heights of joy to the depths of betrayal. And then her father had given her the ultimatum. Choose a partnership with him or a life with the man she loved.

Shaking off the memory, she crossed to the liquor cabinet. She stooped over and the hairs at the nape of her neck pricked. Without glancing up, she knew Mitch had entered the room. Brandy in hand, she met his blue gaze.

"That's not necessary."

"Is that your decision or your brother's?" she asked quietly.

"Carey hasn't always made the best decisions."

There was real regret in his voice, and sadness. Her gaze traveled from his black hair to his forehead, his mesmerizing eyes, the long scar, his sensuous lips. "Does he have a problem with alcohol?"

Mitch glanced away and she realized he'd been regarding her as intently as she'd regarded him. "He says he doesn't."

She knew she was poking and he might tell her to butt out any second. One thing she'd learned was that he was a private person. So instead of following the inclination to move closer to him, she stayed where she was so she wasn't crowding him physically as well as emotionally. "You don't believe him."

Mitch picked up the letter opener on the desk, balanced it on his finger, then set it down. "I've seen him drunk."

"That doesn't mean he's an alcoholic."

He glowered at her. "You sound like Mom."

"If you're worried about him, why don't you talk to him?"

"I'm not worried. I learned long ago worry doesn't help with Carey."

Exasperated, she couldn't control her voice when it rose. "For God's sake, Mitch, stop pretending you're made of stone."

Silence stretched across the room until he said, "Maybe I am."

The softness of his statement jarred her. The urge to shake him, to make him drop his stoic facade was too determined to ignore. She was still disappointed he hadn't kissed her earlier at the hospital. Angrier still that on the ride home he'd pretended it hadn't almost happened. He was certainly in control of his on-off switch and she wanted to rattle him.

Slowly, she approached him, stopping only when the toes of her shoes touched his. She stood there silently, her eyes fastened to his, her awareness of his breathing somehow controlling hers. Energy, so palpable she could touch it, zipped back and forth. He didn't blink when she raised her hand, nor did he try to stop her. Gently, she let the pad of her forefinger rest on the tip of his scar. His chest rose and fell faster but he remained motionless, expressionless. With tender care she traced the rosy brown mark to his jawline. His skin was firm, taut, hot to the touch. Was it always that hot? Or did standing close to her like this have something to do with it?

A hint of beard shadow teased her finger as she let it linger. His eyes blazed with an inner fire, belying his frozen stance, and she knew if she got too close, she'd melt.

"You're not made of stone, Mitch." She moved her hand from his jaw to his chest and let it lie over his thumping heart. "In here, you feel as much as I do. You love your mother. You're fond of my father. And I've seen you play with Mandy and enjoy every minute."

He clamped his fingers around her wrist and lifted her hand from his chest. "Don't try to manipulate me."

She'd never been more aware of another human being, of the feel of his fingers on her skin, the hardness of his chest, the heat penetrating his Oxford shirt, his scent that reminded her of dusky night. And she felt something she couldn't name. A feeling that was exciting but uncomfortable, too.

So uncomfortable, her reply was shakier than she'd like it to be. "I'm not. I'm just trying to show you you're the same as the rest of us."

He dropped her hand as if the last thing he wanted to do was touch her. "I don't play games, Laura."

"I think you do," she challenged, not allowing the erotic sensations he invoked or a nameless sensation influence her to back down. "You play a game with yourself. If you pretend you don't feel something, then you think you don't. It's a no-win game."

Mitch tore his gaze from hers and moved quickly toward the door. "I'll go start the hot chocolate. Don't forget to close the liquor cabinet. You wouldn't want Mandy exploring it."

As soon as Mitch stepped into the kitchen, he stopped and drew in a heavy breath. What was wrong with him? When Laura touched him, he felt as if he could explode into a million pieces. He always responded to life's challenges with his head, and his head controlled his body. Usually. But not around Laura Applegate Sanders. She messed up his head and aroused his body. He was still experiencing it. The softness of her fingers on his cheek, the imprint of her hand on his chest remained.

He hated feeling vulnerable. It was a feeling he'd avoided in the last decade. He remembered the first time he'd experienced vulnerability. He'd only been five years old, too young to understand his father's black moods occurred after he'd been drinking. One night he'd heard his mother and father arguing. Carey had been sound asleep, but Mitch had snuck out of bed.

His mother was upset. He heard her say, "They called again today. If we don't give them some money this month, they're going to turn off the electricity. The landlord's having a fit because we're two months behind in rent. Mitch needs clothes to start school—"

His father's fist had come down hard on the table. "If you'd done what you were supposed to, we wouldn't have a second kid to worry about. Maybe we should give him to the state and let them put him in a foster home."

Tears had streamed down his mother's face. "Never. I love Mitch as much as Carey. And I'm going to keep my family together. If you'd stop drinking and gambling our money away, we could pay our bills!"

"I still say one less mouth to feed would help better than anything."

Mitch had crept back to bed, a horrid, miserable weight making it hard to swallow and breathe. His father didn't want him. He'd never wanted him. And this man had the power to send Mitch away. Mitch remembered crawling into his bed, curling himself into a ball and shaking with fear. But the fear had transformed into determination and a promise to himself and his mother. He would never give his father reason to get rid of him. He'd be good and quiet, and as soon as he was able, he'd get a job. And some day, he'd take care of his mother so she didn't have to worry about paying the bills or having enough money.

He'd kept his promise for the most part. There were a few times when he couldn't stand hearing his father verbally abuse his mother and he'd come to her defense. But other than that, he'd stayed out of his father's way. Carey had gotten into enough trouble for both of them. But then,

Carey never had to worry about being sent away or not being loved. In their father's eyes, Carey could do no wrong. When he'd stolen a car for a joyride when he was fourteen, Sam Riley had excused his son's behavior, saying it was pure male fun. Right. Even Mitch was guilty of saving Carey from the consequences of his actions to protect their mother. No more. It was time for Carey to realize he needed more than charm to get through life.

Mitch took a saucepan from a bottom cabinet and slammed the door. As he opened the refrigerator to find the milk, Laura entered the kitchen and from her expression he knew he'd better get his armor in place fast.

Chapter Five

"Your mom said she'd like hot chocolate, too." Laura removed four mugs from the wooden tree.

"I can take care of this," Mitch said. Acting casual seemed to be the best way to go.

"Or I can do it, and you can visit with Carey."

Casual went out the window. "Stay out of it, okay?"

Laura took cocoa from an upper cupboard. "I have plenty to do keeping my nose in my own affairs. But whoever is in this house is my concern, too. Carey said he doesn't know how long he's staying."

"Long enough to get what he wants." At Laura's arched brow, Mitch poured milk into the saucepan. "About nine months ago, Carey came home and said he might stay if he could find a decent job. Mom was ecstatic. He didn't look for a job. He found as many poker games as he could and managed to gamble away Mom's social security check.

She'd given it to him so he could put a deposit on an apartment."

"He didn't pay her back?"

Mitch gave a humorless laugh. "Are you kidding? He apologized, then told her he was meeting a friend in Virginia. They were going to discuss going into business together. Like always, she forgave him and wished him luck."

Laura used the tip of a spoon to flip the lid from the cocoa. "What did you want her to do?"

Mitch sighed. "I don't know. But at least hold him responsible for the money. I warned her not to lend it to him."

"You've lent him money?"

One thing he'd learned about Laura. She was as persistent as a tornado sweeping through Kansas. "More than I care to count. And he's never paid it back. So I don't do it anymore. But Mom's so gullible...."

"She loves him."

Mitch stirred the milk with a wooden spatula, more for something to do than because it needed stirring. "Love doesn't excuse mistakes."

"No, but it accepts them. You wouldn't love your mother like you do if she were any different. I believe it's a parent's job to love unconditionally."

His eyes buckled to hers. "And it's the child's job not to abuse that love."

"I wonder what your definition of abuse is. I owe my father respect, but not my life."

"I thought we were speaking about Carey."

She planted her hands on her hips. "Hah. That comment was directed at me, too."

"If you feel you did the right thing, why are you so defensive?"

"You make me feel defensive. And we *were* talking about you and Carey."

He looked away. "I'd rather not."

"Obviously," she muttered.

"I don't want to argue with you, Laura."

"Of course not. You want everything your way. Just like my father." She spooned cocoa into one mug after the other.

He was about to repudiate her statement when she swung toward him and extended her hand. "Let's call a truce. At least for tonight. Nora's glad to have both her sons with her."

"Carey and I are like oil and water."

"You don't have to mix. Simply be sociable."

He felt a smile coming on despite the tension between them. She was one little minx. "I think somebody else wants *her* own way."

She grinned. "Could be you're right."

His hand engulfed hers. As soon as their skin touched, heat zipped down his spine. Involuntarily, his thumb caressed the side of her hand, noting its silky skin, its tiny indentations, its warmth. "A truce. Maybe it will last longer than tonight."

"I doubt it. I want you to take me to the store tomorrow and show me the ropes. If you won't, I'll learn them myself."

When he would have pulled his hand away, she gripped it tighter. "Truce still on for tonight?"

She could challenge and defy him in one breath and turn sweet as honey in the next. Lord, was she good! He'd have to be better. "All right. The truce is still on for tonight."

He pulled his hand back slowly. The branding contact of her touch told him he had to be careful. Very careful. Or he could lose more than his investment in Ray's business.

The store was traditional, conservative, like a thousand other jewelry stores Laura had entered over the years. Somehow, she thought it would have changed since Mitch had become her father's partner.

She felt Mitch's eyes on her and sensed he was waiting for a comment. He hadn't worn a coat and the fullness of muscle beneath his blue cable-knit sweater was as attention-drawing as anything in the store. With an effort, she kept her mind on business.

Glancing at the imported crystal and porcelain, the cases separated by gem types, solid gold, and more functional pieces like watches, she said, "It hasn't changed."

He raised his chin defensively. "The jewelry business is stable."

"There are trends that can raise sales." She picked up a Lladro figurine and reverently caressed the blue-gray dress of the collector's item.

"And when trends quit, we're left with inventory that doesn't sell."

Carefully, she set the slender woman onto the glass display shelf. "The Harrisburg store has the same merchandise?"

"No. But my clientele is different."

He thought of the store as his. Did her father think of it that way, too? She faced him squarely. "How is it different?"

"I do have some of the most recent designs," he admitted. "State senators and representatives want the latest fashions for their wives. We have hordes of state workers who window-shop on their lunch hour, see something they like and stop in. But I have my share of traditionalists, too."

As Laura passed along the cases, Mitch introduced her to the assistant manager. Laura smiled and said, "It will be a pleasure working with you."

Sonya Harrison, blond, slender and at least five foot ten, wore enough jewelry to decorate Manhattan for Christmas. Her smile was brittle. "Mitch said you'd be here six weeks."

Laura looked directly into her eyes and tried to assure her her position wasn't in jeopardy. "I want to help you run the store smoothly until Dad returns. There won't be any major changes and I'll probably be in the office more often than on the floor with you."

"I thought Mitch was in charge."

This wasn't going to be easy on any front. "I hope to take some of the burden from Mitch so he can concentrate on the Harrisburg store and his exhibition. I've worked in the jewelry business on my own for six years, Sonya. I've been around it all my life. Of course, if I have questions, I'll check with Mitch. But I'm sure you and I can handle the daily routine without bothering him. Don't you?"

"I guess." The blonde's brown eyes sought Mitch's.

He was absorbing the exchange patiently as if taking bets with himself on how it would go. He nodded. "Laura will be working with you. I'll have the final word."

He asserted a quiet authority that challenged Laura to make unilateral decisions. If she did, there'd be hell to pay. But she'd learned in the past paying the devil was better than losing her self-respect. She unbuttoned her poncho, shrugged it off and slung it over her arm. "I imagine my father will have the final word when he's able. I'm going to toss my coat into the office, then look around the store more closely to get a feel for the merchandise. Or would you prefer to show me the record-keeping setup first?"

Mitch's face was impassive. "Take your time. I have work to do. The more you understand what we display, the more of it you'll be able to sell." He headed for the office.

Laura's temperature rose. He'd better learn right now she was going to be more than a glorified salesclerk. If her father wanted that, he could hire someone temporarily and Laura could stay at the house with Mandy. She followed Mitch, ready to do battle.

He had flicked on the computer. When he heard her step into the office, the flap of her coat falling onto a wooden surface, he parked in the swivel chair and faced her. "Do you think we should hire someone to help with repairs and sizing? Ray was doing all of that here.''

''You're asking *my* opinion?''

Mitch rubbed his hand across the back of his neck as if he was tired. "Laura, put your hackles down. I'm hoping you can be of help. But I do have the final say. Now can we co-operate on that level?''

Suddenly she realized how much responsibility was resting on his shoulders. He didn't complain about it, he simply took care of it. That was nice. Doug had made decisions but procrastinated when it was one he didn't want to deal with or when it interfered with life's more exciting dimensions. She'd taken care of details like calling the plumber and getting the cars repaired. Mitch wouldn't shove off on someone else something he didn't want to do.

''I'd rather cooperate than lock horns. You have a stubborn streak three miles wide.'' *And an unnerving effect on me.*

She thought he'd be irritated, but his lips twitched. "And you don't?''

She suppressed a grin. "Of course not. I simply have a mind of my own.''

Before he could make a smart comeback, she asked, "Would it be easier to send repairs to an independent?''

The depth and changing moods of his eyes fascinated her as he gave the idea some thought. "If it wasn't the Christmas season, I'd take them to the Harrisburg store. But we're backed up as it is and it will only get worse.''

Laura looked at Mitch's face, admiring its planes and angles…its character. "Dad knew a Mr. Johnson who had his own store in the east end. Maybe he'd help us.''

''He retired last year. But he might be bored by now. I'll call him. That's a good suggestion.''

She beamed. Mitch's approval was important to her. She didn't want it to be, but it was. And as before, when she thought about her reaction to him, she felt a wave of an elusive emotion. She couldn't put her finger on it yet, but it made her uncomfortable. It was unusual for her not to be able to pinpoint her emotions. That only added to her unease.

She lifted her hand in an "I'll be back" wave and quickly went into the store area.

The whisper of Laura's slacks as she walked tempted Mitch to watch her leave. Since when had his hearing picked up a sound that soft? He sank back into the chair and stretched his legs out in front of him, staring at his toes instead. Was Mrs. Sanders good-intentioned or sly? A well-meaning meddler or a manipulator? Somehow, she seemed to turn every situation to her advantage. That nettled him. Because he didn't always come out on top? On top. Damn, would he like to...

He slapped his hand on the chair's arm so hard his palm stung. More than once this morning he'd had to direct his attention away from the rise and fall of Laura's breasts under the fuchsia and turquoise sweater. The turquoise wool slacks had pleats and plenty of material but still managed to show her curves too well.

And that hair. It seemed to draw the sunlight to it, making her complexion as delicate as the porcelain in the store. So was he upset with her because she could look fabulous in a brown gunnysack or because he couldn't keep his mind from picturing what was underneath? Both. He'd even taken a wrong turn driving to the store.

"Distraction, thy name is Laura," he muttered tersely.

It wasn't simply her looks. It was something more basic. Something about her personality that made him feel he lacked...he wasn't sure what. But something vital. Emotions stirred, alarming him because they were unfamiliar.

He pulled his legs in and sat up straight. He wanted to keep a careful distance from her because he still didn't know if he could depend on anything she said or did. He had to protect Ray. He had to protect his own investment. He had to protect more than that. When he was close to her, he couldn't think straight. He wanted to kiss her.

Sheer craziness, Riley. Keep alert. Track what she says and does. Examine her motives. Call her on her mistakes. And never underestimate her. That could be fatal.

With a cautious look, Sonya had given Laura the keys to the display cases. Perusing each one, she glanced up with a ready smile when a customer came into the store. She felt at home in this environment, sure of herself. Handling the gold, watching its buttery glow under the lights and the sparkle of precious gems thrilled her. She saved the case with the sapphires for last because she enjoyed them the most.

She lifted out a velvet tray and stared at the rings with longing. Jewelry was beautiful, but she loved handling it more than owning it. Except for the sapphires. Sometime, when Mandy was older, their finances in good shape...

Choosing a ring with fifteen, deep brilliant-cut sapphires in an S shape, she slipped it on her finger. Too big for the fourth digit, she switched it to the middle finger and pushed it on. It was tight but splendid.

She jumped when a voice behind her asked, "Sampling the inventory?"

Mitch's chin almost touched her shoulder as he leaned toward her. The hairs on her neck stood at attention. Oh, Lord. Every time he got this close, she felt like jumping out of her skin. She was quickly discovering Mitch wasn't a "type." Mitch was Mitch. How she ever had the audacity to approach him the way she had last night, she'd never know.

Gulping in a draft of air, she blurted, "Wouldn't I like to! Sapphires are the most mysterious yet the most practical. Can you imagine them surrounding a blue topaz? The Caribbean surrounded by midnight sky."

He seemed surprised by her suggestion. "Maybe you should think about designing."

She shook her head and backed away a few inches. "No, I don't have the imagination. I just know what I like. And I like this ring too much to wear it any longer."

When she tried to slip it off, it wouldn't budge. She gave Mitch a sheepish smile. "I might have to keep it."

His long stare judged her before his words. "Don't you think before you act? We always size a customer before we try to slip a ring on her finger. You should know better."

She twisted the ring around but only succeeded in making her finger red and swollen. "I get excited around jewelry. I merely wanted to see how it looked."

"Well, now you see. And now it's stuck. How inconvenient."

They'd been friendly in the office. Sort of. What had happened to make him suspicious again? Doubts and misconceptions shadowed his eyes. Did he think she'd keep the ring? That she'd done this on purpose? Wise enough to know nothing she could say would change his mind, she decided only her actions in the next six weeks would prove she could be trusted, that she wouldn't manipulate him or the circumstances for her own benefit.

"This isn't a major catastrophe, Mitch. Don't you keep lotion nearby for situations like this?"

"I've never had to—"

She pointed to the shelf below the cash register. "Maybe Sonya does. That looks like lotion."

With a speculative look, he stooped to retrieve the plastic bottle and handed it to her.

Laura squeezed a small dab of the pink liquid into her palm, applied it to her finger, gave the ring a twist and slid it off.

Her gaze and Mitch's caught, and his expression shook her. There was primordial desire there that stopped her breath because she felt it, too. But she could see he resented feeling it and that made him sharp. "I know you're an intelligent woman, Laura. But from what I've heard, your judgment takes second place to your impetuous nature."

Her patience melted like a snowflake on a hot iron. "Have you always lived your life with a step-by-step plan? Hasn't anything ever thrown it off?"

"My father's binges threw it off plenty. So did Carey's escapades. But I always managed to get it back on track."

She heard pride, but she also heard grief. She hadn't meant to remind him of days better forgotten. The sadness on his face squeezed her heart until she felt it, too. She wanted to wrap her arms around him and make it go away.

Softly, she said, "Being on track doesn't have to mean being bored, or not having fun."

"I've never been bored."

"Have you ever had fun?"

"Of course."

"When?"

His eyes were shuttered to keep her from seeing too much. "My first ride on a roller coaster."

"That's it?"

"Of course not."

"Well? What else?"

He gave her a menacing look but answered her question. "Horseback riding."

"And how long's it been since you've done that?"

"Laura—"

"How long?"

He riffled his hand through his hair. "About two years."

She shook her head in exasperation. "Do you have fun at Christmas?"

"It's pleasant."

"What do you do?"

He appeared ready to wring her neck as he stepped closer. "Last year Mom made dinner and your dad joined us."

He smelled of wind and fall and everything basic, earthy and male. Curiosity pushed her to keep at him. "Did you sing carols, trim a tree, play in the snow?"

"We're adults, Laura. We ate dinner and spent time talking. The inquisition is now over. My free time isn't the issue, your judgment is. Make sure you use it wisely when you're in this store."

She saluted sharply. "Yes, sir. As soon as I wipe off this ring and put it away, you can introduce me to your records. If the record-keeping is as rigid as your life, it'll be simple to learn."

He gripped her elbow firmly. "Laura..."

She gazed down at his fingers—long fingers that were stern yet gentle as if he was afraid she'd snap if he pressed too hard. Knowing she was dabbling with the dangerous but unable to resist, she flashed him a smile as dazzling as the sapphire ring on her hand. "Careful. Sonya's watching. We wouldn't want to start any rumors, would we?"

His answer was a fake smile as he glanced at the assistant manager and released Laura's arm. "The bookkeeping is black and white, honest and not open to misinterpretation. Maybe you can learn something from it."

As clearly as she knew her name, Laura realized nothing would be easy with Mitch—not work, not the subject of her father, not the time they'd spend together. They were attracted to each other, fighting it, neither of them knowing exactly why. This might be the most interesting six weeks of her life.

Saturday morning Laura frowned at the computer screen. She'd become familiar with the numbers, the lists, the inventory. She'd analyzed the projected sales for December, also looking at profits for the year at both stores. She was surprised at what she'd found. The York store was falling behind. It was making a profit but not like Harrisburg. Automatically she'd asked herself what to do about it.

Watching the clientele had helped. They were older, steady customers who'd been coming to the store for years. She'd also examined the Christmas ad campaign—what there was of it. That was another problem. She'd bet that sapphire ring out there that Mitch's ad campaign included special publicity about his exhibition and brought in all age groups. She'd also bet his ads were more comprehensive year-round. Had he looked at the differences in profit margins? Had he discussed sales techniques with her dad?

Ideas began clicking. November and December were the months to pick up new customers. If the store offered something unique, a service—Ladies' night, Men's night, a new line to pique interest.... She'd have to talk to Mitch about it with a clear head, without being distracted by the tension between them.

"Are you ready?" Mitch asked, sticking his head into the office.

Sure, not be distracted. Fat chance when his voice echoed through her and his appearance accelerated her heart rate. "Did Dad call?"

"Yep. He can't wait to get home. Discharge papers are signed. He just needs our chauffeur service." Mitch's smile was free and wide. Ray's recovery meant a lot to him.

Laura was concerned. "He seemed anxious last night. As if he's afraid to come home. But he insisted he didn't want a private duty nurse."

Mitch's smile faded but his expression was still relaxed. "I think he's more concerned he won't recover as fast as he wants to. He was delighted by Mandy's visit."

"She's a little afraid of him."

Mitch shrugged. "He's a stranger."

Laura switched off the computer and stood. "So were you, but that didn't stop her from being curious and friendly."

"What do you think the problem is? Maybe it was the hospital setting."

"I hope that's all. Sometimes I feel like I'm watching her too carefully, looking for signs of withdrawal again. If she misses George and Anne too much, we might have to— Never mind. I'm worrying too much."

"I've heard that's a parent's prerogative." A partial smile chased away Mitch's seriousness.

Laura crossed to the old-fashioned clothes rack and took her poncho from a hook, trying not to be apprehensive about bringing her father home. They hadn't been together in that house for six years.

"What's wrong?"

For someone who seemed to close off his feelings, Mitch certainly was aware of hers. She suspected he was still analyzing her—or at least attempting to. If she evaded him, he'd think she was hiding something.

She groped for an explanation that wouldn't put disapproval back in his eyes, but gave it up when she found gaining approval and being honest didn't always go together. Slipping on the poncho, she said, "Dad's not easy to live with under the best of terms." When Mitch started to speak, she stopped him. "You asked me what was wrong. I'm worried. I don't want to upset him. But just being in the house with him brings back memories, some I'd rather forget. He and I have to establish a new relationship. I'm not sure either of us is ready for it."

Mitch stuffed his hands in his front trouser pockets. "Can I say something now?"

"Not if you're going to tell me I'm the one who has to make all the concessions." She stood silently waiting.

His blue eyes darkened and she couldn't understand their message. It didn't seem to matter because he turned his back on her. "Let's go."

As Mitch helped her father into his house, Laura felt like crying. She should have realized she'd be a fifth wheel. The only time her father had paid attention to her after her mother died was when she'd gotten into trouble. He'd thought grounding or cutting off her allowance or forbidding her to see her friends would solve the problems. He'd never realized she wanted his love, his time and his attention.

Why should he be any different just because he'd had bypass surgery? While she was growing up, he'd used his work to close her out. Now he could use Mitch and the years in which they hadn't talked to keep her at a distance. Was she wrong not to have made further attempts to resolve their differences? Possibly. But her letters had been returned unopened the first year. It had hurt too much to be rejected over and over.

Her father had looked to Mitch at the hospital to help him into the wheelchair, to pick up the suitcase, to drive him home. Laura had sat in the back seat, trying to make conversation, but not doing much better than the weather, something they had thoroughly discussed on each of her visits.

Nora met them at the door and ushered Ray into the living room, motioning toward the wing chair. "Would you like to go to your room and rest? I'll bring lunch up to you. Mitch and I discussed the diet your doctor gave you. I made chicken salad with low-fat dressing."

Ray gave Nora a wan smile. "To keep you from running up and down the stairs, I think I'll stay in the housekeeper's quarters." He looked at Mitch. "The sofa in there opens up. Could you sleep there a few nights in case I need something?''

Laura could see her father was scared and uncertain about being home. She wanted to hug him, comfort him, tell him he'd live a long, happy life. But he was looking to Mitch for help, not her. She glanced at Mandy sitting on the sofa, watching everything with wide eyes, and felt very much like her daughter looked—awkward, unsure, wondering what came next.

Making an attempt to help, Laura offered, ''I can help Nora, Dad, if you want to stay in your room. The bed's probably more comfortable. We could put a bell—''

''Ray can probably relax better down here,'' Mitch interrupted. ''He'd have his own living room and TV and the kitchen right outside. I think his idea is a good one.''

Laura protested. ''We haven't cleaned it or aired it out.''

Nora intervened. ''Give me fifteen minutes.''

Laura expected a smug look from Mitch, but didn't get one. He strode over to Mandy and crouched down in front of her. ''Maybe this afternoon you could keep your grandfather company. I bet he'd like to look at your new books.''

Mitch had bought Mandy five books and an elephant puppet to go with one of them. When he presented the gifts to her, his face had lit up as if he was the one receiving a present. Laura had been touched by his thoughtfulness. But he'd brushed her thanks aside, saying he just wanted Mandy to feel at home. Now he was promoting the relationship between grandfather and granddaughter. Laura should be doing that herself.

''Honey, do you want to help us get a room ready for grandpa?'' she asked, to include her daughter.

Mandy jumped off the sofa and stuck her hand in her mother's. ''Okay. Can I show him my puppet?''

Ray boomed, "Sure you can. We'll get to know each other this afternoon when your mom and Mitch go to the store."

Her hand tightened around Laura's. "Mommy, you're not leaving, are you?"

Laura read the unspoken message. *Don't leave me alone with him.* Laura swallowed, suddenly at a loss.

"I'll go to the store alone if you want to stay with your dad and Mandy," Mitch suggested easily.

Laura didn't know if he was trying to keep her away from the business or if he was being sensitive to Mandy's needs. It didn't matter. Her daughter came first. "That'll work for today." She hugged Mandy. "While Grandpa rests, you and I can explore the tree house."

"Super!"

When Ray frowned, his heavy brows steepled. "You be careful with her, Laura. The gardener checks it but..."

"I won't let anything happen to her," Laura said firmly, then wished she hadn't been so abrupt. She should be glad he was taking an interest in his granddaughter. She wished she could stop feeling defensive around him.

A few minutes later, Laura helped Nora make up the sofa bed while Mandy fluffed pillows in the bedroom. Nora tucked in the corner of the sheet. "Don't feel bad Ray wants Mitch's help. Man-to-man he feels more...easy."

"He's pushing me away."

Nora looked as if she wanted to say something.

Laura flipped the sheet under the mattress. "You can be honest with me. I need all the help I can get with Dad."

"He doesn't know how to act with you any more than you know how to act with him. Mitch and Carey are the same way. That's why Carey hasn't been around when Mitch is here."

Laura shook her head ruefully. "I wish life had a road map."

Nora moved to the foot of the bed to fold it away. "Give yourself time. You've only been here a week."

And in that week, Laura already thought of Nora as a friend, the older woman she had lacked in her life. "I only have five more."

"You're a determined young woman. Ray's not as crusty as he makes out to be. You'll find a way."

Nora's words rang in Laura's ears throughout lunch. She could see her dad's fatigue, and conversation was minimal. Mitch had been quiet and keeping his distance the last few days so there was no help from that quarter. By the end of the meal, Laura needed to escape the confines of walls. She invited Mandy to go with her to the tree house, but her daughter wanted to help Nora make a low-calorie dessert for supper first. Ray retired to his room with Mitch so Laura grabbed her coat and headed for the backyard.

The late October wind tossing her hair, the sunlight on her face, gave Laura the sense of freedom she'd left back in Independence. Without conscious thought, she headed for the rose garden and the white marble bench where she and her mother used to sit. Looking into the woods beyond, she remembered the stories of the enchanted forest her mother had woven for her. Beautiful stories with happily-ever-afters and love and hope.

Laura could almost hear her mother's voice, the vitality it carried, the crooning love. Why had she died so young? It had been a long time since Laura had asked that question. About her mother. About Doug. The two people who had loved her had left her. Or were they taken away? It didn't matter. They were gone.

Tears spilled from Laura's eyes and ran down her cheeks. Both had given her joy, both had filled her life with love.

After her mother died, her father hadn't been easy to love. Unbidden, Laura remembered that night in his study six years ago.

Chapter Six

Laura had come home from school, expecting that Christmas break to be the happiest of her life. Instead, her fiancé had told her Ray Applegate had tried to buy him off.

Betrayal stabbing her heart, she'd confronted her father in his study. "Doug says you offered him ten thousand dollars to get out of my life! Is that true?"

The deafening silence in the oak-paneled room answered more effectively than words. Tears pricked in her eyes. "Daddy, how *could* you?"

"I won't let you marry him, Laura. He's a bum with no future. A painter...with a ponytail and beard." Ray Applegate rose to his feet and stood behind his massive desk like a sea captain facing a mutinous member of his crew.

All Laura saw was her father trying to destroy her dreams. She moved closer to him, facing him head-on, damning the barriers between them. "Doug's a commercial artist, too. They make a good income."

Her father shook his head. "He only wants to marry you to get the family money. Once you're married, he won't work a day. Mark my words."

Why couldn't her father see the obvious? That she loved Doug and he loved her. For years she'd longed for the kind of bond she was experiencing with Doug, for someone to love her so completely. As young as sixteen, she'd wished on the moon for that one person who would love her forever. Why couldn't her father accept what she wanted from life? Why couldn't he accept her and love her?

Her fingernails cut into her palms. She had to convince him she knew what was best for herself. "I love him and he loves me. He proved it when he didn't accept your check."

"He proved nothing of the kind. The boy's just waiting for the bigger chance. He's using you."

Tears rolled down Laura's cheeks. "If Mom were here, she'd understand. She'd like Doug."

Ray's face flushed red. "I won't let you live the same capricious life she did. It killed her."

Laura's hands went out in a pleading gesture. "An icy road killed her. Not her acting. Not her singing. Why can't you let me live my own life like she did?"

"You are *not* going to make a stupid mistake."

Her chin lifted defiantly. "You can't stop me. I'm twenty. I don't need your consent."

Ray's arms dropped to his sides and he clenched his fists. "You want a partnership with me, don't you?"

He knew she did. She'd wanted to work beside him in the jewelry business since she was four and had held her first diamond in her hand. "Of course, I do. I've been studying the past two years so I can repair jewelry, be an expert on the quality of gems, settings. When my apprenticeship in Philadelphia is finished—"

"You marry that boy and there is no partnership. There will be no job. You can have either a partnership with me, marriage when you're mature enough to handle it, and enough money to put your children through college and leave you set for life, *or* an uncertain marriage to someone too immature to know what love is."

She couldn't believe her ears or her father's cruelty. "If I marry Doug, you'll disown me?"

"That's right."

She remembered her mother's death and the way her father had closed off his emotions. She remembered him snapping orders rather than making an effort to understand. She remembered his censure when she started to bring home C's instead of A's. She remembered how he'd become more and more strict to try to control her and how she'd defied him even more. She remembered wanting to enter this room to talk to him, but being afraid to do so. She remembered all the trouble she'd caused because she wanted his attention and some proof he loved her, not rules and regulations, but caring and love.

Then she thought about Doug—the affection he wasn't afraid to show, his generosity with his time, his love that had no strings. She didn't want to lose her father. Losing one parent had been difficult enough. But she couldn't give up Doug. She loved him too much. And she desperately wanted the future they'd planned.

"What's your decision, Laura?"

Her father's attitude was unbending. He was giving her no choice. Her anger dissipated and she was left with a hollow happiness because her father wouldn't be part of her life. She said softly, "I'm marrying Doug."

Hoping her father would stop her, she turned toward the door. But he didn't call her back and he didn't follow her. He let her walk out of his study and out of his life.

A sparrow landed on one of the rosebushes and brought Laura back to the present. That scene had played six years

ago. What could she do now? How could she prove to her
dad she was worthy of his love? That question startled her
and brought fresh tears. After all these years, she still felt
she had to prove something. The pain in her chest bowed her
head.

Leaves covered the brick path, muffling Mitch's footsteps. Laura was sitting sideways on the cold bench, her chin
almost in her lap. She was lost in thought, unaware of his
approach. When she brushed her hand across her cheek, he
thought the breeze had tickled her. But then he saw the wet
sheen glowing on her face in the yellow sun and he knew
she'd been crying.

Like a hand closing around his heart, guilt for all the
censorious thoughts he'd had about her overtook him. Then
compassion, along with something more potent, surged in
his veins. She was so saucy, laughed so easily, seemed so
carefree, he'd forgotten she could be disturbed and upset.
Sometimes he thought his distrust actually wounded her.
Was that possible? If her capacity for happiness was so
great, it only made sense so was her capacity for sadness.

His loyalty to Ray made Mitch wary and protective. He'd
seen the older man's pain over the years, the lonely holi-
days when Ray had admitted he wondered where his
daughter was and what she'd made of her life. He'd seen
Ray's yearning to be connected to her again but also the
sense of betrayal because Laura had cut her father out of her
life and never cared enough to look back.

But Mitch couldn't help responding to Laura. He liked
her laugh. He more than liked her joy. Even if they could
find common ground, even if she *wasn't* calculating to take
over her father's business, Mitch wasn't what she needed or
wanted. He was nothing like her husband and never could
be. Adventure was a risk. Mitch didn't like risks. Spontaneity demanded flexibility. He felt safe with a schedule.

Living day by day required an impulsive spirit. He planned for the future and wanted a stable life. Yet when he was near her...

As he stood behind her now, her perfume wafting around his head, her hair glowing like spun gold and exotic stones, her sadness reaching out to him like the moon's pull on the tide, desire roared like an express train racing through a tunnel and made him quake. God help him, he wanted her. He wanted her wildness, her free spirit, her joy. He wanted to kiss her, taste her, touch her until she wanted him just as much. And then she'd wrap herself around him and he'd know heaven.

That couldn't happen! Wouldn't happen. Ray was like a father, and Laura and Ray were at odds even if the tension wasn't in the open. And Laura? Mitch still didn't know if she was a threat, a partner or a woman biding time until she could return to her life in Ohio.

He saw her shoulders shake and he couldn't keep from laying his hand on the back of her hair. Laura went still, then relaxed as his thumb circled her temple. Eons could have passed until she finally looked over her shoulder. Her gray eyes drew him in and surrounded him like a warm velvet blanket.

She was slipping past his defenses. That scared him.

Despite the fear, the sleek track of her tears drew his hand. Tenderly he brushed one wet streak. "What's wrong?"

She cleared her throat but it was still husky. "Indulging in self-pity, I guess."

She lowered her head and he suspected tears filled her eyes again. Though he'd only known her a few days, he already realized she wasn't the type to feel sorry for herself. He lifted her chin with his knuckles. "Are you homesick?"

"I do miss Anne and George. But that's not it entirely. Coming back here brings back so many memories and feelings. I...miss my mother. And Doug..." Her voice caught.

His gut knotted and a wave of protective compassion brought a lump to his throat. He didn't want her to hurt or need. The faint blue shadows under her eyes hadn't been there when she opened her door in Independence. Taking his hand from her face reluctantly, he sat down beside her, his need to be close to her vying with his need for distance.

His thigh rested against hers; the contact seemed necessary and right. "It's tough to lose someone you love."

"You're talking about your dad?"

How could he tell Laura about his father when he'd never told anyone else? But there was so much empathy in her voice, he felt compelled to answer. "Yes. I tried to love him. He was so...erratic. I never felt my love was returned. I felt he resented me for being born. But when he died, a part of me died, too." The admission seemed strange on Mitch's lips. He'd never put it into words before.

Laura leaned her shoulder against his. "Children can sense the truth. Adults don't give them enough credit."

Somehow he knew she'd understand, that she wouldn't tell him he'd been wrong and his father had loved him as all fathers should. He also sensed something about her childhood bothered her and it had nothing to do with her mother's death. "Who didn't give you enough credit?"

"Dad." When Mitch didn't react adversely, she continued. "My mother was a singer and actress. She loved music and people and trying every new food or amusement ride she could find. Dad loved that part of her, but he also resented it. I think he looked on her as an exuberant child he had to channel. Sometimes she wouldn't let him do it, and he'd get angry. He'd watch her when she was with a group of friends as if they'd spirit her away from him. He never wanted her to try out for plays too far away."

"He was afraid he'd lose her."

Laura lifted her hands in agitation. "She loved him. Anyone could see it. She didn't have her eyes set on New York, she just wanted to experience life."

Her daughter had inherited that trait. "You were young. Could you know that for sure?"

Laura let the question linger before answering. "I wasn't too young to know she loved me and Dad. What was he afraid of?"

Somehow Mitch knew. "Of not being enough."

Laura's eyes widened. "I've never thought of Dad as . . . insecure."

"No man's secure around the woman he loves."

She shifted on the bench, her knee bumping his as she faced him more squarely. "Love should make you secure. Nothing's safer than knowing someone loves you for who and what you are."

Mitch felt his whole body tighten. "You and your husband were like that?"

"We started out that way."

Mitch didn't see how he could ever shed his mask completely. He hid his feelings. In the past when he'd shown them to his dad or "friends," they'd been belittled. Men shouldn't feel sad, or scared or lonely. God forbid they should cry. His father had slapped him once for that. Men were ambitious, successful, stoic and logical. Weren't they?

Before he could find the answer, Laura's next question distracted him from trying. "Have you ever been in love?"

Their gazes caught and he knew he'd never been in love the way she meant. Not heart, body, mind and soul. Why did this woman reach his deepest places and encourage responses he'd kept secret even to himself?

"I've thought myself in love. Two years ago I almost asked a woman to marry me."

"Almost?"

Her expectant gaze urged him to continue. "At the time I figured my hesitation concerned making a name for myself, insuring a good income for the future."

"You were going to ask her after you'd done that?"

"I told myself I was. I'd become Ray's partner and was getting ready for my first exhibition."

The breeze picked up the ends of her hair and blew them across her cheek. "What happened?"

He almost smiled. Laura wouldn't think of *not* asking the sticky questions. "She earned her masters in chemistry and decided to get a PhD. She accepted an assistantship at Stanford."

"Her career was more important than you?" Laura seemed concerned and puzzled too.

"I don't think Denise compared the two. We both realized we were together for convenience rather than love. We didn't talk of her not going or looking for someplace closer."

Laura tilted her head until the sun created a halo on the crown. "Or you moving out to California to make a name?"

"Ray and the business meant too much to me at that point." He'd finally found his niche, respect and a bond with the father figure he'd never had. No, he wouldn't have left. It had nothing to do with being a male or a chauvinist. It had to do with finally finding where he belonged. Laura had left all of her sense of belonging to go with her husband. He couldn't understand that. But if they got into that subject, they'd argue. He didn't feel like arguing. He would like to know more about her marriage, though. It sounded as if it might not have been ideal after all. But right now he was simply enjoying sitting beside her and the connection between them.

They sat in silence for a while. Laura finally broke it. "My dad doesn't need me here."

"What makes you say that?"

"He has you. And now Nora. He's not looking to me for anything."

"You're wrong." He couldn't prove it, but he knew she was.

"You saw him this morning, Mitch."

Laura looked down at her hands and he knew she was hurting. He also knew why. Ray turned to him out of habit. "I've been here the last four years." He said it as a fact, not to make her feel guilty.

Her voice quivered. "I'm a grown woman and I still have this longing to earn his approval."

Mitch was so tempted to put his arms around her. But he didn't. Instead he shared a secret. "I do, too."

Her head came up and they stared at each other, knowing a bond had formed between them.

Before they could explore it, Mandy came running down the center of the yard, yelling, "Mommy, Mommy. I want to see the tree house now."

Mitch stood. "And the cycle goes on."

Monday evening Laura came home from the store, damp from the pouring rain she'd run through, but excited and bubbling with an idea she knew would work. It would be her way of gaining her dad's approval, upping profits, and showing Mitch she could manage along with the best of them.

His taciturn comment had ended a conversation that had given her insight into his character. She'd felt close to him for the first time since coming to York. And with all her heart, she hoped he didn't regret anything he'd shared. He was so afraid to open up. He might not admit it, but he wanted to be loved as much as anyone she knew—maybe more.

She didn't know exactly why, maybe it was his father's doing, but Mitch's childhood had clouded his emotions and when they became clear, he pushed them away. Yet he had great insight into himself. He had substance and honesty. And their talk had filled her with... Hope? For what? That they could work together while she was here? Something more? *Fat chance, Laura Sanders. You have a life in Independence.* Mitch as much as said he'd never leave this area. Besides, she couldn't live in York. Once he recovered, her father might try to control her life. Again.

After she hung her poncho in the foyer closet, she dropped the folder with the material she'd worked on all afternoon onto her father's desk in the study and went in search of Mandy and Nora, looking for Puffball as she went through the house. Where Puffball was, Mandy couldn't be far behind.

Laura wondered if Mitch was home. He'd gone to Harrisburg yesterday to ready the store for Christmas. So he said. Maybe Nora knew what time he planned to return.

Laura found Mandy and Nora playing a card game with Ray. He was looking more comfortable today, more sure of himself. He waved to Laura. "Your daughter's too good at this. She keeps winning."

Laura hugged Mandy and ruffled her hair. "Good for you." She addressed her dad. "How do you feel?"

"Like I've been through a war and the other guy won."

Nora spoke up. "Now, Ray. You said each day you feel a little stronger. He's doing fine. The nurse is coming tomorrow to start him on some easy exercises. We took a walk around the house twice this morning before the rain started. You'd be proud of him."

"The doctor said I control my own destiny," Ray muttered. "So I'm going to do everything he tells me and get on with life. It's just rough going right now."

One thing Laura had always admired was her dad's determination. She cupped his shoulder in her palm. "You're doing terrific. Like you always told me, if you're persistent enough, you can do anything."

She thought his eyes were shiny when his rougher, callused hand covered hers, and she felt as if she'd crossed a barrier between them.

Laura joined the card game and noticed a ring on Nora's finger. She remembered Mitch's words. "A cluster of rubies and pearls. When my father gambled it away, she cried and cried." He must have recreated it for her. He'd kept his promise.

Mitch arrived an hour later. His gaze connected with Laura's and she thought she saw an openness that hadn't been there before. Her worry that his sudden decision to go to Harrisburg to avoid her dissipated. After all, the Harrisburg store couldn't run without direction any more than the York one could. She also suspected he'd wanted to give her time with her father.

When Mitch followed Nora to the kitchen to discover what smelled so good, Laura waylaid him in the hallway. As always, being this close to him rattled her. His shirt was wrinkled. He'd tugged down his tie and opened the top button of his striped Oxford; the curly black hairs invited touching. She closed her fingers into her palms.

"Could we talk for a few minutes in Dad's study? I have something to discuss with you."

Mitch's eyes became opaque as he hesitated for a moment, then motioned for her to lead. Their footsteps seemed loud on the wood floor as they walked down the hall.

Mitch waited for Laura to enter the room before him. She picked up the file folder on her father's desk, suddenly nervous. Taking a deep breath, she plowed in. "Someone came into the store this morning who could be the answer to a prayer."

Mitch sat on a corner of the desk. ''I didn't know we'd asked for an answer.''

Okay, so it was an answer to *her* prayer. ''He's an agent for a group of Navaho craftsmen in Arizona. He'd like us to promote their work. The samples were wonderful. The finest quality workmanship in silver, turquoise, coral, onyx. This is just what we need.''

''A few samples of fine quality doesn't mean—''

She went on as if he hadn't spoken, too excited to stop. ''He invited me to Flagstaff to see the craft village and examine all of it firsthand. I could fly out with Mandy—''

That raised Mitch's brows. ''With Mandy?''

''Sure. I wouldn't leave her here. We'd be gone three days tops.''

Mitch came to his feet, defensive and wary. ''You came to York for your father.''

''This *is* for my father. This jewelry is the trend of the future. It's beautiful and affordable. Think of all the new customers we'd bring in. The Southwest trend is catching like wildfire in the East. We might even want to introduce pottery, artwork—''

''No!''

She retreated a step. ''I beg your pardon.''

Mitch's jaw set in a stern line. ''I told you you could help with the store, not revamp it. Lord, I go away one day and your impulsiveness already runs riot.''

Hanging on to her temper was a real problem around Mitch. She modulated her voice into calmness. ''I'm the acting manager of the store in my father's absence. Correct?''

''Acting manager to maintain the status quo,'' he said evenly.

Indignation won over holding her fuse. ''If I'm a manager, I'm going to manage. I'm not going to be a salesclerk or a pawn to do your bidding. I've seen the books. The York store's profits are down significantly. Do you know that? And if you don't, what kind of partner are you?''

Mitch paced to the bookshelves on the far side of the room. He picked up a duck decoy, put it down and faced her. ''That store is Ray's domain. I have no right to interfere.''

''It's not a matter of rights. He should know what's happening. Does he?''

Mitch jammed his hands into his pockets and looked troubled. ''He thought with Christmas, it would turn around.''

She approached him cautiously. ''I saw last year's records. Christmas didn't make that much difference. Look, Mitch. I know my dad doesn't take an aggressive or innovative approach. But the jewelry business has changed in the last five years and he hasn't kept up with the changes.''

''Don't you think I know that? But we have an agreement. I don't interfere with his store, he doesn't interfere with mine.''

Intuitively she knew Mitch was a man of honor and when he made an agreement, he kept it. But there were times . . . ''You're his partner.''

''Ray doesn't like change.''

''Of course he doesn't. But maybe if it's introduced step by step . . .'' Her voice trailed off at Mitch's stubborn expression. ''Maybe I should be talking to him about this.''

The stubbornness turned into protectiveness. ''We're not going to give him something else to worry about.''

''Is that really your reasoning? Or are you afraid I'll show you up? That I'll succeed where you should have taken action before now?'' She knew she was stabbing in the dark. But he couldn't dismiss her one means of making a difference in her dad's life.

''You're incredibly naive if you think in six weeks you can turn the store around.''

"At least that's one of the kinder things you think of me," she said tersely.

"How do you know what I think of you?" His eyes were deep blue, probing, and they touched her as much as the hint of huskiness in his voice.

"I can see it and feel it. Just when I think we're coming to an understanding, you turn judgmental and condemning. You don't always say it, but I can see it in your eyes."

When he stepped toward her, his hands gently took hold of her shoulders. "What would you like to see?"

In that instant she knew she wanted him to like her, wanted whatever he could give in the time she stayed in York. "I want to see acceptance. Open-mindedness. You have too many preconceptions about me."

He dropped his hands and stepped away, as if aware how vulnerable they both were. His words put distance between them again. "I do have preconceptions. I got them from a good source—your father. When you were a teenager, you put him through hell. He didn't even know where you were half the time. Then, when he thought his daughter had decided to grow up, she ran away with a painter and never contacted him."

She understood Mitch had seen her father's pain. But he knew nothing about *her* heartache, loneliness and fears. She had to do something to erase the devastating disapproval in his eyes. "I went through hell, too. I was trying to get his attention. What did he tell you about? The day I hot-wired his car because he wouldn't give me permission to drive it? The night he had to bail me out of jail because a party I attended was raided?"

Mitch's expression told her he'd heard that one, too.

"Maybe he told you I cut classes? My grades slipped? I found a boyfriend who wore a leather jacket and rode a motorcycle? I'm sure it was hell for him because it shook up his established, narrow world. There are two sides to every story, Mitch.'' She prayed he'd want to hear hers, yet she knew he might not choose to because her side might change his opinion of her father.

Mitch's low, quiet tone was slow but unwavering. "You could have contacted him in the last six years."

If she told him she had, he probably wouldn't believe her. His calmness incited a riot of emotions in her. "And he could have contacted me. You have a real propensity for seeing only what's in front of your nose. It's called tunnel vision."

"And you have a propensity for acting irresponsibly and recklessly. Ray doesn't need more headaches or worry about the store. I won't let you damage what he's spent his life building."

Her fingers strained around the folder with her notes until she almost bent it in half. "You're giving me more credit than I deserve. I can't damage much in six weeks."

"You could get a damn good start."

The hope that had sprouted inside her almost wilted. Almost. She never gave up without a fight. Slamming the folder with her ideas and plans for earning her dad's love into Mitch's hands, she said, "Try to keep your eyes open and your brain uncluttered by what a terrible person I am when you read that. If a trip to Arizona, an ad campaign and a promotion that will bring new and younger customers into the store will damage the business, I want to know how."

She spun on her heels and slammed the door as she left her father's office.

After supper, Mitch went to Ray's study. He and Laura had been civil at supper but that was it. He leaned back in the leather chair and opened the folder. Why couldn't she live with the status quo? That had been her problem as a teenager, too. Never satisfied. Always rebelling. At least that was what he'd been told. But in this last altercation she'd said something about getting her father's attention.

Mitch impatiently brushed the paper clip from the clump of papers. Of course, she'd had Ray's attention. She was his only child. Why wouldn't she have it?

Unless Ray hadn't been able to relate to an adolescent, a developing woman. Had he backed off? Did she read that as her father withdrawing his love?

Is that why she wanted to take over now? To get Ray's attention? Well, he'd be damned if he'd let her make a mess of Ray's store just to get his attention. She and Ray would have to work out their differences on some other front. *If* they could.

Mitch flicked open the folder impatiently, planning to give it a quick once-over. But he got caught by the phrasing, the captions, the rough ideas for ads. They were good, all of them. She must have worked like a dynamo all afternoon to get this done. The whole campaign was based on the principle that the sterling jewelry was unique, intricate and affordable for all ages and everybody—sweethearts, sisters, mothers, fathers, brothers.

But a spur of the moment trip to Arizona? Now? He was studying the rate of supply when the study door flew open.

"We can't find Puffball!" Tears rolled down Mandy's cheeks. "Mommy called the cleaning lady and she let her out this afternoon." The child sniffled. "And it's raining and Puffball's gonna get wet!"

Mitch pushed the papers away, stood and scooped Mandy into his arms. He felt at a loss, but he knew he had to do something to comfort her. He did what his mother had always done for him, hugged her close. "Cats aren't like people. They don't mind rain."

"But she's an *inside* cat. And we're not at home. She won't be able to find her way back."

Mitch knew nothing about cats, little about calming Mandy's fears. "Where's your mommy?"

Mandy hiccupped. "She said not to bother you. But she's gonna get all wet, too!"

"She went out to look for Puffball?"

Mandy stuck her finger in her mouth and nodded.

Mitch strode to the kitchen and set Mandy on the counter.

Nora was emptying the dishwasher. "I wanted to go out, too, but Laura wouldn't let me. She's going to get soaked."

Mitch headed for the foyer closet and pulled out his trench coat. On his way out the sliding glass dining room doors, he said, "Don't worry. Everything's going to be all right."

He didn't know if he was assuring himself or them.

Chapter Seven

Mitch saw the blink of a high-powered flashlight near the south corner of the yard. What would they do if they couldn't find the damn cat? How would they tell Mandy? Why hadn't Laura asked his help from the beginning? Did she think he wouldn't care? He'd do anything for that little girl.

He dodged through the pouring rain toward the light. When he reached Laura, she had pulled her wool hood over her head, but she was drenched.

"Give me the light and go inside. You're going to catch pneumonia."

Even in the shadows, he could see a sparkle of defiance in her eyes. "And you won't?"

Don't fight. Be practical, Riley. "Have you been working around the yard?"

She pushed aside branches of spirea to peer into the base of the hedge. "No. I've just been looking wherever a cat might hide. She knows her name, but she hasn't come."

He took Laura's arm as the rain dribbled through his lashes and down his face. "That only means she has more sense than we do. She might be dry in the crook of a tree—"

"That's it!" Laura popped up. "The tree house. Why didn't I think of that?"

He ran beside her in the rain, hoping the tree house was the answer. When Laura tripped over a gnarled tree root, Mitch caught her against him. Suddenly he knew he'd gone to Harrisburg to escape being close to her, to avoid more sharing, more feeling. He wanted to kiss the rain from her cheeks, the tip of her nose, the peak of her lips, but when she regained her balance, he urged her forward.

They reached the tree house and Laura thrust the flashlight at him so she could scramble up the ladder.

"Wait. You won't be able to see." He held the light so she wouldn't misstep and climbed up behind her. At the top he swung the bright streak around the small covered cubicle.

"There she is!" Laura stretched out her arms to the cat.

The animal looked much smaller, and Mitch realized Puffball was as wet, if not wetter, than they were. She meowed sharply and hissed when Laura tried to grab her.

"She's going to fight. Wait a minute." Mitch set down the light and took off his trench coat.

"What are you doing?"

"I'm going to wrap her in it so we all get back in one piece. She still has her *back* claws."

"You'll ruin your clothes."

Of all times for Laura to pick to be practical. With quick, economical movements he wrapped the cat before she could dart away. "They'll dry. Let's get her back to Mandy."

Laura took the light and led the way. Nora and Mandy were waiting with towels in the kitchen. Ray looked on in wry amusement.

Mitch flipped his wet hair away from his forehead and unwrapped the cat on the floor. She was half of her normal size, her hair matted and flat. Mandy ran to her, hugged her and kissed the top of her wet head. The cat meowed twice as if thanking her mistress for her concern.

Laura stripped off her poncho and laid it over the counter. "I'm going to take her upstairs to the bathroom to dry her off."

Mitch's wet sleeves stuck to his upper arms. "I'll carry her up for you."

"Can I help?" Mandy asked.

Laura swept her damp hair back from her face. "You'd be more help if you get your nightgown on and spread a towel for her on your bed. I'm sure she'll want to snuggle after being out in the cold all night."

Mandy studied the drenched cat. "Okay. Maybe she can sleep under the covers with me."

Mandy scampered up the stairs in front of Laura and Mitch. Puffball hung limp in his hands and meowed.

Mitch crouched and settled Puffball on the bathroom rug. Laura's leg brushed his ear as she opened the vanity and removed a towel. "Sorry," she mumbled.

The bathroom was average size but confining with two adults and a cat, especially when the other adult was Laura. "Your slacks are wet," Mitch noted. "You ought to change."

She gazed at his trousers molded to his thighs. The look they exchanged was steamy and sexual. Neither was paying enough attention to Puffball. With a lurch, the cat zoomed for the door and darted down the hall. Mitch took off after her.

Puffball had reached the top of the staircase when Mitch swooped her up and tucked her under his arm. "Gotcha. Believe me, this is for your own good. It won't be so bad, you'll see." When he saw Laura standing in the bathroom with a smile threatening, he felt ridiculous.

Apparently Laura couldn't suppress a giggle. "I talk to her all the time."

The squirming animal kept Mitch from responding. When he quickly slipped past Laura into the bathroom, she stepped inside and closed the door.

This time, he kept a firm grip on the cat. Laura knelt on the floor and toweled Puffball gently but applied enough pressure to soak up the moisture.

Every once in a while Laura's gaze met Mitch's and a surge of energy zipped through him. Inadvertently, his eyes slipped to her damp blouse hugging her breasts. Since when couldn't he direct his line of vision? His grip on Puffball tensed and she meowed.

Laura asked, "Do you want to change positions?"

He shook his head and sat Indian fashion with Puffball across his thighs. If he concentrated on the cat, he wouldn't think about the woman.

Sure. Except when her fingers accidentally grazed his knee, except when her face was so close he could lift her chin and kiss her, except when the scent of her perfume made more potent by the clinging moisture practically inebriated him.

All in all, the process took about ten minutes. But to Mitch it felt like a lifetime. As soon as the cat was as dry as possible under the circumstances, he stood and opened the door. Puffball streaked down the hall to Mandy's room. He noticed Laura had wrapped her arms around herself. He watched her closely and she shivered. It took most of his self-control not to pull her into his arms and surround her with his body heat.

He said, "I'll light a fire so you can warm up. I'm sure Mom already has tea brewing."

As he turned to leave, Laura's voice stopped him. "Mitch, thanks for your help. Puffball's important to Mandy."

"I know." He grinned. "But not even Mandy's going to get that animal to sleep under the covers." When Laura smiled, her upper lip moved to the side in an enticing way. Mitch said abruptly, "See you downstairs."

Laura kissed her daughter good-night, petted a still damp Puffball, changed into her nightgown and robe and thought about Mitch running down the hall after the cat. She giggled again. Somehow, at that moment, he hadn't seemed so straitlaced. And sometimes, when he watched her with those intense blue eyes... How she wished she could read his mind.

The first floor was quiet when she reached the foyer. Listening closely, she heard the soft buzz of voices in her dad's quarters. But not Mitch's deep baritone.

She stepped into the living room and saw Mitch poking at a log on the grate. Flames spurted and spread. Stepping away, he closed the mesh curtain. He'd changed into jeans, and his red-and-black checked flannel shirt looked worn and soft.

He saw her immediately. "Ready for bed?"

The question took on more meaning than it should have. She felt her cheeks flush as her breath caught in her throat. "I decided to be warm and comfortable," she finally managed, sitting on the sofa. She noticed the mug of tea on the coffee table. It had a touch of milk just the way she liked it. Doug had never done that for her. He'd been as independent as she. She didn't serve him; he didn't serve her. Maybe they'd missed something. The caring felt nice.

"The fire should help you warm up."

"Dad and Nora don't want to enjoy it?"

"They're busy playing dominoes." Mitch sat next to her.

Silence seemed preferable to conversation. It was like that with Mitch. She and Doug had chattered incessantly. They were always on the move. With Mitch she could be comfortable sitting quietly. Why was she making these comparisons anyway?

Mitch broke into her thoughts. "There's something I want to ask you."

Her heart beat faster. "Ask."

"The Business Association is hosting a Halloween party on Saturday. Ray thinks we should go. He said you'd know a few of the store owners there. It's at the country club."

Would this qualify as a date? No. Mitch had made it clear this was business. "Years ago, the store owners took turns having the party in their homes. Times have changed. Do they still wear costumes?"

Mitch moved his legs so they weren't so close to hers. "Yes. Can you get something together? I'm renting an outfit from a costume shop. If you want to do that—"

"Everything's probably picked over. I have a few ideas. One of them should work." She didn't say more but waited. He didn't really want to talk about the Halloween party.

"Laura, about our discussion earlier..."

Mitch looked uneasy and she knew he was going to turn her proposal down flat. "It was more of an argument."

"I'm sorry I jumped on you like that." The apology was said quickly but with too much sincerity for her to doubt he meant it.

"About the store or about my dad?"

He sighed and settled back into the sofa. "Let's stick to the store for now."

The easier of the two she supposed. She relaxed into the cushions, too. "You don't want changes, either."

Mitch stretched his arm along the back of the sofa, brushing her hair. "I didn't say that. Change takes thought.

I'm not used to doing something because it seems right. I do research and analyze statistics first."

"That's why I want to go to Flagstaff." She moved her hands with excitement as she talked. "To see the operation myself. I truly think this would be good for the store."

"Your ideas for the sales campaign are good and we still have time to implement them."

It took a moment for his praise to sink in. "You're behind me on this?"

His look was dark, long, and said he knew she was going to protest. "On one condition. I go to Arizona with you."

Her heart sank. "You don't trust my judgment."

"Laura, I have to protect your father's interest as well as my own."

He was doing what he thought was right and she had to respect that. But... "Are you going to be open-minded about this? Because there's no point in flying out there if you go with a negative attitude."

He crossed his heart and smiled as he raised his right hand. "I promise to go with a positive outlook. Satisfied?"

A promise from Mitch even in jest was a promise meant. She smiled back. "For now." His eyes were so blue, his hair damp from the rain. He always seemed to smell like the outdoors.

Mitch fingered a lock of her hair. "This always looks so fluffy and soft."

"It's still damp." She swallowed and her breaths became staggered.

"Are you warm now?"

"Warm and getting warmer." Her heart pounded harder until she could feel it in her ears. Surely he'd lean closer and bend his head...

He leaned closer, but she was glad she didn't close her eyes. Because he didn't kiss her. He moved away.

* * *

Mitch sat across the kitchen table from Ray and methodically presented Laura's plans for the sterling jewelry—as methodically as he had used every iota of self-control to not kiss her last night.

Ray listened without comment and when Mitch finished asked, "And you think this is a good idea?"

"I think it would bring in younger customers who in the long run will come to us for more momentous purchases."

"What you're saying is my clientele is dying off."

Mitch met Ray's bluntness with honesty. "The store could use the promotion and a steady stream of up-and-coming customers, if you're thinking about future profits."

"You've wanted to do something like this for the past year, haven't you?"

"I'm not going to tell you how to run your store."

Ray rubbed his chin. "But Laura will. She sees what she wants to change and she changes it. Like a steamroller. She always was." He closed his eyes for a moment. "Except for the year after her mother died. I hardly knew she was around."

Mitch remembered Laura's tears and her confidences. They were precious to him. They might be precious to her father, too. "She still misses her mother."

"So do I," Ray returned gruffly. "More than I ever thought I could. We had our differences. I wanted a woman who thought home was the best place to be. It wasn't until after we were married I discovered 'home' was much too limited for Patrice. She loved me and Laura, there was no denying that. But she wanted a lot more than us. She wanted to taste everything life had to offer. I had trouble with that."

Ray had never talked about his relationship with his wife. His brush with mortality had evidently given him much to think about. Mitch wondered if Ray had many regrets.

Before he could ask, the older man said with a look of concern, "Laura's just like her mother. Headstrong, willful—"

"Motivated and determined." Why was he defending Laura to her father?

Ray studied Mitch closely. Too closely. "Damn good ideas she has, aren't they?"

"If the jewelry's the quality she says it is, if the craft village isn't a joke, if they can supply what we want, her promotion's good. But I told her I go along to Flagstaff."

Ray's eyes twinkled. "Bet she had something to say about that, didn't she?"

"Not as much as I expected, but I think that's because we've reached an . . . understanding."

"You two are as different as night and day."

"In most ways." But in others, they were alike.

Ray stood, went to the refrigerator and removed a pitcher of orange juice. "What's on your mind, Mitch? You've been itching to say something since you came in here."

Mitch tipped his chair on the back legs, then let it fall front. "Laura thinks you don't need her."

Ray pushed his glasses up on his nose and his cheeks darkened as he set the pitcher on the table. "She's wrong."

"She thinks I've taken her place."

"You're like a son to me, boy. You've made life worth living again. When I lost Laura . . ." He cursed. "Stubborn old fools are the worst old fools. What do I have to do so she won't leave?"

"She's not planning on it. Yet. But it wouldn't hurt to talk to her about it."

Ray sighed and pulled a glass from the cupboard. "We can't talk about serious things. She and her mother always did that. Patrice and Laura were just like Laura and Mandy." Pouring himself a glass of juice, he said, "I'll back her ideas for the sterling campaign a hundred percent.

That'll show her the store needs her and we need her. What do you think?''

Mitch thought Ray needed to tell Laura he'd missed her and wanted her back in his life. But Mitch wasn't in the position to give advice. If Laura felt Ray needed her at the store, she'd stay. For six weeks. She'd made that clear.

"That'll work. For now."

Uncomfortably, Mitch stood in the living room and ran his fingers along the edge of his red cummerbund. He felt ridiculous. The satin blousy shirt and tight velveteen slacks made him feel as if he belonged in a store window.

When the chimes rang, Mitch called into Ray's quarters. "I'll get the door."

It would be Carey. He'd stayed for dinner one evening and heard them discussing the Halloween party. Ray had suggested he go along. Mitch didn't think Carey would accept—he had his own friends and places to go. But this trip he seemed at loose ends and had accepted the invitation eagerly. Mitch suspected the reason was Laura. Carey liked her. And she seemed to like him. That idea tightened Mitch's stomach.

When he answered the door, he was surprised by the traditional costume Carey had chosen—brown suedes and a coonskin cap.

Carey grinned. "Expecting Dracula, were you?"

Mitch shrugged. "I never know what to expect with you."

"That's part of the problem, isn't it, bro? I never do what *you* expect."

Mitch didn't want to rehash the past or get into an argument. He motioned to the living room. "We can leave as soon as Laura comes down."

As if on cue, she appeared on the steps. Both men looked up at the tap of heels on wood floor. Mitch knew he was staring openly but couldn't do anything about it. He felt himself flush as desire took hold of him with a forbidding grip. Her black leotard clung enough to elevate his blood pressure. Sheer black nylon stockings encased her shapely legs. The long black whiskers painted around her mouth, her pinkened nose and the black plastic headband with two black felt ears created the effect of the most fetching cat he'd ever seen.

Carey responded first with a loud whistle. "All right! You know how to make a fashion statement."

Her gaze never left Mitch's as she descended the steps. "It's called improvisation. Actually, it was Mandy's idea. She helped me paint on the whiskers before she went to bed."

Mitch noticed her false eyelashes and fake scarlet nails as she reached the bottom step. "You went all out."

"So did you."

Yep, he belonged in a store window from the way she was staring at him. "I'll go warm up the car. Come out when you're ready."

Laura and Carey carried the conversation on the way to the party. They seemed to have a lot to talk about from riding a motorcycle to craving chocolate fudge.

When they arrived at the country club and costumed guests milled around them, Laura's eyes sparkled. "I haven't been to a costume party in years. This is going to be fun!"

They entered a room where groups of chairs were clustered around squat tables. A Juliet and Cyrano stood conversing at the bar. Music from the ballroom beyond softly drifted in.

Mitch watched as several men studied Laura. He was shaken by a shock of possessiveness he had no right to feel. It confused him. He'd never felt possessive of Denise. These men ogling Laura . . . He'd like to personally put their eyes back where they belonged.

They chose chairs near the doorway where they could peer into the ballroom and watch the dancing. Mitch nodded toward the bar. "Can I get you something to drink?"

Carey answered first. "Tom Collins for me."

Mitch sighed to himself. Of course Carey would drink. He shouldn't have expected otherwise. "Laura?"

"Sprite with cranberry juice if they have it. If not, soda's fine."

Mitch strode toward the bar. Carey nudged Laura's arm. "Did you see that look? As if one drink will start a binge."

Laura felt the need to defend Mitch. "It could."

Carey slouched in his seat and stretched his legs out in front of him. "If I wanted to get drunk, I'd drink straight liquor."

"You don't have to explain yourself to me."

He canvassed her face closely. "No, I don't think I do. What's with you, Laura? I'm sure you've heard about me from my mother and Mitch. And most of what they say is true."

"I had my own reputation to contend with. What I felt inside had nothing to do with what I did on the outside."

"Or it had everything to do with it."

She thought about it. "Yes, I guess that's true. I thought I acted spontaneously, but I had hidden motives."

"Don't we all." He sounded sad. Pulling himself up straight in his chair, he said, "I've been many things, but I'm not an alcoholic."

She knew alcoholics denied their disease, but Carey's pale blue eyes and his determined tone led her to think he was telling the truth. "I believe you."

His expression showed relief. "I wish Mitch would."

"Maybe if you stay—"

"I'm leaving in a few weeks."

"Must you?"

"Yes. York's not a good place for me. I've been in too much trouble here. I'm getting my life together now in Virginia. I like it there. I found a group—" He gazed at her as if he wondered how much he could trust her. Finally, he confided, "I'm not an alcoholic, but I *am* a gambler. I joined Gamblers Anonymous. It's helping. I haven't bet on anything in six months."

"Does Mitch know?"

"No. He wouldn't believe me if I told him. I've lied to cover my tracks so often. I don't blame him. He's always cleaned up the mess. I'm hoping he'll help me one more time. I have a chance to buy into a video business."

"You want him to lend you money."

"This time it's legit and it will pay off."

"But you have to convince him."

"If he'll just listen to me..."

Mitch returned with the drinks and set them on the table. His eyes were rough and turbulent. "It's time to mingle. Laura, would you like to dance?"

He looked as if he wanted to shake her rather than dance with her. But the idea of being held by his strong arms was too hard to resist. She stood. "Sure."

As he led her into the ballroom with his hand firmly in the small of her back, she smiled at Carey over her shoulder. "We'll be back."

Mitch escorted her to the dance floor, nodding to acquaintances on the way. Laura saw a few people she remembered.

Taking the standard position, Mitch folded her hand into his chest. When his fingers skimmed her breast, tingles skidded down her spine and her eyes shot to his. Something unintelligible sparked there. But like a door closing, the blue became shuttered. He removed himself.

She wanted to lay her head on his shoulder, but she felt the warmth of his thighs pressing into hers, the sinews of his arm securing her against him, and the heat and her longing for more scared her. Another feeling gnawed at her....

She gazed into Mitch's blue eyes, looking for reassurance, and almost drowned. Her foot caught on his and she tripped. He caught her to him and she could feel his heart hammering as hard as hers.

He loosened his hold. "What were you and Carey discussing so fervently?"

Had her friendliness to his brother put the storm in Mitch's eyes? "We were just talking."

"He was charming you."

"No, we were talking like two human beings who connect."

"Connect?"

"We have a lot in common."

"Don't I know it," Mitch muttered.

"And that means?" she drawled.

"You're both impetuous and impulsive."

"Those are adjectives, not sins."

"Don't let Carey con you into any of his schemes."

"I can take care of myself."

"You don't seem to be able to stand on your own two feet for long."

She went rigid. "Explain that."

"Your father took care of you, your husband took care of you, and now your roommates take care of you. When have you stood on your own?"

She felt as if he'd clobbered her. He certainly didn't know or understand anything about her marriage to Doug. She pulled away and said sharply, "Yes, I look to other people for moral support. You should try it some time. It would make you more ... human."

Not waiting for him to follow, she found Carey and participated in the conversation he was having with a voluptuous Cleopatra.

Eventually Mitch rejoined them, anger smoldering in his eyes. At least that's what it looked like. A fast-tempoed number had Laura tapping her foot in time with the driving beat.

Carey smiled and nodded toward the band. "Do you want to give it a go?"

One look at Mitch's impassive countenance and she said, "Sure. Let's do it."

They danced one dance after another until she was nearly out of breath. It would have been tons of fun except for Mitch. Every time she turned around he was watching her, a hungry look in his eyes. She tried to be annoyed by it, but it excited her. Doug had never cared who she danced with, never looked up from his conversation while she was on the floor.

Still, she would have given up Oreos for a year rather than admit she was dancing *for* Mitch, trying to tempt him out onto the floor with her. Laura Marie Applegate Sanders wouldn't stoop to such tactics.

The devil in her knew better.

Mitch's emotions simmered under the surface as he drove home from the party. Laura's display of sensual dancing, her quick laughter, her easy rapport with Carey didn't matter. Okay, she aroused him, nothing more. That condition wasn't fatal. As for Carey...

Jealousy was his middle name when it came to Carey. He'd been jealous of his brother's relationship with their father. He'd been hurt by it. But that was the past. And now? Carey would be gone as suddenly as he'd arrived, just like Laura. Life went on. There was no reason to get riled by either of them.

When they reached Ray's, Carey roared away on his motorcycle. Laura exited the car without saying good-night to anyone. Puzzled, Mitch found her in the kitchen pouring herself a glass of milk. In some ways she was so damned wholesome. She hadn't looked wholesome when she was dancing! The memory brought an almost painful arousal.

She took a swallow of milk and set down the glass, a white mustache hanging on her upper lip. Then slowly and deliberately, she poured a second one. "Maybe a good night's sleep will sweeten your disposition," she said in a sugary tone, offering him the milk.

She was taunting him and he knew it. He should go into Ray's quarters and lock the door. He moved closer to her, removed the glass from her hand and calmly set it aside. "You put on quite a show tonight. I don't think it's what Ray had in mind when he suggested you go."

Her cheeks grew rosy underneath the cat whiskers. "I was having fun. Something you apparently don't know how to do."

He took two steps closer until he stood in front of her. "Just like I don't know how to be human?" He hadn't realized how deep that jab had cut until this moment.

"Exactly." Her gray eyes dared him to react.

His restraint snapped. He didn't plan it; he didn't think about it. He pulled her to him and crushed his lips to hers. And in that instant he knew. This was what he'd wanted to do from the moment she'd opened her door. He'd kissed enough women in his life to know what a kiss could do. The problem was those women hadn't been Laura. They hadn't been fiery and passionate and totally captivating.

Bolts of heat shot through him like night lightning flashing across a humid August sky. His mouth twisted to take hers, then twisted to take more. The storm inside him thundered and threatened to erupt. He wanted to plunge into her, mold to her, until her joy and spontaneity became his. He needed that part of her to complete himself.

Laura's arms went around Mitch's neck as if they belonged there. She leaned into him, aware of his arousal, the dangerous thud of his heart and just let herself feel—his desire, her need, the hard power of his thighs, the strong tightness of his arms, the pads of his fingers on her neck, the exciting sensuality of his body pressed against hers.

Mitch's mouth was bold and demanding. He was so big and imposing. So male. The vibrations between them were pure electricity. Man meeting woman. Man wanting woman. Woman wanting man. He ground against her erotically. She'd pushed him too far, but she didn't care. This was what she wanted. His passion. His feelings. His strength.

But Mitch apparently had different ideas. Pushing her away, he dropped his arms as if she'd scorched him. He took a long, deep breath and closed his eyes. Opening them, he said, "I'm sorry."

Laura was stunned. "Sorry? What for?"

"I usually think before I act, especially about consequences. The consequences of this can only mean trouble."

The piercing intensity of his blue eyes pinned her to the spot. She could still feel the heat from his body. It beckoned to her as much as his expression told her not to get close. "Trouble isn't always something to avoid," she said, stepping closer.

He looked as if he wanted to reach for her again, as if trouble could be worth what they could find in each other's arms. But then he tensed, and whatever he used to protect himself took over.

"In your world, Laura. Not mine," he said grimly and with a last long look disappeared into Ray's quarters.

Tears flowed to Laura's eyes along with the emptiness his retreat caused. She brushed away a stray one and bit her lower lip.

Seeking refuge in the mundane, Laura carried her glass to the table and sat. Kissing Mitch was as glorious as she'd expected it to be. And yet there was something else her feelings and desire for him triggered. Suddenly, she realized what it was. Guilt.

Why? Because she still felt married to Doug? She'd always be connected to him. She'd never forget him. There was a special niche in her heart filled with him and pictures of their life together. During lonely nights, her heart had ached for him. But the aching was almost gone and in its place had come peace and the knowledge he'd want her to get on with her life. She knew that intellectually, and she'd never felt the need to test it emotionally. Until now. Until Mitch.

Even with Doug, the attraction hadn't been this strong. They'd started out as friends who'd shared dreams and a zest for living. With Mitch... Were they friends? Sometimes she thought so. Other times the attraction seemed to get in the way. It was weird. Mitch was fighting it. Until tonight, she'd been fighting it. Because of Doug? Because of her father? Because of the business? She'd always run toward life, not away from it. Maybe if she embraced what was happening, Mitch could do the same. Maybe that would relieve the tension between them.

Maybe it would make it worse.

She heard noise in the hall and wondered if Mandy was awake and needed something. But it was Nora who came into the kitchen, not the four-year-old.

She pulled the belt on her chenille robe tighter. "Did you have a good time?"

"I danced quite a bit," Laura hedged.

"With Mitch?"

"Mostly with Carey."

"That boy knows how to have a good time. He learned early from his father. Sam was lots of fun when he was young and sober."

"Mitch needs to learn how to let go."

Nora pulled out a chair and sat down. "He never had the chance. Too much responsibility too soon because Carey didn't do his share. Truthfully, he made the burden worse. Carey was older and should have known better. But he learned Sam's tricks."

Carey was trying to change his life. He'd sounded desperate for Mitch's help. Laura hoped his desire to change could weather a refusal from his brother. Still, she was more concerned about Mitch than Carey.

"Mitch doesn't trust easily."

"No. But he trusts your father."

"He told me about Denise." Laura didn't feel guilty for fishing.

"She was too much like he is. You know, organized, settled. No zip between them. Now, you and Mitch..." Her voice faded.

"There is no me and Mitch. He doesn't want it. I'm not sure I do, either. We'd be asking for complications."

"You can't always plan these things out with your head, can you?" Nora asked dejectedly.

Laura suspected Mitch's mother was talking about herself. "You and Dad seem to get along well."

Nora picked up her glasses lying next to the lead crystal salt and pepper shakers and toyed with the side piece.

"He likes your company," Laura added. "Last night he told me he's never met a better domino player."

"We come from different worlds. He's ten steps above me."

Laura patted Nora's hand. "That's not true. You're as good as he is."

"He's always had money—he's educated."

"Education doesn't always come from going to school. He'd be the first one to say hard work is more important. You've worked hard, Nora, and I'm sure he respects that."

"You're not against me and Ray being...friendly?"

"Of course not."

Nora put down the glasses and stood. "It would never work. I'm not good enough for him."

"Why do you think that?"

She sighed. "I just know I'm not."

"Nora—"

"Don't you worry about me. You concentrate on teaching Mitch how to have a good time. I'm going to bed. Good night, child. I hope your dreams are pleasant."

Laura sat in the kitchen a while longer absently toying with Nora's glasses. Teach Mitch how to have a good time? Maybe if she bought Disneyworld and held him captive there for at least a month.

Putting Nora's glasses on for fun, she made a face at herself in the oven window, then noticed something odd. She was no optometrist but she'd swear Nora's lenses weren't prescription.

Why would Nora wear spectacles that were clear glass?

Chapter Eight

"I like flying in airplanes," Mandy concluded, popping a peanut into her mouth as she peered out the window.

"You're getting to be an experienced traveler." Laura uncrossed her legs, trying to stay closer to Mandy than Mitch. He took up his whole seat and then some. She was constantly bumping his arm or his foot and pulling back.

Just as he'd pulled back from their explosive kiss. The four days since Saturday night had dragged long and slow. It was evident he wanted nothing to do with her. He'd avoided her both at home and at the store. She thought she knew how much rejection hurt. After all, she'd had practice with her father. But Mitch's rejection took the pain to another level.

"Mommy, can we get a camera and take pictures of clouds when we come back?"

"Honey, we have a camera at home."

"But we need one *here*."

"She has a point."

"Excuse me? Did you say something?"

He misunderstood her irritation. "I understand you can't buy Mandy everything she wants, but pictures of the pueblo and the jewelry could be useful. Ray would be interested."

"I suppose it would be a good idea," she agreed grudgingly.

"Can I take pictures?" Mandy asked with hope in her eyes.

"Sure." Mitch smiled one of those smiles that turned Laura's heart upside-down because they were so rare. "You can even help me pick out a camera. I've always wanted one and never bought one."

Laura felt her irritation subside. Sometimes she forgot Mitch had grown up poor.

Mandy's grin said she liked Mitch as much as Oreos. Stuffing the foil packet with peanuts into her pocket for safekeeping, she plucked her favorite storybook from the pocket of the seat in front of her, bounced out of her seat, slid past Laura and looked up at Mitch. "Will you read this to me?"

Lifting Mandy onto his lap, Mitch said, "Sure."

He never refused Mandy anything and seemed to enjoy every minute he spent with her. He was a gentle man who chose the best way to talk to a child to be understood. He'd make a good father. Laura didn't need a genius IQ to realize where that thought was leading. She watched her daughter curl into the crook of Mitch's arm and lay her head against his blazer. Mitch gave her a quick hug, opened the book and began to read.

Laura listened to *The Velveteen Rabbit*. Mandy knew the tale by heart. But Mitch's deep baritone gave the poignant story new meaning as he related the hopes and dreams of a velveteen bunny who was sad because he wasn't plush or furry. Mitch told how a stuffed bunny became "real" from a boy's love.

When Mitch finished the last sentence, Mandy turned to Laura and said, "The boy's love hurt the rabbit because he loved him so much he rubbed the bunny's fur off. George said Grandpa hurt you. Was that because he loved you so much?"

Laura blinked. And she thought Mandy had asked tough questions before. To give herself time to form an answer she asked, "When did George say that?"

"When you were packing. He told Anne he was afraid Grandpa would hurt you again. Will he hurt me, too?"

Mitch frowned, both of his arms sheltering Mandy. Instead of defending Ray as Laura thought he would, Mitch asked, "Is that why you're afraid to be alone with your grandpa?"

Mandy bobbed her head.

Laura leaned close to her daughter. "Grandpa would never hurt you, sweetheart. George meant . . ." She was still at a loss to explain something so complicated.

Mitch stepped in. "Grown-ups argue sometimes. Their feelings get hurt. That's what George meant."

"Did Grampa's feelings get hurt, too?"

Amazing how children could cut anything down to the bare essentials. Laura answered, "I guess they did."

Mandy absorbed that. So did Laura until she realized leaning closer to her daughter had moved her closer to Mitch. She could smell his after-shave, feel his intent gaze...

Squirming from Mitch's lap, Mandy asked, "Can I go to the bathroom?"

Laura smiled. The small cubicle had fascinated Mandy from the first time she'd visited it.

A flight attendant coming down the aisle must have overheard. She said, "I'll take you."

Laura checked with her daughter. "Would you rather I come?"

Mandy looked at the attendant and her friendly smile. "No. I'll go with her."

Laura watched her daughter sashay down the aisle, holding the attendant's hand.

Mitch said, "You're lucky. She's a wonderful child."

"I know. And you're perceptive. I hope Mandy won't be afraid of Dad now."

"I think she understood."

"George is usually more careful. He probably didn't know she was there."

"Probably."

The strained silence vibrated between them.

At the same time, they spoke each other's names. Laura waited for Mitch to go first.

"Do you think we can enjoy this trip?"

When she turned to face him more directly, her arm brushed his. But she didn't move it. "I'd like to. How can we?"

"By forgetting Saturday night happened."

His solution didn't seem workable to her. "You must have a short memory."

"Laura..."

She knew that exasperated warning. "Unless I pretend you didn't turn me inside out, we can't have a pleasant time."

"Can't you make anything easy?"

"Easy's a matter of perception." When he rolled his eyes, she asked, "What would make this trip easy for you?"

"If we could cooperate."

"We cooperated Saturday night," she said sweetly and earned a scowl. Did she taunt him on purpose because of some perverse streak or to pull an impulsive reaction from him? She didn't know. Taking pity on him, she agreed,

"Okay. That means we don't fight and we don't kiss. Fine. I can do that. If I don't agree with you, I'll keep quiet and go eat a chocolate bar. And if I feel like kissing you..."

His eyes darkened.

She shrugged. "I'll take three deep breaths."

His lips twitched and he gave in to the smile. "You're impossible."

She straightened her skirt and folded her hands in her lap. "That's a matter of opinion."

When he chuckled and shook his head, the tension evaporated. She just hoped deep breathing was therapeutic because she might be doing a lot of it.

They arrived in Flagstaff in the early evening. Laura was transported back in time to another era. Although the city was the largest in northern Arizona, it had a rugged, western atmosphere. Because of the Navaho and Hopi reservations nearby, native Americans were common on the streets. So were cowboys from surrounding cattle ranches. She felt as if a caravan of covered wagons should come rolling down the street.

She wholeheartedly approved of Mitch's choice of hotels. Simply put, it was comfortable and welcoming. She and Mandy explored the photographs of Indian festivals on the walls while Mitch checked in. They met him and the bellboy at the elevator. After they arrived at the fourth floor, to Laura's surprise, the bellhop opened the door to the room, then proceeded to deposit all three suitcases inside.

Laura began, "One of those goes into the next room." When the bellboy looked confused, Mitch took Laura's arm and led her inside. "There is no other room. This is a suite with two bedrooms. Yours has two double beds. I thought this would be more convenient if we want to discuss business."

If she didn't know better, she'd think he had an ulterior motive. But he'd made it very clear kissing wasn't on the agenda so nothing else would be, either. She walked into the living room. The decor was pleasing with the well-known peach, russets and turquoise, hallmarks of the southwestern motif.

"Laura, is this all right?"

The bellboy waited for his tip and the okay to leave the luggage. The sudden concern in Mitch's eyes told her if she had reservations, he'd get another room for her.

"It's fine."

Mitch tipped the bellboy and closed the door. "I'm sorry if you're upset. I just thought since you live with George and since I've been staying in the same house with you, sharing a suite wouldn't be a problem."

Mandy was investigating the knobs on the television. "Honey, you can take your bag of toys into the room with two beds, okay?"

Her daughter took her Barbie Doll canvas bag and ran off to find her room.

Laura faced Mitch. "Do I look upset? Did I say there was a problem? Do you have a guilty conscience maybe?"

His stance grew defensive as he crossed his arms over his chest. "Why should I?"

"Because you didn't consult me first."

Mitch uncrossed his arms and stuffed his hands in his pockets. "You could be right."

"Could be?"

He grimaced. "You are. I didn't think about the arrangements I made until we checked in. I assumed this was the best plan and I did it. You're not upset?"

One of the things she liked most about him was his strength never to shirk responsibility. "Of course not." She walked to the window and waved her arm to encompass the scenery outside. "We're here. That's all that matters. I wouldn't care if we had to camp out and sleep in the same tent." She grinned. No, she wouldn't mind at all.

"Don't push it," he muttered, his eyes growing dangerous.

Letting the subject alone, she went to check out her room.
Then she took three very deep breaths.

As Mitch drove the rental car toward the Navaho reservation, he appreciated Mandy's oohs and aahs and Laura's
fascination with the countryside. It was an unbalanced land
where shepherd families, according to the season, lived in
mud-chinked hogans or brush shelters. It didn't seem
strange to see Navaho rangers welcoming tourists to a tribal
park complete with a campground. Somehow, the old and
the new appeared to mesh.

Red sandstone slabs reached toward the turquoise sky.
Mitch could understand how the surroundings influenced
the creative flow of art in the Southwest. Clumps of juni-
per, salt sage and rabbit brush added green to the variety of
earthtones. He could sit out here for days, sketching ideas,
forming designs, soaking up inspiration and peace.

The Navaho reservation was vast but Laura's directions
were specific. She did have an organizational streak. He'd
seen a glimpse of it in her outline for the sterling promotion. Just when he thought he knew her, another facet of her
personality intrigued him. She was too complex to catalog.
Not for the first time, he wondered exactly what had tran-
spired between her and Ray before she left six years ago.

Mandy skipped along beside Laura asking question after
question as they walked through the pueblo. She pulled on
her mom's arm as they passed a Navaho woman in traditional dress—velveteen blouse, full cotton skirt, and an
abundance of silver and turquoise jewelry. "Isn't she
pretty?"

Laura agreed. "Yes, she is."

Mitch's gaze moved from the woman to Laura and
skimmed her salmon-colored pantsuit. "So are you."

She looked surprised, and he marveled that the compliment had slipped out so easily. She also looked pleased. They'd been getting along well. He congratulated himself on his attitude last night. After buying a camera, sightseeing in Flagstaff and stopping for pizza, they'd settled in easily. Tired from the trip, after three games of cards they'd all gone to bed. No hassle. No fuss. No undue temptation. The trip was going to go smoothly personally and professionally.

Laura stopped outside a hogan where a tribesman was working under the brilliant sun. She picked up a ring of inlaid stones and shell while Mitch examined a cuff bracelet with burnished silver geometric patterns. "Is this what the agent showed you?"

"Similar." She turned her attention to a necklace of turquoise beads. "It was the concha belts and squash blossom necklaces that really caught my eye."

"But you want to incorporate less expensive pieces, too, don't you?" He fingered a string of tiny silver beads that shimmered. It was called liquid silver.

She gave him a smile almost as bright as the sun. "I want all of it."

He laughed. "After we see *all of it,* we'll have to make a list and break down the number of pieces we want of each."

"It could take forever if *I* have to decide."

"We have all night. I thought Mandy might like to go to the Lowell Observatory after an early supper. When she goes to bed, we can work."

Laura looked away, down at the table in front of her, and he wondered if she was thinking about them working together alone. "That sounds good," she said over her shoulder.

They'd be occupied with business. It would be no different than working in the store. "I thought tomorrow we could take a Jeep ride through—"

At her smile, he stopped. "What?"

"You are a planner, aren't you?"

She didn't sound critical. "What did you have in mind for tomorrow?"

"I haven't thought about it. I was going to see where today led."

"If you don't want to ride into the cliffs—"

She laid her hand on his arm. "It'll be a great experience for Mandy. But maybe we could play the rest of tomorrow by ear. Sort of go where the sun leads?"

He enjoyed her touching him and it was more than the elemental response his body gave. "You might have to teach me how to do that." He was beginning to believe she could teach him lots of things.

She held up her index finger. "Step one. Relax and forget schedules. At least until we get back on the plane day after tomorrow."

Mitch found following the sun wasn't as difficult as he imagined it would be. He simply followed Laura.

She led him through every nook and cranny where visitors were allowed in the pueblo, peeping into a beehive oven where bread baked, examining and watching an elderly Navaho woman weave a rug on a loom, walking far enough away from the hubbub to scan shepherds herding sheep on a far hill.

She talked to everyone she saw, smiled at those who didn't speak English. When she learned about the ruins of Wupatki National Monument east of Flagstaff, they went there next. She was as curious as Mandy.

Mitch enjoyed watching her move, gesture, laugh. She opened up a world to him he'd ignored for too long. He scheduled his life too well and didn't allow time to look at the sky. This sky couldn't be ignored. It was too intensely blue, too expansive, too beautiful. But if he took the time to look at the sky in York, it might have its own beauty.

Later that evening, Laura smiled as Mitch sat forward on the sofa and checked the list they'd made. They'd called room service for a second pot of coffee—this time decaffeinated. Laura had tucked Mandy in two hours ago. Since then, she and Mitch had looked over the lists of choices of jewelry pieces, discussing salability and their sales campaign.

Their sales campaign. She liked the sound of that. She liked standing beside him, working with him, watching his tenderness with Mandy. Even when they disagreed or argued, some bond tied them together. And suddenly she knew she was falling in love with him. That scared her.

She took a deep breath. Thanks to her mother, she'd never been frightened by feelings. That wasn't true for Mitch. When he didn't like what he felt, he shut it off. What did he feel? Laura was afraid to ask.

He'd been more relaxed today than she'd ever seen him. But now with Mandy in bed and the intimate silence of the suite surrounding them, they were more aware of each other and less relaxed. She could tell by his movements, the tension in his body. Passion rose whenever they were in the same room. They didn't have to argue. They didn't even have to touch. It was just there—vibrating, sharp, nipping at all her senses, slicing through whatever was in its way. She didn't know why. But she'd come to accept its presence and revel in it. She wished Mitch could.

He put his cup down with a click. "Are you satisfied with what we've decided?"

"The quantity or the ads?"

His head came up and his stare was direct. "Both."

"I understand your reasoning to temper the first shipment. As long as we have the option to add to our inventory when we need it, that's okay."

"But you'd like five more squash blossom necklaces."

"I'd like ten more." At his wry look, she shook her finger at him, almost hitting his chest. "You wait and see. I bet we sell out when we have Ladies' Night."

He caught her finger as amusement danced in his blue eyes. "I hope we do."

She went still as the heat from his hand warmed her all over. But she pushed a question past the sudden tightness in her throat. "You want my ideas to work?"

The nerve in his jaw jumped. "If you're successful, Ray and I will benefit."

So it was strictly for business reasons. Not because he cared. She swallowed. "I see."

His eyes dropped to the pulse at her throat, the gold chain with the dangling rose, the swell of her breast under her sweater. His chest rose and fell as he let out a draft of air and tenderly rubbed her wrist with his thumb. "I want this to work for you. I know it's important because you think you have to succeed to earn your dad's approval."

He did care about her. "I've never had my dad's approval. Not as an adult."

Mitch's fingers slid up her forearm to her elbow. As if in a trance, he moved them to her shoulder and slid them under her hair. "A very beautiful adult."

She swayed toward him, not wanting the cherishing note in his voice to diminish or the exciting light in his eyes to fade. Her lips parted on a small sigh.

When he groaned and drew her to him, she knew desire had won over logic. This kiss was different from the first. His lips were hungry but not bruising, demanding but not angry. He greedily tasted her, but savored the contact as if he might not experience it again. When the pressure became more frustrating than satisfactory, his tongue slid along her upper lip and teased it until she parted it from the bottom one and he slipped inside. He was hot and strong.

Her heart beat so fast she couldn't think. Three deep breaths were the last thing on her mind.

She wanted to feel his passion break loose. This was the real Mitch, the one who yearned to be free. She wanted to experience everything he had to give and she wanted to give back . . . needed to give back.

She brushed her tongue against his, chased it into his mouth, and brought her hands up to caress his face. She felt the scar, wondered again how he'd been hurt and tried to imagine whatever pain he'd experienced. Winding her arms about his neck, she held him tight, close, wanting to make his pain, his reserve, his doubts go away. With her fingers laced in his thick hair, she massaged his scalp with the same fervor and energy she invested in their kiss.

His arms surrounded her as he slid her onto his lap. His hand caressed her hip. She gently nipped his tongue, unable to break away to tell him how excited she was, how thrilling his touch was, how wonderful this closeness was. When his hand sneaked under the back of her sweater, goose bumps broke out all over and she couldn't even imagine how she'd feel if he touched her more intimately.

His palm came to rest boldly on her breast. She felt as if she'd explode. She squirmed on his lap as his finger played across her nipple, sending jolts of need to her womb. Underneath her thigh, she could feel how hard he was and how much he wanted her. She wanted him, too. She wanted to feel him, touch him, hold him.

Mitch couldn't think, couldn't reason, couldn't do anything but feel. The feelings and sensations were strange, some forgotten, some never before experienced. Laura's power to arouse him was exasperating, frustrating, exquisite. Why couldn't he control the rush of feelings? And why was he lured by her excitement? Why couldn't he keep away from her? Because she was everything he wasn't?

He remembered how she'd looked at the observatory with the black sky and brilliant stars framing her profile. The moon she'd wished on had flirted with the blondest strands of her hair. He'd known then tonight would be much harder to deal with than last night. He'd been right. All he could think of was kissing her, wrapping his body around her.

As the lacy piece of material gave under his fingertips, he didn't care about why he couldn't keep away from her. He didn't care about logic. He forgot about her background. He felt her desire as intensely as he felt his own. It was like hot lava—smoking, bubbling, flowing over them both.

His fingertips appreciated the upper moon of her breast as he lost himself in her softness. He wanted more. He wanted now. He wanted Laura.

He wanted too much.

He couldn't have Laura. Now would lead to tomorrow. Tomorrow would lead to too many complications to contemplate. All because he'd given in to... to... feelings.

Disgusted with himself, he jerked away and pulled his hand out from under her sweater. He took in harsh breaths that brought with them her sweet scent. Torture.

Mitch felt a blush creep up his neck. Damn it all. There was no graceful route to get out of this one. If he'd been a drinking man, now would be the time for a triple shot. But he didn't depend on liquor. He didn't depend on anything or anyone but himself.

When Laura saw his expression, she moved from his lap to the sofa. She looked flustered, disappointed, hurt, and sexy as hell with her hair mussed like that and her gray eyes wide. Not trying to hide her discomfort, she rearranged her sweater and pulled it down to her waist. Then she waited.

"I don't know what to say."

"Give it a shot."

Her tone was husky but annoyed. Anger shook him. It was connected to what had just happened. He tamped it down, knowing this situation wasn't her fault but his.

"I don't think so."

She threw her hands in the air and tossed her hair back from her rosy face. "Sure, pretend this didn't happen either. Face reality, Mitch!"

"I am. That's why I stopped. You don't need this any more than I do. We're different, Laura. Like January and July, fire and ice. Besides that, you're Ray's daughter. I can't..." He swore.

"Don't tell me what I need. Apparently *you* need to hide behind your relationship with my father and however many other excuses you can think up."

Her lashing out hurt, and he didn't know if she was right or not. "I'm not hiding behind excuses. Sex isn't something I play with. *You* seem to jump right in. And I wonder why. Do you think you can get to Ray's business through me?" He saw her flush but didn't know if it was anger or hurt. He'd asked because it was suddenly very important for him to know.

She exploded off the sofa, her hands balled into fists. "If you have to ask, you don't deserve an answer. I'm sick of your suspicion and doubts. Today I thought we'd finally—"

"Connected?" he asked with a calm he wasn't feeling. He'd just driven a giant wedge between them. He needed space and time to resolve what he was thinking and feeling.

"Yes. But obviously you don't feel the same way." She shook her head as if she didn't understand him at all. Then she sighed, rubbed her hand across her brow and moved toward her room. At the doorway, she faced him. "Do you still want to take the tour to the cliffs tomorrow?"

He mowed his hand through his hair. "I think Mandy will enjoy it."

"At least we agree on that." Laura went into her room and closed the door.

Chapter Nine

Laura shifted the bag of groceries from her right arm to her left as she opened the door of her father's house. Before she could cross the foyer, Mitch appeared and took the bag from her. "I could have gone for groceries."

"No need. It was on my way." Lord, how formal she sounded! One thing she and Mitch had never been was formal.

Mitch shrugged, and a lock of black hair fell over his forehead. Laura itched to smooth it back, remembering the feel of it between her fingers. She'd missed him. He'd spent his days and nights in Harrisburg since their Arizona trip and this was the first she'd seen him in four days.

For Mandy's sake, they'd maintained a strained, civil, bordering on trying-to-be-friendly tone after the fiasco in their hotel suite. Mitch's accusation that she was using him to try to get control of the business had hurt terribly, but it had also given her a glimmer of understanding.

No wonder Mitch was fighting his feelings so hard. Who would want to fall in love with a woman who would do something like that? Nothing she could do would prove she wasn't manipulating him. He had to risk trusting her. She didn't think he'd had much practice risking or trusting.

She unbuttoned her poncho, wishing she could bridge the gap between them, wanting to, needing to. "I called Nora to check on Mandy's sniffles. She mentioned she needed a few staples."

"I got in about an hour ago. I read Mandy a story and she coughed a few times. So I called a pediatrician and he explained her runny nose could be from the change in altitude and temperature. He said to call him back if she gets a fever. Otherwise, the over-the-counter decongestant you're giving her is okay."

Before Laura could respond, he added, "I know you're a good mother, but I was worried and called him to ease my own mind. She's taking a nap now. I thought it would be good for her and she didn't argue."

Laura was touched, not angry as he seemed to expect. Mandy's welfare seemed to be as important to him as it was to her. "Thank you for caring."

Neither of them moved. After a moment of uncomfortable silence, Mitch spoke. "I'll take these to the kitchen. Your boxes of clothing from Independence arrived, but one of them was broken open. You might want to see if anything is damaged." He strode to the kitchen as she went into the living room, leaving Laura feeling cut adrift.

There were two cartons, one with some of Mandy's winter clothes, the other with Laura's. Laura's box had a deep gash in the side and the top slit was broken open. Lifting the flaps, she removed a sweater that didn't look any the worse for the accident. Underneath it lay a framed photograph of her, Doug and Mandy. Anne must have thought she needed something familiar to hold on to.

Laura sat on the recliner and slipped off her poncho and heels. Holding the picture in her hand, she ran her thumb over Doug's face. Sometimes she couldn't see it clearly now when she closed her eyes. He was her past.

When she looked up, Mitch stood in front of her. Could this man be her present? Her future?

"Is anything damaged?" he asked.

"I don't know. I didn't get very far."

He nodded at her hands. "That's a good picture."

In it her arm was wrapped around Doug's waist, his across her shoulders. A two-year-old Mandy stood at their legs. "We were at a picnic."

Mitch's eyes searched her face. "Were you always that happy with him?"

"We were happy a lot. But..."

Mitch sat on the sofa and waited.

"You're going to laugh."

His eyes said he wouldn't.

"I was the practical one."

"Would you tell me about it?" he asked quietly.

This was one of those times when she felt a bond between them, when she knew they *were* friends. "After Mandy was born, I couldn't pick up and go quite as easily. I had her to think about. I breast-fed and Doug couldn't help with that. I suppose he felt removed from her immediate care."

"That didn't have to happen. There's a lot a father can do."

Somehow she knew Mitch wouldn't be the type of father to sleep while the baby cried. Or the type of father who would resent the time and care a mother gave to her child. He'd be proud of it.

"Was he a good father?"

She was honest because she sensed it was important to Mitch. "When he wanted to be. But he could be easily distracted. I never completely trusted him with her."

"He sounds irresponsible and selfish," Mitch muttered.

Laura bit back a defense, knowing ideas of responsibility didn't always jibe. "You thought I was irresponsible. You still might."

Mitch met her gaze directly. "I know you better now. You're impulsive but not irresponsible—especially not with Mandy. How could you be happy with someone who didn't put her first?"

Mitch wasn't criticizing, he was trying to find out about her life. "Doug had good qualities and faults, too. If you had known him— He was so easy to be with. When we started out, he loved me for who I was, not what he wanted me to be. And that's the way I loved him." Though in the months after Mandy's birth that had changed. When Laura could no longer be footloose, Doug was less accepting of her "mother" role.

Mitch picked up on one part of what she'd said. "Loved?"

She understood. He was asking if she was still in love with her husband. "He's gone, Mitch. Just like my mother. My life has to go on." Meeting and caring for Mitch had brought that home even more.

Before Mitch could respond, they heard footsteps in the foyer. Ray, in gray sweatpants and sweatshirt, entered the living room. Laura had rarely seen him in anything but a suit, even when she was a child. Since he'd started walking with Nora and exercising with the rehab nurse, he seemed to enjoy casual clothes. He looked relaxed, more approachable.

He took in the photograph in Laura's hands and her serious expression. But he didn't comment on either. "Nora says supper will be ready in half an hour. Mitch, let's go to my office and discuss your sales campaign for Christmas. And, Laura, I'd like to speak to you—"

"*His* sales campaign?" Laura asked with raised brows.

Mitch said calmly, "We worked on ideas together in Flagstaff."

Ray gazed at Mitch intently. "But you had your ads for Harrisburg set up months ago."

"I know. But I might incorporate Ladies' Night and Men's Night as Laura suggested."

Ray rubbed his chin. "I see. Well, then, we'll save that for after supper. Laura, can I talk to you for a few minutes now?"

Her gaze went to the stairs.

"If Mandy wakes up, I'll get her ready for supper," Mitch assured her.

Laura laid the photograph on top of the box and followed her father to his office where Ray immediately sat down in the monstrous leather chair behind the desk. She stood, rather than dropping into the captain's chair in front of the desk. She wouldn't let him make her feel like a delinquent sixteen-year-old again. Though she did feel at a disadvantage in her stockinged feet. "What did you want to talk about?"

"You and Mitch work together well."

She sent him a puzzled look. "Sometimes, but what does...?"

Ray smiled. "You're intelligent adults with your own ideas. Of course you won't agree on everything."

She waited.

"Have you considered staying in York permanently?"

Consciously or not she had, especially since she realized she was falling in love with Mitch. But his feelings were the deciding factor, and the way it looked now... "I have a life in Independence," she hedged, wondering where this was leading.

Her father propped his elbows on the desk and put his hands together, steepling his fingers. "What if I said I'm thinking about retiring and I'd like you to take over the York store while Mitch takes Harrisburg."

Her heart raced and her stomach tightened. What she'd always wanted was in her grasp. But did she want it now? If she accepted, would her father think he could run her life as he'd tried to before? What would happen to her independence if she lived in York? And what about Mitch? What would this mean for him?

"I thought you and Mitch were partners."

He nodded. "We are."

"What would I be?" she asked bluntly.

Ray disconnected his fingers and folded one hand over the other. "I could have a lawyer draw up a three-way partnership."

He was so controlled. She couldn't read him. Was this purely a business proposition? Or did having her in York mean something to him? "Mitch will lose money."

He shook his head emphatically. "Not in the long run. If your ideas work, the York store will be on par with Harrisburg. You have the energy to pour into it. I don't anymore. In a few years, you might even want to open a third store. That would be a challenge, wouldn't it?"

"Mitch will resent me." He already thought she wanted to horn in. If she said "yes" to her dad's offer, it would mean certain death to any relationship she and Mitch might have. She couldn't push in. If Mitch wanted her to stay, he'd have to ask her himself without coercion from Ray, without being trapped in a partnership he hadn't chosen.

"Mitch would see merit in the idea," Ray argued. "Remember, he's the one who brought you here."

"I know," she said, unable to keep the sadness from her voice. It would have meant so much more for her father to have called her himself.

As if guessing her thoughts, he said, "I never thought you'd come. Not after I didn't answer your letters."

Laura's throat tightened. Her dad had never explained himself. "Why didn't you?"

Deep lines emphasized Ray's age and what he'd been through in the past few weeks. "I was still angry about—" He stopped. "I thought you'd come running home."

Laura sent him a disbelieving look. "When you didn't bother to answer me?"

"Where else would you go? Once you were home, I thought we'd settle our differences."

She couldn't help wondering if she became a partner and did something he disapproved of, would he disown her again? She couldn't deal with that a second time. But if she brought that up, they'd have to discuss why she left. They were just starting to mend their relationship. She didn't want to put a wall between them again because of a past that couldn't be changed.

Her father's face was expectant.

"I'm sorry. I can't accept your offer," she said tightly, wishing it could be different.

Ray didn't ask why, just as he hadn't asked what she was feeling after her mother died, just as he hadn't asked her how she felt when he cut her out of his life. "There are other changes I want to make, too. If I have a fatal heart attack, I want Mitch to have more than the partnership."

She couldn't imagine her dad not sitting behind this desk, not barking orders. Even when she was in Ohio, she'd known he was somewhere. If he died... Tears pricked in her eyes. She blinked, swallowed and tried to speak, but her father's next words forestalled her.

"If you're not interested in moving back to York and becoming a partner, I'm going to make a new will." Ray's chair squeaked as he leaned back. "You will, of course, inherit the house and my personal possessions. You would also receive a stipend from profits. But I want to leave the business to Mitch if you don't want to be a part of it.''

If he'd expected her to be shocked, she wasn't. It was only fair. Mitch had worked beside her father for the last four years. He was more than a partner to Ray. He'd become a son to him as well. Laura didn't feel jealous, but she did feel an overwhelming sense of loss. Personal loss.

She didn't need the business; she was happy with her life. Mitch did need it. It was his future and she couldn't take it away from him. Staying in York was impossible, unless . . .

Unless Mitch trusted her wholeheartedly and asked her to stay himself. Fat chance. "If you feel you need to, have the papers drawn up."

"You won't reconsider?"

She wondered if this was simply a ploy of Ray's to shake her up and make her change her mind. "Not as things stand now."

He gave her a probing look, but didn't press. "I won't do anything until you leave. I've waited this long, I can wait a little longer. Then if you change your mind . . ."

Tears welled in her eyes. Was this her dad's way of reaching out? Why couldn't he ever admit he cared for her? Loved her? "I'll let you know," she murmured, then turned away from her father and left the office.

She needed to see Mandy and hug her. She needed to talk to George and Anne, to reassure herself she belonged in Independence with people who loved her, who trusted her and who depended on her.

Mitch paced the kitchen, trying to make himself immune to the pleading in Carey's eyes. "I can't give you the money."

"Can't or won't?"

"I've given you money before."

"This is a loan."

Damn! First the mess he'd made of the trip with Laura, now this. He hadn't been able to think of anything but Laura since the night he'd almost made love to her. Every time he looked at her, remembered the way she'd felt in his arms, under his hands, he wanted to scoop her up, carry her to his bedroom and make love to her until his need for her was fulfilled. Maybe if he went ahead and did it, he could get her out of his mind. The more he fought the attraction, the more it gripped him. But he didn't believe in using a woman, and that's what it would be.

Just like Carey was trying to use him for the umpteenth time in their lives. Carey had lessons to learn. He wouldn't learn them if Mitch continued to give him handouts and clean up the consequences. "How many loans have I given you?"

Carey blushed and mumbled, "I don't know."

"Guess." His brother had to face facts.

"Nine, ten, twelve. I don't remember. But I guess you have them all written down in a ledger."

A stab of pain jabbed Mitch. He loved Carey. Their father's behavior and attitude had put a wedge between them, just as Carey's mistakes had put Mitch in the position of rescuer. Did Carey resent that? Couldn't he see everything Mitch had done, everything he was doing now was because he loved Carey?

"No, I haven't kept track. Carey, you need to take responsibility for what you do. Go to work. Save the money before you spend it. Then you don't have to answer to anyone."

Carey dropped his head and ran his hands over the edge of the table. "Just one more time, Mitch. I promise I'll never ask you again."

It wasn't the asking Mitch minded, or the giving; it was the wasting. He regretted his own weakness where Carey was concerned. He'd bent over backward to show his brother he didn't blame him for the accident. Had he been wrong?

Mitch said the words he had to say. "I won't give you the money."

Carey's pale blue eyes filled with supplication. "Do I have to crawl?"

Mitch's heart turned over in his chest. "Don't do this."

"Right. Don't make life any harder for you. You've hated me since I . . ." He stared at Mitch's cheek.

Mitch stood perfectly still. It hurt to swallow. "I *don't* hate you. I didn't then and I don't now."

Carey's chair scraped as he pushed back and stood, his words angry. "Don't worry, *brother.* I'll never ask you for anything again."

Carey exited the kitchen and Mitch heard the front door bang. He felt as if he'd lost someone, and he wondered if this was how Ray had felt when Laura walked out of his life.

Mitch ran the knife down the middle of the box and lifted out a silver-plated tray.

Laura came into the office and went straight to the small refrigerator in the corner. She took out a container of yogurt and turned without meeting his eyes.

"Is that lunch?" Mitch asked. He hated the tension between them. This was his first day back in the York store with Laura and they were being so careful around each other it hurt.

"You could say that."

When she lifted her gaze to his, he couldn't tell what she was thinking. That was unusual. The fact that he'd put the shuttered look there generated guilt. "Let's take a break and have a nice lunch. The bistro in the next block has fresh croissant sandwiches."

"You want to have lunch with me?" Her tone was puzzled.

"Sure. We're both hungry." He pulled his topcoat from the coatrack and handed Laura her poncho, then frowned. "This is what you wore today?"

"It's all I have here."

"I thought Anne sent winter clothes."

"She forgot my coat. This is fine."

Mitch didn't agree, but he held his tongue. Winter hadn't waited for Thanksgiving as it usually did in south-central Pennsylvania. The last week had been unseasonably cold.

Thanksgiving. Two weeks away. This year with Laura and Mandy here, maybe Ray could enjoy it.

As soon as they stepped outside and the wind whipped them, Mitch muttered, "It's only thirty-two degrees out here." He cupped her elbow. "Let's take a detour." Turning her around, he headed her down the street in the opposite direction.

"Where are we going?"

"This will only take a few minutes." At her perplexed look, he said, "You're the one who likes surprises. Come on."

Keeping her head down against the wind, apparently Laura didn't realize where he was taking her until the Indian bell over the door tinkled behind her and plush carpet softened their steps. The smell of leather wound around them and she sent Mitch an inquiring look.

He guided her to a rack with full-length leather coats and pulled out a rich forest-green one with a hood. "Try it on."

Mitch had bought his jacket here. This coat was as supple and soft as his. Leather would suit Laura perfectly. It would enhance her sensuality. Of course, that might not be such a great idea. He had enough trouble with her appeal now.

"I can't afford this," she protested.

"It's a gift." Her gray eyes softened and he wanted to tug her into his arms and simply hold her.

"I can't accept it."

He could see she wanted to and not simply because she needed a coat, but because it came from him. "If Anne and George gave you a present, you wouldn't give it back, would you?"

"That's different. Why would you want to give me a present when you think the only reason I want to get close to you is to take control of the business?"

The hurt in her voice was evident and Mitch felt lower than a sinkhole. He looked around to see if anyone was listening. Across the room the salesclerk was ringing up a sale at the cash register. Two ladies were at a nearby rack. "Must we have this conversation here?"

"If you want me to try on this coat, we must."

He sighed and turned his back on the two women. "Laura, to tell you the truth, I don't know what I believe anymore." He thought about things differently since he'd met her. He knew he'd never been in love with Denise. He realized he'd denied most of the pain in his childhood. He acknowledged he kept his feelings hidden. And now, he wondered what had actually happened between Laura and Ray.

"I'm not trying to take control of the business," she said. "Dad asked me to stay and manage the York store if he retires. I refused. I'm going back to Ohio in three weeks."

Mitch felt as if he'd been kicked in the gut. Her decision meant she had no ulterior motive; she wanted no part of the business. It also meant she would be leaving. That prospect didn't give him an iota of the relief he once thought it would. She'd become a fire in his blood he couldn't extinguish or ignore. He didn't know if that was interfering with his judgment or directing it.

Recovering, he said, "Then you have to accept this as a going-away present. You need it now. It's early."

Indecision played in her eyes. "Cloth would be fine."

"But not as warm. Trust me. This is just what you need for an Independence winter, too." When she still looked as if she might refuse, he said softly, "Let me do this, Laura. I've given you some rough moments."

She smiled, the first genuine smile he'd seen since Flagstaff. "They're over? You're going to be agreeable and compliant from now on?"

"As much as you are," he quipped. He took the coat from the hanger and held it for her.

She slipped her arms into the sleeves. He lifted her hair, holding it a moment longer than necessary before he let it flow softly onto the closed hood.

Laura wrapped the coat around herself reverently as if it were mink. When she belted it, her hands caressed the leather.

Mitch's breaths became shallower. He'd like to wrap himself around her as closely as the coat, mold to her, stroke her. Hell. What would that get him? In three weeks, she'd be gone. Flings weren't his style. And Laura? She lived in the moment. An affair might be acceptable to her. Her response in the hotel suite seemed to indicate as much. But the more he told himself to stay away, the more he was drawn to her.

"What do you think?" he asked, loving the way the deep color emphasized and complemented the golden highlights in her hair.

She turned around, her eyes sparkling with silver lights. "It feels wonderful!"

He pointed to the side wall. "Go look in the mirror."

She walked toward the three-way mirror, the coat swaying around her as if it was made for her. It moved with her, against her, for her.

After facing the mirror head on, she turned to the left, then to the right. Her smile grew wider by the minute. Pulling the hood up, she buttoned the collar to achieve the full effect. She put her hands in the pockets; she pulled them out. Pirouetting in a circle, she let the leather slap against her calves.

Returning to where Mitch was standing, she let down the hood. "It's a beautiful coat."

"You look beautiful in it." The huskiness of his voice surprised him.

Her eyes combed his face. "I *could* use a new winter coat, I suppose."

"It's yours."

"No, that wasn't what I meant. What if I pay half?"

"Nope." When he saw her open her mouth to protest, he added, "But you can pay me back another way."

Instantly she was wary. "How?"

"My jewelry exhibition is Friday night. Go with me to Harrisburg." The look in her eyes made his heart jump crazily.

"That's it? That's not a payback. I'd love to see your work. I've wanted to since I arrived."

"You'll be giving me moral support," he said, trying to make the deal sound two-sided.

"As if you need it. Dad told me last year you sold every piece that one night."

"This year might be different. The public is fickle."

Her fingers lovingly stroked one lapel as she looked down at the deep green leather. "And you think this is a fair trade?"

He kept a serious expression. "Absolutely."

"I'll accept the coat on one condition. You let me take you out some night."

There was a daring light in her eyes. "To dinner?"

She laughed and drawled, "Maybe. Or maybe something else."

"Like . . . ?"

"Let me think about it. Is it a deal?"

Deals with Laura were happening more often. He was especially pleased with this one. "It's a deal."

Laura's stomach rumbled. She smiled and unbuttoned the coat.

"Aren't you going to wear it?"

"If the salesclerk cuts off the tags." She glanced at the price again. "Mitch..."

He dropped his arm around her shoulders and shepherded her toward the cash register. "We made a deal. Now that you won't freeze, let's go to lunch."

At five-thirty, Laura waved to Mitch as he drove away after dropping her off at the house. He had to pick up his dry cleaning. She opened the front door and hung the new coat in the closet, holding on to the feeling of hope it gave her. She loved touching it. Whenever Mitch wore his, she wanted to run her hands over it. But not as much as she wanted to run them over him.

They'd connected again. Was it because she'd told him she was leaving? Did he now feel he could trust her? She still sensed he was intent on keeping some distance between them. Because of her father? Or was it more personal?

Did intimacy and love frighten him? She so much wanted to show him love was meant to be experienced and shared. True, love could hurt. But it was magical and wonderful, too.

She shut the closet door and homed in on voices in the sun-room. Just outside the door, she realized the voices belonged to Nora and Carey, not Nora and her father. She was just about to turn around and see if Mandy was with her grandfather when Laura heard Carey's raised voice.

"Mitch wouldn't give it to me. Ma, I need the money to get my life on track. Won't you talk to him and convince him to make the loan?"

"When Mitch sets his mind, he doesn't change it. If he thinks he has a good reason, nothing I say will make a difference. You know that."

"What am I going to do?" Carey's voice sounded desperate.

"I have some money. It's only a third of what you need. I've been saving what Mitch gives me."

"He'll pop his cork if he finds out."

"You decide, Carey. It's yours if you want it."

He was silent for at least a minute. "I'll take it."

"You won't do anything foolish?"

"No, Ma. Your stake is going to change my life. You'll see."

Laura heard his boots cross the ceramic floor and she guessed he kissed and hugged Nora.

"You go back to your crocheting. I have things to do."

Before she could move, Carey came out of the sun-room and saw her. They stared at each other silently.

"I'm sorry. I didn't mean to eavesdrop. It just sort of happened."

"Please don't tell Mitch."

"You should tell him and prevent the fireworks."

Carey seemed to cringe at the word. "It's not necessary. Why stir the pot when you don't have to? When I turn the money into what I need, I'll pay Ma back and the case will be closed. No arguments, no fuss."

"Turn the money into what you need?" Laura hoped she was wrong about what she was thinking. "What are you going to do?"

"I'm going to take one last chance."

"Tell me you're not going to gamble again."

He held up his hand and lowered his voice so his mother couldn't hear. "Just one more time. And it won't be gambling. I have friends at the track. I'll wait for a good solid tip."

"You're lying to yourself, Carey. There are no solid tips. Don't you know that by now? Call someone from Gamblers Anonymous. If I can't talk you out of—"

"I have to do this." His hand rested briefly on Laura's shoulder. "It will be all right. I know what I'm doing."

Laura knew all the words in the world wouldn't change his mind. "For your sake, I hope you do."

His fingers tightened. "Promise me you won't tell Mitch."

"That's a hard promise to make."

"Trust me with this, Laura. Please."

She doubted if anyone had trusted Carey in the past few years. He needed that, maybe more than he needed the money, though he didn't seem to realize it.

Knowing she was probably making a mistake, but unable to deprive Carey of the faith he needed, she pledged softly, "I won't tell Mitch." But a corner of her heart protested and she wondered if she'd just sunk her foot into quicksand.

Chapter Ten

When Laura entered Applegate Jewelers in Harrisburg with Mitch, it was immediately clear this was Mitchell Riley's exclusive domain. The sign on the door stating Automatic Surveillance Cameras On Premises was only one of the many ways this store differed from her father's.

Pale blue plush carpeting formed a muted backdrop for the angled cases of wood and glass protecting the store's inventory. The store echoed class and quality, just like Mitch. He'd unbuttoned his suit coat and brushed it back; his hands were stuffed in his pockets.

"I like the atmosphere here, Mitch."

He grinned. "Not too formal and stilted?"

"No. It's elegant."

Mitch cupped her elbow. "I want to show you my workshop before I introduce you to everyone. You can leave your coat in there."

He'd been friendly since she'd accepted his present, but she hadn't seen much of him the past few days. He'd been here, preparing for this. Tonight he was also friendly and pleasant, but keeping his distance, too. He was being careful not to get too close or touch her too often.

Laura followed him to the back of the store into a short hall. He opened the door to the right and flicked on the light.

She stepped over the threshold and blinked, letting her eyes adjust to the bright incandescent lighting. With difficulty she switched her attention from Mitch to the workroom. A sink stood under a four-by-four-foot window with workbenches on either side. Vats next to the sink were used to dip the jewelry after the pieces were worked on. A hood hung over the soldering area and there was a switch to turn on the fan to ventilate the room. Small tools—rifles, screwdrivers, tweezers—were lined up on each worktable.

This workroom was similar to her father's but more modern. Cabinets with supplies lined a wall. In the corner stood a polishing machine. The tan walls and beige industrial tile floor added lightness to the room.

Laura crossed to a workbench, picked up a bracelet mandrel used to hold a bracelet while it was being worked and set it down. Gold wire-rimmed glasses lay open on the pocked and lined surface. She picked them up. "Are these yours?"

"Uh-huh. I need them for close work."

She remembered Nora's glasses and their very weak prescription. "I didn't know you wore glasses."

"I keep a pair here and a pair in my glove compartment so I have them when I need them."

She carried the glasses to Mitch. "Put them on. I want to see how they look."

"Laura . . ."

"Come on," she urged, holding them out to him.

After he adjusted them on his nose, she swiveled his head to the side. Lightning struck when her fingers touched his jaw. She felt the jolt go through him too, when the muscle in his cheek jumped.

Lowering her hand, she took a deep breath to steady her knees. "Very distinguished. I like them."

He turned his head so his eyes caught hers. The primitive desire there caused her pulse to thud.

He broke the circuit of sensual energy by taking off the glasses, folding them carefully, and laying them back on the workbench. Then he unnecessarily straightened a file folder. "I'm glad you approve."

Laura's intuition told her it wasn't just the sexual tension between them that was bothering Mitch. "Are you nervous?"

He rubbed his thumb along his chin and she saw vulnerability in his blue eyes. "Now's the time for that moral support."

Laura unbuttoned her new coat and slid it over a stool to keep herself from hugging him. "What's bothering you?"

He shook his head as if disgusted with himself. "I know it's stupid. I created what *I* wanted to create. And it shouldn't matter if anyone else likes it and wants to buy it. But it does. Oh, not so I can make the sale, though that's important. But because if someone wants to own it, that means they understand my concept of beauty and appreciate it."

Laura stepped toward him. "I know what you mean."

The bond between them at that moment was so strong, she felt paralyzed. Until Mitch reached out and brushed a strand of hair away from her cheek. Then she felt so activated she could hardly stand still.

His eyes swept over her face and down her magenta sweater dress. His gaze scorched her as it touched her throat, her breasts, her waist, her calves. She trembled.

Mitch took a step back, but his voice was grating and sensual. His eyes darkened with the passion he wouldn't set free. "It's time to face the public."

She wished he'd face his feelings. "I'm ready when you are."

Mitch introduced Laura to his assistant manager and three salesclerks. All of them urged her to find a place near the hexagonal case with the black velvet covering so she'd have a good view. She squeezed close, bumping elbows with the man on her right and shoulders with the woman on her left. Laura smiled in apology but wedged closer.

When Mitch tugged the covering away from the glass, a hush fell over the crowd. Jewelry was a language. It stated what a person felt about herself or himself—if he or she was confident, reserved, stylish or traditional. Mitch expressed himself through the medium of this language with the same passion that had broken through in their hotel suite in Flagstaff. Each piece was an intense, individual statement. His work captured attention, stimulated curiosity and interest. It ranged from the deceptively simple to the obviously complex.

There was a Pegasus pin fashioned from copper...a silver owl sitting on an ivory branch...a fan created from gold, studded with abalone...another gold piece pierced and filed to create the illusion of a web...a sleek gold panther with a black pearl eye.

To the right side of the case were the more expensive pieces with precious gems—brooches, pendants, earrings. The crowning achievement at the very center of the case was a monarch butterfly pin designed from baguette diamonds, amethysts and emeralds.

Mitch's collection wasn't a reflection of present vogue. It was unique and timeless. Each piece emanated vitality and was meant to be worn and treasured for a lifetime. Laura felt tears swim in her eyes. His jewelry revealed a facet of Mitch that had no other outlet. She was proud to know him.

The hush changed to a low hum as the customers moved around the glass. Laura stepped back and walked toward Mitch.

Beside him, she murmured, "They're beautiful, Mitch. So beautiful. You should be very proud."

When Mitch faced her, he saw the shimmering depth of her emotion and knew she understood. She hadn't been mouthing platitudes earlier. She really understood that his heart and soul and passion were here . . . in his work. "This is what I love to do. That's a year's work in that case, a year of stealing time when I could find it. My memory's a storehouse of colors, shapes, textures, lines and forms that are aching to come out. If I could, I'd do nothing but design."

"If you'd give your assistant manager more responsibility and hire someone to help with repair work, maybe you could."

"I've thought about that. But I'd have to be absolutely sure . . ." He stopped. He wasn't comfortable with a risk in his business life any more than in his personal life.

"Sure of what?"

"It would have to be worthwhile creatively and financially. The market *has* changed over the years from a few people buying large jewels to a multitude buying smaller investments. That's why there's been a rise in quantity production and chain stores. But there still are those customers who want and value the unique. I have to make sure the local market is big enough to warrant more of my time."

She touched his arm. "You have the market. Look around you. You're a success, Mitch. You can do whatever you want."

She made him feel like a success, like the world was at his feet. She was as shimmering as any of the gems he'd ever handled, as vibrant. She fairly hummed with life.

Mitch's assistant manager tapped him on the shoulder. Reluctantly he shifted his gaze from Laura to the younger man who had been running the store in Mitch's absence.

"Mrs. Waltheim wants to talk to you about designing another butterfly in different colors."

"Go ahead, Mitch," Laura encouraged. "I'll look around."

As Mitch talked to patrons, Laura circulated, admired the designs and watched Mitch. Several times she caught him watching her. The potency of that gaze was enough to make her giddy.

When everyone had left, Mitch activated the security system and Laura fetched her coat from the workroom. He locked the door and glanced at his watch. "It's early. Would you like to see my apartment? Or do you want to get home?"

"Mandy's cold is gone. She's sleeping by now. I'd like to see where you live."

"I bought a small bottle of champagne in case I had something to celebrate." He looked sheepish, like a boy revealing he still slept with his teddy bear. "We sold everything, so we have reason."

"Even if you hadn't sold everything, you'd have reason."

He seemed embarrassed, as if praise was foreign to him. She took his arm. "I'm ready for bubbles to tickle my nose."

His look said tickling her *nose* might be the last item on his list.

The silence between them was rife with expectancy as Mitch drove through the capital city to Front Street along the Susquehanna River. The moonlight bounced in a rippling strip from the horizon to the water's edge. Laura was filled to the brim with anticipation but wasn't sure what she was anticipating.

Mitch drove into a parking garage, then escorted Laura to the main door of the apartment building. The security guard nodded as they walked in the front door. The elevator took them to the tenth floor and Laura stood to the side as Mitch unlocked the door, flipped the light switch and motioned her ahead of him. He was always a gentleman. He did it without thinking, and it made her feel special.

The apartment was beautiful, apricot, rust and navy the predominant colors. Deep carpeting in a light shade of rust led down two steps to a sunken living room. The extra-long quilted sofa and two black leather wing chairs curved around a white stone fireplace. Laura could see through an archway where an oak and bronzed glass table and chairs sat under a Tiffany lamp. She guessed the kitchen lay beyond.

"Make yourself at home," Mitch suggested as he crossed to a rack stereo system and flipped on the tape deck. Soothing strains of a jazz saxophone floated out. He disappeared into the dining room. "I'll be right back."

Laura descended the steps into the living room, tossed her purse on the end table and sat on the sofa. Mitch returned with glasses of champagne. The sofa gave with his weight as his thigh brushed hers.

He handed her a glass and raised his in a toast. "To success."

"To *your* success," she corrected.

He clinked his glass against hers and they took a sip at the same time, their eyes locking.

Mitch slowly set his glass on the coffee table. "What do you think of my place? Do you like it?"

She took another sip, loving the zip of the bubbles. "Who wouldn't? It's fabulous. But does it ever looked lived-in?"

"Lived-in?"

"Newspapers on the floor, sneakers under the chair, half a glass of soda on the table."

Mitch's broad shoulders lifted and fell. "I like order. There wasn't much of it when I was a kid. Mom tried. But Dad... Any order she managed, he destroyed. He didn't respect her or our home—" He stopped abruptly. "I don't want to talk about him. Not tonight."

She set her glass next to his. "Can I ask you something?"

"You can ask."

He waited, but didn't look guarded as he sometimes did. "Why wouldn't you dance at the Halloween Party?"

"I did."

"Once. A slow one."

"I'm not Carey," he said almost angrily.

"I would never confuse the two of you."

"Because he knows how to have fun?"

There was so much hurt there. She wished she understood it and could learn what had caused it. "Because your eyes are two shades darker than his."

He was taken aback, not expecting that kind of answer. After a moment, he confessed, "I don't know how to dance like that. I never learned."

She should have guessed. Nora had told her Mitch had worked since he could find neighbors or store owners who needed something done. He hadn't had time for proms, football games or learning the latest dance moves.

Laura smiled. "It's never too late."

He scowled. "I've seen men out there looking like roosters flapping their wings. No thanks." The mellow music wound about him and a potent darkness gathered in his eyes. "This tape is my favorite. Would you like to dance now?"

"I'd love to."

His grin was crooked as he took her into his arms in the middle of the room. When their bodies touched, the grin vanished. His body tensed and for a second she thought he was going to put space between them. He seemed to make a decision. Wrapping his arms around her waist, he pulled her closer.

Laura's arms circled his neck eagerly. He was tall. She was short. He was strong and wide and encompassing. She was a reed in his arms.

When he looked down at her, she knew something was going to happen. Something important. He bent his head, his lips molded to hers, and she felt as if she'd finally come home. His tongue teased her lips, urgently, hungrily, as if he couldn't slow himself down or wait another moment for the intimacy he'd been avoiding. The taste of champagne on his tongue was heady. His texture, his heat and his desire became hers until the kiss exploded with more need than either of them could handle.

Mitch pulled back, his breath as hot as the steaminess of the kiss when he whispered, "I don't want to fight this anymore. I can't."

His tense and yearning body told her more clearly than words how much he wanted her. "You don't have to."

His hands caressed her bottom, pushing her closer. Her imagination created pictures of legs intertwined, arms embracing, lips kissing. She was a teenager again—free of responsibilities, chains or restrictions. His tongue filled her mouth. She wanted him inside her, satisfying the need he created so easily. She pushed against him and he groaned. His forward thrust promised fulfillment. He curled his tongue in her mouth, sweeping and arousing until she responded wildly, invading the cavern beyond his teeth. He drew on her until she thought she'd faint.

Need careened through her like a flash flood sweeping the land. She couldn't swim against the raging currents of desire any more than he could. She didn't want to. Should she analyze the feelings? Should she pretend Mitch was experiencing more than desire? Passion was one thing. Passion with deep-seated feelings was another. Could she tell the difference or was she fooling herself?

An aching need coalesced in her to erase his sadness, to give him joy. But could she? If they continued this, would he embrace their passion or regret it? Suddenly, she felt afraid. What if making love put a barrier between them again? Her hands tightened on his shoulders.

The throbbing of Mitch's body reminded him his needs were physical, not emotional. But the tugging on his heart contradicted logic. He felt Laura's life flowing into him, her vibrancy, her fiery spirit. And he felt whole. How could he? Why did he react to her like this?

The shimmering stroke of her tongue on his lips was like liquid fire. When she sought his heated depths, he opened his mouth, waiting for more.

But she retreated, hesitated, and he wondered about her unaccustomed shyness. This was wild, impulsive Laura. Why was she tentative and . . . scared?

He opened his eyes and lifted his head. "What's wrong?"

The cloudy doubts suddenly left her eyes and she pulled him back down, gliding her tongue across his lips, once, twice, taunting him. She could make him crazy this way.

"Laura, kiss me again," he murmured, his voice a raspy caress.

"I am," she said softly. Coming to him a third time, she slipped the tip of her tongue between his lips.

He dragged in his breath and waited. She brushed over his teeth, then dashed inside recklessly. That broke his control. He made a sound of satisfaction, of need. To deny her was to deny himself. He was damn tired of that. He lifted her off her feet so they fit together perfectly.

She moved, brushing the ridge of his arousal, making his knees shake. What about this woman made him feel weak and vulnerable, yet strong and invincible at the same time? The sensuality of their bodies touching led him to forget questions he had. Doubts about the future fled. This woman was his . . . now. Laura.

If he said her name, it was lost in the kiss. She was trembling as she strained against him. She kissed like she did everything else—wholeheartedly. She held nothing back.

He swung her into his arms, amazed that he needed to feel strong and protective as he carried her to his bedroom. He laid her gently on the bed, turned on the light and quickly slipped off his jacket and tie.

"I want to undress you," she said with such longing he almost ripped off their clothes to rush toward the end result. But he didn't intend to rush with Laura. He intended to enjoy.

He sat on the edge of the bed and tried to remain composed as she started with his shirt. He watched her hands on him as her fingers created need and more need and he locked his jaw. By the time she undid his belt buckle and reached for his zipper, he was shaking.

Her clothes took less time because he couldn't wait to see her. When she was naked, then he'd move slowly. But her skin glowed in the mellow lamplight, undermining his resolve. He lay beside her and tasted her neck first. It wasn't nearly enough. His hand found her breast. Her first soft moan was the only one that hit the air. He swallowed the rest in a profound kiss that broke out sweat all over his body.

Slow it down, Riley. Slow it down.

He tore away and smoothed his palm over her nipple, his eyes holding hers. She cried out. She was the most passionate woman he'd ever met.

When she blushed, it surprised him. "Don't hold back. I want to hear you as much as I want to see and touch you."

She smiled and raised her brows, even though her cheeks were still flaming.

He grinned and admitted huskily, "Almost as much."

Her understanding washed over him. "I don't want you
to hold back either. Pretend you're designing. Pretend—"

"I don't have to pretend anything, Laura. Because when
I touch you, when you touch me, there's no armor left. You
penetrate it all too easily." As soon as he said it, he knew he
shouldn't have. Now she had power over him. He'd live to
regret it.

But regret wasn't on his mind as her hands caressed his
face, then his shoulders. Every touch peeled away more of
his layer of self-protection. As her nails scraped lightly
through his chest hair, he made a low sound of pleasure
from her touch, but it was mixed with pain—pain from
feelings that crashed against each other without him knowing what they were. Laura buried resolve, rules, reality.
There were only her soft hands, her sweet taste, his
arousal—hard, hot, demanding.

He cupped the weight of her breast in his hand and his
thumb circled slowly. "So soft." When he rimmed the rosy
circle and she moaned, he murmured, "Fragile and
unique." At last his thumb went up one side of her hard-
ened nipple and down the other. "So ready." His eyes bored
into hers. "Are you ready for me, Laura?"

Laura tried to break out of the passionate haze. But staring at his incredibly male shoulders, broad chest and powerful arousal made it almost impossible. She had to forget
his physical attributes because his immediate question demanded more than a blurry, careless answer. What would
their coupling mean? Was she ready to accept the complications, the consequences, especially if he never came to
love her?

The answer was simple really. She loved him. Nothing else
mattered. "I'm ready."

The surge of need on his face startled her, but he didn't try
to hide it and she was glad. She wanted to tell him he could
trust her with his heart, but she never got the chance.

His eyes were alive with passion. She loved the thought she could incite it. Her body pulsed with feminine life. He reached for her and she reached for him.

He touched her everywhere but where she wanted to be touched most. It was the most exquisite form of torture, an extraordinarily exciting way to bring her to full arousal. She quivered as the keening yearning between her legs swept through every limb to each nerve and became a pulsing need. Unable to keep still, to try and assuage the emptiness, she threw her leg over his hip and moved against him.

He marveled, "You are so passionate . . . so responsive. I can't wait."

She lovingly enclosed him in her hand and he growled a primal sound. "Don't wait. I want you now."

Quickly, he slipped on protection and rose above her, his passion evident in his tight muscles, his slick body, his expression. She knew he tried to restrain himself but with the first touch of her accepting him, he entered her with masterful strength.

She arched to take all of him and the spiraling began, one circle after another as he thrust again . . . and again. All she could do was hold on for dear life. He set a frenzied pace that conveyed how much he wanted her, how badly he needed her. She hugged him with her thighs, scraped her nails across his back and gloried in the love she felt for him.

She began a steep ascent to another plane. Colors swam in front of her eyes, iridescent colors—colors like jewels flung against the sun—fiery ruby, explosive diamond, shimmering sapphire, brilliant emerald. She was suspended in the sky until all the colors combined into an eye shattering, resplendent star. The beauty was so overwhelming she cried out with wonder and awe.

Seconds after, Mitch shuddered and collapsed on top of her.

He slid to his side a few minutes later and held her. But when she turned to look at him, he wasn't smiling.

Chapter Eleven

Shattering. That's the only word that filled Mitch's mind. God, he felt as if he'd given Laura his life's blood. What was worse was that he wanted to do it again, needed to do it again.

But he wouldn't. Feelings he couldn't sort were bursting inside him.

"Mitch?"

Her eyes were luminescent, her face flushed. He remembered exactly how she'd looked as he'd aroused her and brought her to climax. But he didn't know what she expected now. He didn't know what he expected. Only one thought kept running through his head like a computer printout that wouldn't quit.

He voiced it. "You're leaving in three weeks."

"What does that have to do with tonight?" she asked.

"If we keep this up, we'll both hurt when you go. Do you want that?"

"I don't want to hurt any more than you do. But what we shared tonight was—"

"Incredible," he cut in. "Don't you see how much more difficult that makes everything? There's Ray to think about, and Mandy..."

"What about us, Mitch?"

She was trying to pull something from him. Something he couldn't give. It had to do with trust and love and he didn't know if he could give either. Voices echoed in his head. His parents arguing. His father saying he wished Mitch had never been born. Carey and his father laughing over a ribald joke and not including Mitch. His mother trying to convince him his father cared about him, but shushing him whenever Sam Riley was drunk or in a bad mood. Denise leaving to take a job across the country and not being overly upset by it. Where had that thought come from? He'd told himself he didn't care.

Trusting the feeling between himself and Laura was as foreign to him as sailing on the Indian Ocean. Laura grabbed what she wanted and lived every ounce of life out of it. But caution had always been his guide. Maybe a brief affair was enough for her, but it couldn't be for him.

She was waiting for an answer.

He tenderly brushed her cheek, not wanting to hurt or disappoint her, but knowing what he needed to do to protect her and himself. "Once wasn't enough. But three weeks won't be any better."

"So you'd rather have nothing more than the beauty of what we shared tonight?"

Mitch pushed himself up against the headboard, closed his eyes and rubbed his hands over his face. "I don't know."

She stroked his forearm. "This doesn't have to be as hard or complicated as you think. Your feelings will guide you."

Passion stirred again at her touch. He wasn't used to letting his feelings guide him any more than he was used to following the sun. "It might be easy for you, but it will never be easy for me." He ignored the longing to take her in his arms. "We'd better get dressed. It will be midnight before we get to York."

He saw the same yearning he was feeling on Laura's face. Before he did something about it, he shifted away and dropped his legs over the side of the bed. It was going to be a long drive.

Gnarled branches reached up to an azure sky as Laura took a long, vigorous walk Sunday afternoon. The November breeze pushed puffs of whipped cream clouds against one another. She'd been wired since Friday night. Silence had never been as thundering as it was in the car when Mitch drove from Harrisburg to York. Making love with him had been . . .

Tears pricked in her eyes whenever she thought about it. Their souls had fused as well as their bodies. But he wouldn't admit it or face it. Since her father was getting stronger, Mitch had said he'd stay in Harrisburg until Thanksgiving to prepare the store for the Christmas rush. Yes, he was needed there, but it was also a convenient excuse.

Mitch had been gone a day and she missed him already. She couldn't stay in York without him asking her to stay. But he couldn't ask unless he acknowledged his feelings and trusted them. He wasn't used to doing that.

Laura was surprised when she rounded a corner and saw her childhood home. She'd been almost jogging instead of walking. Still brimming with energy she couldn't burn off, she wandered around the front walk to the backyard. When she was a teenager, she'd sit at the stream and let the babbling gurgles and its constant flow soothe her. Maybe it could do that now.

Cutting catercorner across the grass, she thought she saw movement by the stream. Tree trunks blocked her view. Maybe she'd spy a deer.

But it wasn't a deer. It was her father and Mandy. Curious, she moved closer.

Ray held Mandy's hand, gently swinging it back and forth as they stared at the water swirling over the rocks. Laura approached them and heard her dad ask, "Are you cold, honey?"

The little girl shook her head. "Uh-uh. Mommy says fresh air is good for me—just like love and sunshine."

Laura held her breath, wondering how her father would react to what he used to term "romantic nonsense."

"Your mommy's right. Did she ever tell you how she and your grandmother would come here to the stream and wade in their bare feet?"

"She must've forgot. Didn't you stick your feet in, too?"

His answer was slow in coming, and sad. "I was too busy."

"Too busy to play in the water? Didn't you *want* to?"

"I wanted to. But I was too busy for too many things in those days."

"Was it a long, long time ago?"

His expression was indulgent as he smiled down at his granddaughter. "Before you were born."

"Maybe Mommy and I can come back when it's hot and we can all put our feet in."

"I'd like that very much. But you live pretty far away."

Laura thought she heard a huskiness in his voice and suddenly realized how much it meant to him for her and Mandy to be here. And it had nothing to do with the business. Her dad might never say he regretted their estrangement, but he did. In the few short weeks they'd been here, Mandy had become an important part of his world.

Since the conversation she and Mitch had had with
Mandy on the plane, Mandy and Ray had been together
more often. Mandy was no longer afraid of him. When
Laura came home from the store, more often than not, she
found Mandy nestled on Ray's lap while they watched cartoons or he read her a story, rather than helping Nora in the
kitchen.

Had Laura ignored their budding relationship purposely? She was happy for her daughter but part of her hurt
because she'd never been that close to her father. Had he felt
left out because she and her mother were so in tune? And
then when Patrice died, he was at a loss? It made sense now.
As a teenager, she hadn't possessed the insight to see it.

Laura walked slowly toward her father and daughter.

Ray heard her approach and looked over his shoulder.
"Have a good walk?"

She nodded. "This kind of day makes you forget how
ugly November can be."

"Mommy, can we come back when it's hot so we can play
in the stream with Gramps?"

Laura's eyes found her father's. If she hadn't reached out
enough in the past, she needed to do it now for all their
sakes. "Would you like that, Dad?"

His eyes glistened. "You're welcome here anytime." As
if embarrassed by his obvious emotion, he took a more formal stance again and shrugged. "I certainly have enough
room." Clearing his throat, he dropped Mandy's hand.
"I'm going in. You two staying out here?"

"We could. Or we could go inside and play a game of
Candyland."

"*Candyland!*" Mandy shrieked.

Ray smiled. "Sounds good to me. Then we can bother
Nora as she makes supper."

"Or we can help her."

"I'm all thumbs in the kitchen," Ray grumbled.

"Thumbs are good for mixing meat loaf," Laura teased.

"You think she'd let me try?" Ray looked as hopeful as Mandy when she asked for something she was doubtful she'd get.

Laura grinned. "I'm sure if Nora doesn't let you mix it, she'll let you add the bread crumbs."

Ray returned the grin.

Laura knew instantly when Mitch returned. It wasn't the sound of the door or his footfalls or even the sound of his voice minutes later. She'd sensed his presence.

She looked down the front of her sweatshirt and grimaced. It was liberally decorated with streaks and spots of flour from the pie dough she'd mixed. She and Nora were getting ready for Thanksgiving the next day by making apple pie and a special pumpkin custard pie recipe for Ray.

When Mitch came into the kitchen, Laura's head came up and all thoughts of flour and pies were forgotten.

His gaze took in Nora peeling apples and Laura holding the rolling pin. "Ladies, don't you know it's eight p.m.? The day should be winding down."

"Laura wanted to help so we got supper out of the way before we started."

Mitch walked over to his mother and snatched a piece of apple from the bowl. "Where's Mandy?"

Laura wanted to run to him, throw her arms around him and tell him she'd stay in York to nurture the feelings growing between them. Instead, her hands trembled as she folded the pie shell into quarters to lift it onto the pie plate. "She got bored with us. She's with Dad watching *The Charlie Brown Special*." Her eyes caught his. "She's been asking about you."

"I missed her. I bought her two more books and another puppet. Maybe she'll sleep with this one, too."

Did you miss me? Laura wondered, then pushed the question away. "She'll like that. Dad said she took the elephant to the park today. But he got a bit sandy from the sandbox." Laura felt awkward, not knowing what Mitch was feeling, if he was feeling anything.

When Mitch tried to sneak another wedge of apple, Nora slapped his hand. "*Whole* apples are in the refrigerator."

Mitch's grin was boyish. "But these don't have the peel."

His mother shook her head and handed him the quarter she'd just peeled. "Here. That's it or we'll never get finished."

He popped it into his mouth, crunched, chewed and swallowed. "I'll unpack and give Mandy her books."

Even the way he chewed was sexy... Laura took a deep breath. "How long are you staying?"

"The Friday and Saturday after Thanksgiving are our two busiest days of the year. If you think you can handle the store here alone, I'll go back to Harrisburg Friday."

At least he was giving her professional capabilities a vote of confidence. "I can handle it." She didn't know if she could handle being close to him all day tomorrow and not touching him.

Two hours later, Laura took the apple pie from the oven and set it on a cooling rack next to the pumpkin custard. The hairs on the back of her neck prickled and she knew Mitch was watching her. She turned and the power of his gaze took her breath away. She remembered the first time she'd skydived from an airplane. This was the same breathtaking, free-falling sensation. He wasn't hiding anything now. His stare was loaded with possessiveness, passion and longing.

Thoroughly rattled, she dropped a pot holder. Before she could move, he strode across the room, stooped and picked it up. He handed it to her and their fingers touched.

His hand engulfed hers, pot holder and all. "The pies smell delicious."

She was amazed he could act so...so normal when everything inside of her was screaming to him to take her in his arms.

"Laura?"

She found her voice. "What?"

"Don't look at me like that."

Tears came to her eyes. She pulled her hand from his and faced the counter. "What do you want me to do, Mitch? Pretend I don't want you to hold me or make love to me?"

She heard his oath but his hands were gentle as he took hold of her shoulders and turned her around. "I don't want you to pretend." He attempted a smile. "Besides, I don't think you'd know how."

Somehow her hands ended up on his chest. She could feel his body heat beneath the flannel shirt and his heart thumping. The longer her hands rested there, the faster it beat. She couldn't find any more words. She just stared at him, not hiding the longing she felt.

With a groan his mouth swooped down on hers and his arms went around her. The kiss was as fulfilling as it was passionate. His urgent lips trapped hers, then separated them. When his tongue delved inside, she let him sweep her into a passionate hurricane she didn't want to abate.

It was astounding how everything about him aroused her, enervated her, yet surrounded her with a safe cocoon. He was so stable, solid, dependable. And the passion? She'd never felt anything like this before. As his finger slid under her hair and he tilted her head to deepen the kiss, she pressed against him.

Mitch drowned in Laura, her softness, her scent, her sweetness. He had never known such fierce desire or the excruciating emptiness that being away from her caused. Her joy poured over him, mending all the broken places. His body's aching couldn't be relieved with one act, with one day, with a few weeks. Damn reality! He pushed his chest against her breasts and spread his legs to hold her closer.

He couldn't keep his hands from moving over her shoulders, down her back, under her hair again. He needed to feel the softness of her skin. When she chased his tongue into his mouth and stroked him, he took a hank of her hair between his fingers...

Something caught. Something tore. Laura made a sound and it wasn't from pleasure. He broke the kiss and lifted his head. Bringing his fingers together he felt the string of gold.

"Hold still a minute," he mumbled, his voice still thick from his passion.

He caught the chain, held both ends and stepped back, taking it from her neck. There was a small red mark on her throat where the golden rose had pulled tight when he caught the chain in her hair.

He touched the spot with his thumb. "I'm sorry."

"It's okay," she whispered, her eyes still glazed from the kiss.

He examined the rose. She wore it often and he wondered, not for the first time, if it had been a present from her husband. "I can repair the chain. But it might be better to get a new one, a fine rope instead of a link so it's sturdier. If you want to keep wearing it."

She became more attentive. "Why wouldn't I?"

"I don't know what it means to you but..."

"Dad gave it to me for my eleventh birthday."

"Ray?"

She nodded.

"And you've worn it since you were eleven?"

She nodded again.

"You love your father, don't you?"

"Yes. I tried to stop, but I couldn't."

"When you left, it wasn't only your fault." He'd become more and more sure of that in the past two weeks.

"No."

"Do you want to tell me what happened?"

"It might be better if you heard it from Dad."

He brushed her cheek with the back of his hand, surprised the need to hold her close was still so strong. He wasn't used to it yet. "Are you afraid I won't believe you?"

She smiled. "No. I just think it's better if he tells you himself."

He could respect her reasons, whatever they were. "All right. If there's an opening, I'll ask. But it doesn't matter anymore, does it? What matters is now."

"You've come to understand that?"

Her long intense look made his stomach clench and his groin tighten. Laura was "now" personified. She mattered. "I'm trying to." He suddenly realized he'd crushed her chain in his hand. "I'll keep this and put a new one on it Friday."

He bent forward and tenderly kissed her forehead. Her lips would tempt him more than he could endure at the moment. A war raged inside him. He was trying to give "now" a chance.

"Nora's glad Carey will be here for dinner," Ray said to Mitch as they watched the Thanksgiving Day Parade on television, and varied sounds and smells issued from the kitchen.

"It means a lot to her to have him here." Mitch's legs were stretched on the sofa, one ankle crossed over the other. The parade was as good a diversion as any to keep him from going into the kitchen and taking Laura in his arms or carrying her upstairs. He'd thought about that when he was alone in his bed last night, his sheets knotted from his tossing and turning. But he couldn't do that in Ray's house. He wasn't sure he should do it at all.

"What about you?"

Mitch remembered Ray was talking about his brother being here for dinner. "Since I turned down Carey's request for money, he's not speaking to me. He can't see I did it for his own good."

Ray stared at the television and said low but clear, "That's often a good excuse for wanting to maintain control."

Mitch's head turned to the older man. "What do you mean?"

Ray turned down the sound on the remote. "You want Carey to do what *you* want him to do."

Ray's words rankled. Uncomfortable and no longer relaxed, Mitch swung his feet to the floor. "I want to keep him from destroying his life."

Ray gave Mitch a rueful smile and shook his head. "That's what I thought I was doing with Laura. It didn't work any more than your attempt will work."

Mitch didn't think he could compare himself and Carey to Ray and Laura. But this was the opening he'd hoped for. "What happened between you and Laura?"

Ray ran his hand through his thinning hair. "She hasn't told you?"

Mitch shook his head. "She thought it would be better if you did."

"I'm surprised she can be that fair." He peered down at the toes of his wing-tipped shoes. Without raising his head, Ray said soberly, "I offered her fiancé ten thousand dollars to stay out of her life."

Lord! Mitch had never expected that. Knowing Ray, he thought maybe he'd presented an ultimatum. And knowing Laura, he'd guessed that would have made her do exactly what her father didn't want. But to try and buy off Doug Sanders . . . The betrayal she must have felt!

"What happened?" Mitch asked, wanting to know the whole story.

"He refused the money. But that wasn't good enough for me. I thought he wanted to marry her for a bigger chunk of my money. I thought all I had to do was cut her off from it and he'd be gone. So I told her she had to choose him or a partnership with me."

Mitch was stunned. He'd never expected any of this from Ray. He'd thought her father had maybe forbidden her to marry and in rebellion she'd done it anyway to hurt him. To punish Ray further, Mitch thought she'd purposely stayed away. But that was a fictitious scenario formed because he respected Ray, before he really knew Laura.

"You're looking at me differently. Have I lost you, too, because I was stupid six years ago?" Ray's expression was worried.

"I'm not going anywhere, Ray. Why didn't you tell me all this before? You told me stories about her that led me to believe she was selfish and uncaring, wild and irresponsible."

"That's because I began to believe it myself. I had to. I knew she'd never forgive me so I needed to feel justified."

Mitch shook his head. "I'm surprised she came back with me."

"So am I."

Uncomfortable silence settled between them. Mitch wanted to dispel it. "At least you know she loves you. She'll probably even forgive you if you give her the chance."

"It's probably too late."

"It's never too late if you both try. But I can see why she doesn't want to stay in York." Mitch bet she was afraid Ray would interfere in her life again or try to mold her into what he wanted. How often had she told him how much it meant that Doug had accepted her unconditionally? What a lure that must have been.

Mitch's heart sank. If he'd entertained a last lingering hope she'd change her mind and stay, it died.

Mitch was quiet during Thanksgiving dinner. At first Laura thought it was Carey's presence. Carey always managed to make himself the center of attention. He had a knack for telling entertaining stories. She and everyone else except Mitch encouraged him because it felt good to be together on a holiday and laugh and share. She hoped Carey felt he belonged and would rethink his plan to increase Nora's money.

Her father smiled more than Laura could remember since her mother had died. Laura wished she could openly discuss with him the situation that had torn them apart. But their new relationship was so fragile, she was afraid to try. So she enjoyed what was beginning and tried to build on it.

As they ate dessert, Mandy asked her, "Are we going to call Anne and George? Do you think they're having turkey?"

"I'm sure they're having turkey. Don't forget to ask them who won when they pulled the wishbone."

"Can we call now?" It was obvious Mandy missed their friends.

"As soon as you finish that last bite of apple pie."

"I'm full."

"You can be excused. We'll call as soon as I finish *my* pie."

"Can I push the buttons on the phone?"

Laura straightened the pink barrette in Mandy's hair. "Yes, you can. But not till I can tell you which ones to push."

"Okay." She hopped off her chair. "I'll go see if Puffball ate the turkey Nora gave her."

When Mandy had left the table, Laura looked up and caught Mitch watching her daughter leave the room. She wished she knew what he was thinking. He was tender with Mandy, but firm too when he had to be. Like the night she wanted him to read her one more story when he'd already read two. And he hadn't fallen for the I-need-a-glass-of-water stall tactic either. He'd solved the problem by setting a full glass on her nightstand. He'd make a wonderful father.

The thought created a weight on Laura's heart. She wondered how Mandy would feel about leaving Ray and Mitch. She'd bonded with both of them. Yet she seemed ready to go back to Anne and George. Was life that much clearer for a child? Would Mandy remember these few weeks in York if they left? How would she react if they stayed? Laura didn't want to suggest it until the possibility existed.

She went to get Mandy so they could make their phone call to Anne and George and tell them they'd be home in two weeks.

As the afternoon wore on, Mitch didn't initiate contact. Laura knew it wasn't simply his interest in the football game. She couldn't stand the way he isolated himself from her, especially after last night in the kitchen. Last night had given her hope. But today...

She needed time alone. Using the excuse she wanted to price a shipment of dinner rings that had come in at the store, she pulled her coat from the closet. After a kiss for Mandy, Laura left, saying she'd be back in an hour or two.

She lost track of time as she checked the packing slips and tagged first cocktail rings, then bracelets, then watches. The repetitive actions and silence soothed her, though the weight on her heart didn't diminish.

Sounds at the back door startled and alarmed her. She had locked it behind her, hadn't she? A key turned in the lock and seconds later Mitch stood in the office, a wicker basket hanging over one arm.

"You scared me." His eyes held hers and she sensed he'd come to a decision about them.

"I didn't mean to. It's after seven. I brought a picnic in case you were hungry—coffee, turkey sandwiches, slices of pie."

His thoughtfulness lifted the weight in her chest and she began to hope again. "Thank you. I didn't realize it was so late."

He took off his leather jacket and hung it on the coat-rack next to hers. Jeans showed off his physique in a way dress slacks couldn't. Beltless and well-worn, they hugged his slim hips, molded to his thighs and urged her to remember the sight of his body unclothed. She remembered all too well. Shifting her attention upward wasn't much better. His blue-and-navy plaid flannel shirt was open at the neck and revealed a few of the hairs she knew were scattered across his upper chest.

He moved, taking a blanket from the basket. "I thought we'd make this a real picnic. I couldn't find ants to bring along. It's too cold and they're hibernating."

"Do ants hibernate?"

He smiled. "I'll check it out in case Mandy asks." Scooting a chair to the side, he spread the blanket on the gold indoor-outdoor carpet. Placing the basket in the corner, he sat down. "Come on. The coffee's just brewed."

She plopped beside him. "Did Nora get this ready?"

"Nope. I did. The sandwiches probably aren't as neat as hers would be, but they're as good." He picked up the thermos.

"Why did you do this, Mitch? I would've been home soon. It's almost Mandy's bedtime."

"I know."

"I want to spend some time with you. I like being with you. And after the other night... I want to be with you even more."

She trembled and everything inside her screamed, "Ask me to stay." But it was too soon for that. He was just coming to realize they had something precious between them. What if he didn't realize the extent of it in time? Fear shook her along with desire.

He gently caressed her cheek with his thumb. "Ray told me what he did to you. I understand why you left."

Tears came to her eyes as she thought about the time she and her father had lost. "I had to go. He gave me no choice. If I had stayed, if I had denied my love for Doug to please Dad, I would have never grown up. My father would have had power over me for the rest of my life. I had to live my life, not the life he chose for me."

"I know. I just wish there had been some other way. He spent lonely years. You could have used his support when your husband died."

"Maybe even before," she admitted.

He reached for her and brought her to him gently. She loved his gentleness. She'd seen it with her daughter and felt it in his touch. His invading, sensual kiss left her clinging to him. Tears burned in her eyes. This was exactly what she wanted, where she wanted to be. In his arms. In his life.

"I've missed you," he said simply, his voice raspy as he rubbed his cheek against hers.

"I've been right here."

"But I haven't." He lifted his head. "Maybe the way you live is best. Take today and tomorrow be damned."

She wanted tomorrow, too. "That's not all I believe."

"Shh." He trailed a path of kisses down her throat. "No talking. Not now. Let's just live."

Of course, she wanted to live. She wanted to experience everything she could with him. But today didn't mean half as much without knowing if they had the rest of their lives. But maybe he'd never trust himself enough, or her, to trust tomorrow.

His blue eyes swallowed her as he carefully undressed her, taking the time he couldn't on Friday night. Slow was as exciting as fast, maybe even more so. Once her sweater was over her head, he kissed her shoulder, each touch of his lips a shock that connected to her womb.

She reached for him, but he caught her wrists with one of his large hands. "No, not yet." His voice was as commanding as his gaze.

"I want my turn."

He chuckled. "You'll get it. I want to kiss you everywhere, in every way." While he unsnapped her bra, he nibbled her shoulder. As the fabric melted into nothingness, he brushed his fingers down to her hips and up her back.

She shivered and leaned into him, aroused and wanting more. His lips took one lazy journey after the other until they teased her breast. He flicked his tongue until she thought she'd go mad. And when he reached for the zipper on her slacks, she turned the tables.

She didn't care about slow. She wanted to touch him. This time *she* grabbed *his* wrist and kissed the inside. When he closed his eyes to savor the pleasure of it, she quickly unbuttoned his shirt. She stared a long time. She loved looking at him. Bending forward, she rubbed her chin over his dark nipple.

His breath hissed out.

"Do you like that as much as I do?" she asked.

"I like it," he muttered hoarsely.

She did it again and then used her tongue.

And the exploration continued.

He sucked on her breast and blazed moist kisses on her stomach. She nipped his earlobe and blew hot air across his ribs.

His hands lured and promised as they stroked inch by inch over her hip. Her fingers tantalized and stunned as they charted his thigh.

He probed her secret places. She gasped and arched.

She found his manhood and curled her hand around him. He groaned and pulled her on top of him.

With Mitch inside of her, Laura lost all sense of time and place. She embraced the happiness and knew only Mitch. Their mouths clung as passion met passion and she rose to the summit of a glorious mountain. Up. Up. Up. Until she tumbled over the edge. When she landed, Mitch held her in his arms and she snuggled closer, not wanting the loving to end.

Chapter Twelve

Friday afternoon Mitch stared at the sketch in his hand. Satisfied, he laid it on the worktable. He'd come back to Harrisburg for the day to help with the Christmas crunch, but his sales team was adequately handling the steady flow of customers. So, he'd escaped to work on this. The gems he intended to use winked up at him—eleven midnight-blue sapphires, one pear-shaped blue diamond. It would be a stunning ring.

And he was going to have a stunning weekend. He'd made a decision Thanksgiving Day. If he and Laura only had two weeks, they were going to be the best damn two weeks of their lives. This was the closest to happy he'd ever been. He'd thought the business was all he wanted or needed in life. Since Laura, he knew better. After she left . . .

She'd be back for visits. It wouldn't be the same as . . . A little voice whispered, *If she stayed*. Mitch squelched the sound. She'd bring light and freshness into his life whenever she came back. That would be enough.

The voice became louder and asked, *Would it?*

The following Thursday morning snow began falling. And fell, and fell, fast and heavy. At midafternoon, Laura stared out the store's window at the deserted street. The snow made her think about Christmas. Wouldn't it be wonderful to spend it here with Mitch? They'd spent the past six days never far apart. And Sunday afternoon at his apartment had been . . . wonderful, exciting, and bittersweet.

The thought of leaving Mitch . . . and her father . . . Her dad had seemed depressed the past week. She'd read that was normal after heart surgery. He was feeling better but still couldn't do what he wanted to do, like driving and coming in to work. Hopefully his checkup would be a good one and he could at least think about coming to the store for a few hours at a time. Immersed in his business for most of his life, inactivity wasn't easy for him to handle. Without Mandy and Nora, he'd probably be even more restless and depressed.

A pang of guilt stung Laura. Did her decision not to stay have anything to do with his depression? She hoped not but knew it was probably a contributing factor. If Mitch would realize what they could mean to each other . . .

A chill ran up her spine when she thought about something she'd been trying *not* to think about. What if this relationship was purely physical for him? What if he only experienced the chemistry, not the feelings? What if that's all he'd let himself feel? Why, oh why, had she fallen in love with a man who might be afraid of loving?

That train of thought was hopeless. She *had* fallen in love with him, with his strength, protectiveness and caring. She'd always needed those qualities in her life. Her dad had possessed strength, but not the tenderness or understanding that accompanied Mitch's. Doug had given her freedom and acceptance but not protection and dependability. With him she'd always felt they lived on the edge.

But after Mandy was born, Laura knew she needed more. She had a daughter to love and safeguard. Living for excitement and thrills didn't fit anymore. She'd changed after the birth of her daughter. Doug hadn't. With Mandy depending on her, Laura had longed for someone *she* could depend on.

She could depend on Mitch. That was as sure a fact as the sun coming up tomorrow. She thought about Carey and how different the two brothers seemed to be. Again she remembered the confidence she was keeping. She should tell Mitch Carey had borrowed money from Nora. But what good would the telling do except drive the two men further apart? There was still the chance Carey would reconsider his strategy.

"Do you wish on snowflakes, too?"

Mitch had come up behind her. She smiled as she turned around. "Sometimes."

He grinned. "Let's go home and build a snowman. Mandy will love it."

"What about you?"

"I haven't built one in years. It'll be fun."

Laura was delighted that the word "fun" was now part of his vocabulary. At home, Mitch helped her bundle Mandy in a double pair of pants, hat, winter coat, scarf and mittens. The three of them rolled a giant snowman and with Mitch holding Mandy at the snowman's head, she poked in a carrot nose and two stone eyes. When Laura suggested they create a snowwoman, too, Mandy lost interest and ran inside to see if Nora had finished baking a batch of chocolate chip cookies.

Flakes were still falling intermittently and the sky was darkening with evening's onset.

"It's you and me, kid," Mitch tossed over his shoulder before he stooped to mold a small ball.

Laura bent to do the same.

And quickly jumped up when she felt something cold and wet on her neck.

Mitch was standing a few feet away. She wriggled from the icy discomfort and called, "You'll be sorry. Just you wait."

He chuckled and kept his distance. "You looked so tempting. I couldn't help it. I'm sorry, honest I am." His smug smirk said he wasn't sorry at all.

Laura pretended indifference as she peered through the swarm of snowflakes and watched Mitch diligently add snow to his ball. While he was busy with his task, she quickly fortified herself with three well-packed snowballs.

"Hey, Mitch," she called playfully.

He turned to face her and she threw the three torpedoes in rapid-fire order, one of them catching him on the shoulder, another in the middle of his chest. She pictured his intent immediately and sprinted away. He chased after her with long lithe strides despite the snow drifts. She eluded his first attempt to catch her but not the second.

He dove for her leg, tripping her and toppling them both into the marshmallow-soft snow. He pinned her beneath his long torso as the snow caught on his brows and lashes.

"Say you're sorry," he insisted, the heat from his jeans branding her legs in spite of the cold. "Then *maybe* I'll let you go with just a warning this time."

His hot breath warmed her nose. "Never." She grinned puckishly, her own words making a puff of white smoke in the frigid air. "You deserved it," she added as she struggled to wiggle out from under him. "You put snow down my back," she accused with righteous indignation.

"But I apologized!" He was obviously enjoying her predicament and her sinuous movement. "Now you have to apologize or..."

"Or what?" Laura asked with suspicion, fascinated by the silver sparkle in his eyes.

"Or I'll have to do something drastic. Like this," he said as he placed a light kiss on her lips. "And this," he repeated, his next kiss a little longer. After the third kiss, Mitch released her hands and lifted his head as breathless as she was. "That was quite an apology."

An apology her foot. She brought her hand between them and cupped him. "An apology? Is that really what you want?"

He sucked in a breath. "Laura Marie—"

"Yes?" she asked sweetly, not stopping for a moment.

"You wouldn't want me to...er...embarrass myself."

"If I give you pleasure, that doesn't matter."

He sank down tight against her to still her hand. "It matters because I want to pleasure you, too. I can't do that here. So if I can't..." He kissed her hard. "You can't." He pushed himself away and held out his hand to pull her up.

She gripped his hand. "I've decided where I want to take you to pay you back for the coat."

"Uh-oh. I don't like that twinkle in your eye."

"There's a new club in the west end. I'm taking you dancing."

"Laura—"

"Trust me. You'll have fun. Mark your calendar for Saturday night."

He looked dubious but answered, "All right. I'll go. But if after one fast dance I look ridiculous..."

"You won't. You have a great sense of rhythm."

The grin started in his eyes and spread to his mouth. "You're a handful. You know that?"

"And proud of it." She let him pull her up. Maybe Saturday night would be the night he asked her to stay and share his life.

Laura wished she had a camera. Mitch's face was a study in controlled neutrality as pink, white and blue streaks from the strobe lights shimmered and jumped on the walls and floor of the night club. With his hand on her waist, he led her to a barrel-shaped table in a corner as far removed from the reflective steel dance floor as he could manage. The music blared throughout the room, pouring over the oval bar area as easily as the dance floor.

He stood behind the heavy chair and pushed it in for her, his navy suit coat swaying on either side of her as he leaned forward. She sucked in a breath—cologne, soap, and Mitch. *Cool your jets, kid. You're here to teach Mitch dancing can be fun.*

When he sat down across from her, his neutrality slipped for a moment in favor of a look of sheer discomfort.

She tapped his knuckles. "I promise this will be painless."

His grin was apologetic. "I've only been in a place like this once or twice. It feels . . . strange."

"You and Denise never went dancing?"

"No."

"What did you do?"

He wiggled his brows. "Wouldn't you like to know?"

Her mouth dropped open.

He chuckled and tweaked her nose. "Gotcha."

She was seeing his sense of humor emerge more often. "Are you trying to tell me to mind my own business?"

He took her hand and folded his fingers around hers. "There's no deep dark secret. We went to the movies. We played Scrabble. Actually we weren't together that much. She went her way, I went mine. It's what we both wanted."

She could push a little. Just a little. "What do you want now?"

A shadow crossed his face. "I want to spend all the time I can with you before you leave."

Well, she'd asked for it.

The waitress spotted her two new customers and came to take their order. As she made her way back to the bar to get two club sodas with twists of lime, Mitch leaned close to Laura. "You'd look great in that outfit."

Laura's eyes followed the waitress. Her white satin short shorts and halter top molded to her like a second skin. "You'd like me to wear it dancing?" she asked with a flirting grin.

He growled in her ear. "No way. Bedroom only."

The possessiveness in his eyes excited her. Desire coalesced into a tight ball in her womb. She licked dry lips. Mitch's gaze followed the trail of her tongue.

The driving beat of the top forty hit ended and a slower rhythm took its place. Mitch stood and offered his hand to Laura. "We can start out slow, can't we?"

"Slow was good the last time we tried it."

His blue eyes said he remembered that night in his apartment very well.

On the dance floor, he enclosed her near his body, crossing his hands at the back of her waist. Her arms ringed his neck.

He ducked his head to her ear. "Have I told you how beautiful you look tonight?"

He had a talent for making her feel beautiful and feminine and delicate. Her dress was a vibrant color of teal, blue in one light, green in another. Its scooped cowl neck draped along her collarbone. The dress was one of her favorites. She was pleased he liked it.

Laura let her hand drag from the back of his neck, down the placket of his white shirt to his waist. "You look pretty good yourself." Seeing him, smelling him, having him this close sent her pulse leaping.

His eyes twinkled with amusement. "You'd better watch where you put your hands or we could get into trouble."

She returned her hand to its previous position. "I'm an expert at getting into trouble."

His thighs pressed against hers, subtly guiding their motion. "I know. But I'm beginning to like your brand of trouble." His thumb traced the shell of her ear and she shivered. He noticed her response and a smile whispered across his lips. "You're incredible."

"Because I can't control my reaction to you?"

"Because you don't try. You don't hide what you feel."

Laura's body followed Mitch's instinctively. Dancing with him was almost like making love. She scanned his face, watching his eyes darken to deep ocean blue.

Mitch's breath warmed her neck as he caught her earlobe between his lips. Her knees wobbled. While his one arm maneuvered them into the midst of dancing couples, his other slid between their bodies to the fullness of her breast.

"I love touching you," he breathed.

Her nipples peaked as her breasts grew taut. He'd used "love." That was the first time. Not quite in the context she wanted it, but it was a start. Just as his fingers were starting something they couldn't finish here.

Her breath caught. "I think we'd better watch where you put *your* hands."

His voice was low and husky. "Are you telling me to behave?"

"I guess so," she said wistfully as she laid her head under his chin, but the pressure of his hips against hers triggered an avalanche of erotic thoughts.

They broke apart when the music stopped, but Laura immediately snatched Mitch's arm before he could go back to the table. "Wait."

He waited, but with a frown. When a staccato thump beat on the drums, Laura advised, "Relax. Just let every part of you *feel* the music."

With the same strength of purpose he attacked any problem, Mitch closed his eyes for a moment to do what Laura said. He opened them again and moved tentatively at first. When he moved his hips, they smoothly gyrated with the rhythm of his feet. One strong shoulder rolled back away from her, then the other. He was a natural, possessing the ease of an athlete, coordinating all the members of his body. She could picture him naked—synchronizing his movements to hers. Heat oozed through her like hot honey.

Mitch discovered no one was watching him but Laura. Forgetting his self-consciousness, he watched back. The fluffy mass of her hair brushed her cheeks as she kept time to the music with her head. Her dancing reminded him of how she made love—the way she undulated above him or beneath him. She was uninhibited, joyously sensual. It didn't take much effort to remember her fingers sketching designs on his chest, her moist lips loving him to oblivion, her gray eyes shooting silver sparks as he made her his.

And—damn!—he was thinking of her as his more and more often. It had to stop. She was leaving in less than a week. He'd heard her telephone her supervisor and confirm the date she'd be back at work. There'd been no hesitation in her voice. She hadn't even asked if she could delay her return. If he meant more than a brief affair, wouldn't she have tried? Yet even if she wanted to stay, the memories in York were painful, and although she and Ray seemed to be getting along, there was an undercurrent of tension that stemmed from the past. Hurt still lingered. God knew, he understood that kind of pain.

Enough, Riley! Learn from her. Take what you can get.

As Mitch became more attuned with the music and Laura's steps, they began a primal dance—a mating ritual.

Laura moved provocatively to the right. He moved to the right. He stepped backward. She stepped forward, her eyes grafted to his. When he curved his hands around her waist, the notes vibrated through her swaying hips to his soul. The dance ended and he caught her to him, placing a kiss on her lips embellished with a flourish of his tongue. He wanted her here...now...yet knew the wait could be even longer than tonight. Privacy was elusive.

The music began once more and he admitted, "You could convince me to do that again." He added, "You wouldn't have to try very hard." Anticipation might kill him but he couldn't let go of the excitement.

And he didn't the rest of the night. By the time they left the nightclub, he hoped the icy air would start what a cold shower would finish when he returned to Ray's house.

But as usual, resolve was one thing; Laura was another. After he unlocked the car and they climbed inside, she snuggled close to him. The icy air had done no good at all. Her coat rustled against his. The sound, the feel, was more erotic because of the barriers. He knew what his skin against hers could do to both of them. At a stoplight he turned to look at her. Her smile tugged his head toward hers and he kissed her long after the light had turned green. Luckily, no one was behind them.

The kiss encouraged the need for intimacy their dancing had generated. Mitch finally realized that no amount of winter air or cold water could douse the passion he felt for this woman. To someone who held every aspect of himself with tight restraint, that was an exasperating and overwhelming insight. He'd never thought himself capable of "high" passion—the stuff movies and books were made of. He'd been wrong. He'd never indulged himself with anything. Sure, once he had money in his pocket, he'd lived comfortably. He'd indulged his mother and Carey. But never himself. Maybe it was time to indulge himself with

Laura, to fill himself up with her so that when she left, some of her would linger.

He drove into the garage and when he pressed the remote, the door hummed down behind them. When he switched off the ignition, the silence and the warmth lingering from the car's heater created an intimate pocket of awareness. The glow from a street lamp strayed in one garage window, casting dabbles of pale light mixed with shadow.

His gaze found Laura's and a hot lick of desire taunted him, leading him to forget staid and proper. He took her hand and interlaced their fingers. "I had fun tonight."

She squeezed his hand. "I hoped you would."

"It makes me wonder what else I've missed because of... misconceptions."

"Trying new things is hard."

"Not for you." He lifted her hand to his lips and kissed her palm. His tongue caressed the line down the center. Her small moan crawled across his aroused nerve endings until her pleasure was his. Her scent of flowers wound about him, enticing him closer. His body throbbed with need.

She cupped his chin and stroked his jaw with her forefinger.

"I want you, Laura." The husky tremor in his voice once might have embarrassed him, but it didn't now.

"I want you, too."

It was so simply stated, so simply meant, he couldn't doubt it. He'd told her about his reluctance to make love to her in Ray's home. She understood. "I wish we'd driven to Harrisburg."

"But we didn't." Laura was very still, obviously waiting for some sign from him of what he wanted.

He shifted on the seat and his hands slipped under her hair, cradling her head. "We don't have to go to Harrisburg to kiss."

Her lips were warm under his, the inside of her mouth was hot and slick just like her body when she received him, tightened around him... His groan sounded in his chest.

Laura's fingers feverishly burrowed inside his topcoat, inside his suit jacket, seeking to be closer to him.

Mitch understood the need. He unbuttoned her coat and pushed the leather aside. His lips blazed a trail down her neck to the hollow of her throat where her pulse wildly beat. For him. He felt proud. He felt thankful.

"This is crazy. We're in a car," he muttered as he found the hem of her dress and pushed it up her thigh.

Her hands tugged out his shirt and her skin touched his. "Does it matter?"

When the pads of his fingers felt the edge of nylons and the garter belt, his manhood pulsated so hard he hurt. "Hell no, it doesn't matter," he growled, not caring if they were in the middle of Times Square on New Year's Eve. Need mattered, being inside her mattered, making the most of now mattered. That was all.

Chapter Thirteen

Sunday afternoon, Laura took a long walk so she could think as well as feel. She and Mitch only had a few days left. Last night in the car had been wild and wonderful. But he hadn't mentioned love and he hadn't asked her to stay. Part of her was starting to panic. Her good sense was telling her to give him all the time and space she could.

Laura admired Mitch more than she could ever tell him. Nora had told her how Mitch would stand up to her husband to protect her despite the consequences, like a slap across the face or an angry tirade Mitch couldn't escape. He'd avoided his father whenever possible, but when it wasn't...

The past had left its mark. He liked to take the safe route. And he didn't consider her safe. Because she coaxed him to feel? And in the past that had led to disappointment?

Her promise to Carey nagged at her as she circled the block and started back toward the house. Was she breaking a trust with Mitch by not telling him about Carey? If he found out, would he forgive her? What she needed to do was convince him to talk to Carey. If Carey realized how much Mitch did care... The thought stepped up her pace.

Laura loved the wind, the taste of winter on her lips, the crunch of leftover snow under her boots. As she approached the driveway, Mitch stepped outside. His hair ruffled in the breeze. His disheveled hair and slight beard shadow made him look rumpled and sexy.

Mitch watched Laura as she moved toward him. He couldn't believe they'd made love in the car last night! Their fumbling hands, their clothes in the way, the cold air making their heat that much more scalding, her hands inside his shirt, his hands slipping down her panties... He'd never been that excited in his life. Maybe for the first time he understood the allure of danger, risk, impulse. His body heated up thinking about it, let alone looking at her now. She was beautiful with her hair mussed, her cheeks red. He'd never seen a woman look so good or affect him so deeply.

Laura frowned as Mitch met her in the middle of the walk and he asked, "What's wrong?" He stayed a few steps away. One touch. Just one touch and he'd catch on fire.

"I thought Carey might decide to come over this afternoon. But I don't see his motorcycle so I guess he's not here."

"Carey does what he pleases, when he pleases."

"Have you two ever really talked?"

"About what?" Mitch felt compelled to ask, although it was against his better judgment.

Her hands flew through the air. "Life! Your life, his life, what the two of you think and feel about each other."

What had gotten into her? Sure, he'd tried to talk to Carey. But they ended up arguing. The tension between them had always been there, fed by their father. That was too painful to explain.

Mitch shrugged and fell back on a viable excuse. "Carey's never around."

She became more agitated. "He's around now. He's been here almost as long as I have. You and I have found time to talk."

They'd found time to do much more than that, but he decided not to remind her right now. "Carey and I have trouble talking."

"Like me and Dad." The agitation left Laura. She reached up and traced the scar on his cheek, as if he was the only thing that mattered in the world. "Tell me how you got this."

Her caring brought a lump to his throat. He forced himself to swallow it. "It was the Fourth of July. Carey got a hold of fireworks."

She frowned, her nose wrinkling at the bridge in the way he loved. "How? Aren't they illegal?"

All emotion left his voice as he remembered. "He had friends who knew where to get them. I found out where they were going to set them off. Like always, I thought I'd fix it, stop him, make him see reason."

"But you couldn't?"

"I was too late."

"What happened?"

Mitch shoved his hands deep in his jacket pockets, reliving the fear for his brother. "Carey was too close. He didn't have any protective gear. When he lit the fuse, I pulled him out of the way. We landed on the ground and when the firecracker exploded, some of it hit me."

She touched the scar again as if to make any pain he'd suffered go away. "You were lucky it missed your eye."

"Yes, I was." He stood perfectly still.

"And Carey feels responsible."

"He shouldn't. It was an accident," Mitch explained for the umpteenth time in his life.

"He caused it."

Mitch pulled his hands out of his pockets and started toward the door. "I've been through this before. I don't blame him."

She grabbed his arm. "How could you not?"

Mitch stopped. "He's my brother!"

She said gently, "That doesn't mean you weren't and aren't angry with him for it."

He wished she'd stop playing psychologist but he realized she thought she was helping. He sighed. "I might have been when I was a teenager. Kids can be cruel. But I've always felt more protective than angry. That's what's led us to where we are today. I don't know what I could have done differently. I could have stood back like I'm trying to now, but he needed me."

She released his arm. "He needs you now, too."

Mitch's hand mowed restlessly through his hair. "He needs money and he sees me as the all-beneficent giver. I can't give it to him this time, Laura. If I do, he'll never grow up. I can give him advice. I can give him support. Hell, I could even give him a job if he wanted it."

"Have you told him all that?"

"He won't listen. We end up arguing. He thinks I hate him."

"And you don't."

The understanding in her eyes melted all his defenses and reached to the emptiness she had begun to fill. "If anything..."

"What? What's between you and Carey besides an accident?"

"Our father's between us. He loved Carey. He didn't love me." The hurt in his voice was so evident, he felt like a child exposing his soul.

Laura wrapped her arms around his chest and held tight. Mitch blinked back sudden tears. He'd thought he'd shed them all when he was five.

After a few minutes, Laura leaned back. "I wonder if he loved either of you. Maybe he tolerated Carey because he didn't cross him and he pretended to get along. But if he let him get away with everything you've said, if he didn't try to discipline, or hug him, he didn't love him any more than you."

"He didn't want to put Carey in foster care."

"Mitch!"

"I cost too much. I heard him and Mom arguing one night."

The words had come out in a spurt. Laura was stunned. No wonder Mitch didn't trust love. No wonder he was afraid to feel. What that must have done to his self-worth! His life.

"Oh, Mitch."

He broke her hold and stepped back. "I don't want your pity."

His face was taut, his jaw clenched. His tight fists added to the telling picture. He didn't want her to see him expressing this much emotion, this much vulnerability. And part of him resented her for bringing it all to the surface.

She stepped up to him, knowing he wouldn't retreat because he was a strong man, not a coward. But he didn't have to be so tough, and someone had to teach him that.

Laura framed his face with her hands and smoothed over the tense lines around his mouth with her thumbs. "I don't pity you, Mitch. I hurt for you." She couldn't suppress the tears welling in her eyes any more than she could suppress the love in her heart. She didn't say the words because he wasn't ready to hear them. When she gave her "I love you" for the first time, she wanted to be believed and cherished, not doubted or analyzed.

She could feel the change in him happening slowly, the knowledge seeping through him that she truly shared his pain and wouldn't mock or belittle what he saw as weakness. His shoulders lost their rigidity as his arms came around her to pull her close.

He rested his chin on top of her head and his husky baritone vibrated through her when he spoke. "What is it about you that makes me say out loud things I've never told anyone? Things I've hardly admitted to myself. I've spent my life trying to forget."

"That's the problem. You've been burying instead of healing. Talking about it and sharing it helps start the process. If I hadn't had George and Anne to talk to after Doug died, I'd still be blaming myself—"

"Why?" He pushed back and gazed down at her, still holding her securely.

"Because we'd argued before he left. He wanted me to go sailing with him. Mandy had had an earache the day before and I didn't want to leave her with anyone. I certainly couldn't take her along. He didn't understand that. He said he was tired of coming second, that it had been that way since she was born."

"It *should* be that way," Mitch erupted.

"Not entirely," Laura disagreed. "There are times when a child comes first and there are times when a husband comes first. I knew that with my mind. But the smaller the child, the greater the immediate needs. And after Doug left, I felt so guilty, like I was a bad wife, like I could have made him feel more important. And when I never got the chance to see him alive again—"

He sifted her hair through his fingers and stroked soothingly. "The guilt took over."

"Yes. Until I talked about it over and over again with Anne and George. They knew me—they knew Doug. They didn't judge. They could be objective and help me get some perspective. I finally realized his death wasn't my fault. He chose to go sailing. He chose to stay out in the storm."

"If he had cared more about you and Mandy, he wouldn't have gone. Period."

Mitch's protective instincts were aroused again. He would put his wife and child first. But she had to be fair. "I don't know about that. I do know Doug and I were growing in different directions. But because I loved him, I blamed myself for what happened. Just like you blame yourself. You couldn't *do* anything about your father. He had a disease, Mitch. That's what alcoholism is. He couldn't love you—not like you needed to be loved. It's not your fault your mom stayed with him. It's not your fault Carey got into trouble."

His hands stopped stroking. "I felt it was. I felt responsible."

"Children in alcoholic families often do."

"How do you know so much?"

She grinned. "I watch Oprah and Donahue."

His brows arched and he looked disbelieving. "As if you have time."

She shook her head. "I do. Anne tapes them and we watch the good ones after Mandy goes to bed. But it's not only that. I know a couple of people who've faced the same problem."

Mitch's hands rested on the warmth of her neck. His fingers were cold but his palms were hot. "George or Anne?"

"I'd rather not say."

He kissed her forehead. "I understand. Confidences are important."

She hoped to heaven he felt that way once he knew about Carey.

They walked inside together. After shedding their coats, they went to the living room. Mandy was sitting on the floor in front of the fireplace dressing her doll. But Laura's eyes shot to Ray and Nora on the sofa. She could have sworn they'd been holding hands. Nora's cheeks were flushed; her father looked like the cat who had swallowed the canary.

Laura's eyes switched to Mitch. How would he feel about a relationship between his mother and her father? How did she feel about it? Seeing the smile on her dad's face, she didn't have to think about it long. He wouldn't be lonely anymore.

Nora stood and excused herself. After a puzzled look from Mitch and a shrug from Ray, Laura followed Nora to the kitchen.

Nora was crouched in front of a lower cabinet, shifting saucepans.

"Need some help?" Laura offered.

Nora kept her head down. "No. I'm looking for a muffin pan. Thought I'd make some biscuits to go with the stew."

"Nora?"

"What?"

"Are you upset about something?"

Nora took the muffin pan from the side of the cabinet and stood up. "No. What would I be upset about?"

She was pulling one of her son's tricks. Only she wasn't as good at it. "You could have stayed with Dad. I can mix flour, milk, shortening and baking powder."

"There's no point in me staying with your father. Nothing can come of it."

"Why? If you enjoy each other's company..."

"Laura, I told you before I'm not good enough for him."

"Bull!"

That made Nora smile. "Maybe your father and I can be friends. But that's it. Believe me. I've been around a lot longer than you. Some things don't change."

"What things?"

"Things that have nothing to do with you, things you couldn't understand."

"I understand Mitch had a rough childhood. I understand you held your family together as best you could."

"But you can't understand why I had to stay with a man who had no strength in him, a man who didn't love his children, a man who was drunk more than he was sober." Nora's eyes were filled with sadness and regret.

"Why did you stay?"

"Because I was afraid not to." Nora turned away, ending the conversation.

Laura pulled the canister of flour forward on the counter, knowing Nora was hiding something private. But she couldn't figure out what.

When Carey entered the store Monday afternoon, Laura's heart plummeted. The grin on his face, the air of excitement about him, portended trouble. She glanced over her shoulder. Mitch was still in the office.

Carey waited for Laura by the porcelain display as she gave a customer change and gift wrapped the small box. After she wished the woman a merry Christmas, Carey motioned to her to join him.

Sonya was taking care of a client who'd come into the store a few moments before. Laura went to Carey.

He shifted from one foot to the other as if he couldn't stand still. "This is it." He fumbled in his jacket pocket and opened his hand to show her a scrap of paper with scribbling on it. "I'm going to show my brother he's not the only one who can be a success."

"Placing a bet won't make you a success," she whispered sharply.

He spared her a quick surprised glance and his brows knit together in a frown. "Turning judgmental on me, too? I didn't expect that from you."

She softened her tone, afraid he wouldn't listen if she came on too strong. "Think about what you're doing, Carey, and why you're doing it. What if this doesn't turn out the way you expect? Are you going back to gambling for a living?"

He looked blank as if he hadn't thought about it. "Of course not. I told you one last time is all it'll take."

"And if the tip doesn't pan out? If this wonder horse happens to get indigestion today or something else happens and he loses?"

"That won't happen."

She shook her head. "In some ways you and Mitch *are* alike. You can't see what's in front of your nose." She was leaving in two days and it looked as if Mitch was going to let her fly out of his life without a word to stop her. The tension and the possibility of not seeing him again were getting to her.

Carey swore and rubbed his hand over his face, a gesture she recognized as one Mitch used when he was upset. "Mitch and I have the same parents. That's it. And what I see is that money will make me his equal."

"Is that what you really want?" Laura demanded.

Carey raised his hand impatiently. "What I want is for him to admire me the way I admire him. What I want is for him to know I regret the trouble I caused and all the mistakes I made. When Dad was alive, it's like I knew who I was. I was his son. And even though he wasn't the best father, I felt . . . anchored . . . like I knew I belonged. After he died, I was lost. I didn't know which end was up. Mom was working all the time to keep a roof over our heads. She took in sewing at night, too. Mitch did everything right. He helped her and watched out for both of us. I didn't know where I fit, *if* I fit."

Laura stepped closer to him and touched his elbow. "I understand, Carey, I do. When my mother died, the whole world turned upside down. Nothing was the same."

Another customer came in the door along with a blast of cold air. The interruption broke their bond of understanding.

Carey stepped back. "I'll let you take care of business. I have to get to the track before the fourth race. See you at supper." He gave her a thumbs-up sign she didn't return.

After the door closed behind Carey, Laura asked herself one question again and again. Should she tell Mitch?

Ten minutes later, she was still agonizing when Mitch came out of the office, the worry lines around his eyes deep. "Can I see you inside?"

She followed him, her heart thumping madly. Maybe he was going to ask her to stay. Or maybe... Had something happened to her dad? Had he spent too much time in the store yesterday and overtaxed himself?

"What is it? It's not Dad? He hasn't—"

Mitch grasped her shoulders gently, his gaze telegraphing reassurance. "No, Ray's fine. He's going to be stronger than ever. You got that?"

Laura nodded and felt color come back to her cheeks. "What is it then? You look worried."

He gave her a small smile as if to thank her for noticing. But then his concern wiped it away. "Mom called. She's afraid Carey's on his way to the track. He asked her for money and she gave him her savings." Mitch thumped his fist on the desk. "I can't believe she gave it to him. How *could* he have taken it?"

When Laura didn't move, when she didn't respond, Mitch tensed. "Did you know about this?"

Dread began climbing through her body. "Carey was just here..."

"In the store?"

She nodded.

He stepped away as if he'd been burned. "You knew he was going to the track?"

She nodded again.

"And you didn't stop him?" he exploded.

"How was I supposed to stop him?" she shot back before thinking.

"You could have come for me!" His exasperated expression asked her why she didn't think of that.

"And what would you have done? Tied him down?"

He jerked his jacket from the coatrack. "Maybe. I'm sure as hell going to do something like it when I catch up with him. I just hope I can grab him before he places the bet."

That was the worst thing Mitch could do. Yes, money was at stake, but so was Carey's decision whether to stay straight or not. If Mitch took that choice out of his hands... "Maybe he won't," she said quietly.

"Are you crazy? He's been gambling since he was twelve. But this time it's more than odd dollars he's going to lose— it's Mom's life savings."

She couldn't stay silent any longer. If Carey wouldn't tell Mitch, she had to. It could make the difference. "He hasn't gambled for the past six months, Mitch. He's a member of Gamblers Anonymous now and he hasn't placed a bet since he started attending the meetings."

Mitch's one arm was in the jacket, the other free. He froze. "When did you find this out?"

"The night of the Halloween party."

Mitch slid into his jacket absently.

The news didn't seem to affect him and she had to make sure he understood. "He's trying to start a new life. When you wouldn't give him the loan, he became desperate and decided a good tip was his last chance to—"

"You've known about this? All along?" Mitch reared back as if she'd punched him. His face was frozen and rigid. Betrayed.

Laura knew if he'd ever thought about asking her to stay, if he'd ever admitted to himself he loved her, if he'd ever trusted her, she'd just destroyed it all by being loyal to Carey. She had to explain, to try to erase the awful expression from Mitch's face. It was so...cold.

She forced herself to take two deep breaths to steady her body and contain the panic she knew would be evident in her voice. "Please try to understand."

His eyes narrowed with suspicion. "How long have you known?"

Her knees shook. "A week or so."

Mitch shook his head in disbelief. "I thought we'd come to an...understanding. I thought we meant *something* to each other."

If she said she loved him now, he'd never believe her. She leaned against the desk for support. "We *do*. I didn't want to keep this from you."

"Just like you didn't *want* to stay away from Ray for six years?"

The fierce degree of his anger rocked against her and she felt sick to her stomach. She'd thought Mitch had come to terms with that and didn't blame her any more. Heaven knew she still blamed herself enough for them both. But she had to stay in the present. "I learned about Carey's loan by accident. I overheard his conversation with Nora and he knew I heard. He pleaded with me not to tell you."

Mitch violently zipped up his zipper. "And he's so damn endearing, you agreed."

"No! He was so desperate, I agreed. All he wants, Mitch, is to show you he's changed. He's trying to compete with you. He wants you to see he can be a success. He wants you to respect and admire him the way he admires you."

"He told you that?"

"Sort of. He's trying to get your approval."

"He's never wanted anything from me but money and a quick fix for his problems."

"Maybe you haven't looked deep enough. Maybe you haven't really talked to him." Her gaze clung to his, pleading with him to understand.

"Talking can't solve everything. I haven't seen you and Ray talking all that much. Don't you practice what you preach?"

"Dad and I have settled our differences."

"You've formed as uneasy peace. You haven't talked about why you left, have you?"

Guilt stabbed her. "No."

"Actions speak louder than words, Laura. I know that's old, but it's true. My mother might lose her life savings because of you. And I've lost..." He stopped as if the admission would cost him too much.

"What have you lost, Mitch?" Once the question hung between them, she wasn't sure she wanted to know.

"I was beginning to believe deep feelings weren't a bad thing. I was beginning to believe two people could share more than their bodies and trust wasn't a tiger that could eat you alive. I was beginning to believe you were a risk worth taking. But I was wrong about all of it. Carey trusted you, but you didn't trust me. I did trust you, and you betrayed that trust. And when trust is destroyed, it can't be repaired."

"Mitch..."

"There's nothing else to say."

Damn his stubbornness and his barriers! He was locking her out again. "Yes, there is. You don't understand Carey, and you don't understand me."

He brushed past her and would have kept going but she grabbed his arm. "Do you think he wanted to be a wild teenager? Do you think I wanted to be rebellious?"

Mitch stared at her hand until she removed it, but he didn't step away.

Tears sprang to her eyes as she tried to explain. "Your dad confused Carey as much as he did you. But Carey felt connected to him and wanted to please him. When your father died, he felt lost. He didn't know where he belonged. Nora was working most of the time. You were the perfect son doing everything right. He wanted attention and didn't know how to get it. That's exactly how I felt. I needed to know somebody loved me."

His eyes burned into her. "Your father loved you. And Mom and I loved Carey."

She shook her head. "But don't you see? We didn't *know* that. Carey needs your love and emotional support now as much as he did when he was younger. Can't you tell him—?"

"Fix your own life, Laura. And stay out of mine."

The pain in his eyes was as great as the sorrow surrounding her heart. She wanted to cry, *Don't leave. Don't do this to us.* But in her anguish she realized part of him wanted to prove he was right, that she wasn't meant to be trusted or loved.

Because he was afraid of loving. He was afraid of risking, afraid of being rejected. She'd been living under the illusion he'd come around, he'd admit his feelings, he'd ask her to stay. She'd been wrong. Self-protection was more important to him than love.

He strode out the door and this time she didn't try to stop him. The damage had been done and there was no turning back.

Chapter Fourteen

Laura answered the phone on the first ring. It could be Mitch....

"Laura, it's Carey."

She closed the door to the office.

"Are you okay?"

"Better than I've been in a long time. I'm at your dad's. I gave Ma back her money. When I got to the track, I turned around. You were right. One bet could lead to others."

"I'm proud of you."

"That means a lot."

"I'm sure Mitch is, too."

"I wouldn't know. He's not back from the track yet. He's probably still looking for me. I'll be gone in a few minutes."

"Gone?"

"I'm going back to Virginia and start a new life. I can't invest in the video store, but I can get a job somewhere. With my track record, I'd be great in sales."

"You should stay until you see Mitch...."

"Give it up, Laura—I have. I just called to say goodbye. You take care of yourself and Mandy."

"I will." Tears clogged her throat.

"I hope it works out with you and Mitch. I can't promise I'll stay in touch. I'm not good at that kind of thing."

Carey's mind was made up. There was nothing she could do about it. Only Mitch could. "Good luck."

"You, too. You've been a good friend."

When Laura put down the receiver, tears rolled down her cheeks. She'd gained a friend in Carey, but she'd lost more than a friend and lover in Mitch. She'd lost her heart.

Mandy came into Laura's room the next morning and jumped on the bed. "Are we really going home tomorrow?"

Laura flicked the brush through her hair, carefully styling it around her face. She didn't know why she bothered. She was staying home today to pack, to pick up their tickets, to spend time with her dad. After breakfast, Mitch would be gone if he wasn't already and he certainly wouldn't be speaking to her. He'd made that clear last night. Dinner had been a silent, tense meal, only made bearable by Mandy's chatter and Ray's attempts to force conversation. Nora had been upset because Carey had left. Mitch had been solicitous of his mother but coolly formal with Laura. He responded with natural warmth to Mandy, but whenever his gaze landed on Laura, it was icy blue.

Laura hadn't slept last night and her head pounded, but she was determined to make her daughter's last day in York as enjoyable as possible. She sat on the bed next to her.

"Yes, we're leaving tomorrow. How do you feel about that?"

Her daughter smiled the smile that always warmed Laura's heart. "I want to see Anne and George. But I'm gonna miss Nora and Gramps. And especially Mitch. I like him as much as George."

That was the highest honor Mandy could give. "I know you do."

She bounced on the bed and played with a string on her jeans. "But he'll be here with Gramps, won't he? We can come back and visit both of them. Think he'd like me to send him pictures I draw?"

Laura let the idea of visiting Mitch pass. "I'm sure he would. But you can ask him today when you see him." She was sure Mitch wouldn't go back to Harrisburg without saying goodbye to Mandy.

"Can I help you pack the suitcases?"

"If you want to."

Mandy hopped off the bed. "Can I do it now?"

Such energy. Laura wished she could scoop some of it up and spread it over herself. Her sleepless night was going to make this a long day. She checked her watch. "There's time before breakfast. It would help me a lot if you take everything out of your drawers and put your clothes on the bed." She'd have to pack the suitcases carefully to get everything in. By the time Mandy emptied her drawers, she'd be tired of the idea.

Laura pulled Mandy's suitcase from the closet and opened it on top of the bed. Mandy was happily emptying the drawers when Laura went downstairs to start breakfast. Using an egg substitute and skim milk, she could make her dad French toast. And maybe she could make them all something special for supper and give Nora a break. Besides, it would give her something to do. Time on her hands was the one thing she didn't want today.

Laura was beating the eggs with a fork when Nora entered the kitchen, wearing a rose jogging suit and a sheepish smile. "I forgot to set my alarm. I'm sorry."

Laura wondered if Nora had spent a restless night also. They had talked about Carey last night and although Nora missed him, she'd agreed he was on the right track. They'd avoided the subject of Mitch as if they'd made an unspoken agreement.

Laura added pepper and minced onion to the egg mixture. "There's nothing to be sorry about. I have this under control. You can sit and talk to me."

Nora pulled out a chair, stared at it, and pushed it back in. "You know I don't like to sit and watch. What can I do?"

Laura motioned to the books on the other side of the kitchen. "You could check the cookbook for the Chicken Cacciatore recipe and tell me what ingredients we don't have. When I pick up our tickets, I'll stop at the store."

Nora gave her a blank look.

Laura pointed. "It's the red one on the shelf."

Nora went to the shelf and pulled down the book. She looked at it as if it might bite her. "What did you say it was called?"

"Chicken Cacciatore. If you check the index in the back...."

Nora turned to the back of the book. "I can't find it."

"I'm sure it's under *chicken*." Laura switched her attention from the eggs to Nora. Tears glistened in the older woman's eyes.

Suddenly Laura suspected what was wrong.

The nonprescription glasses, Nora never having the time or inclination to read Mandy a story, Nora letting Laura make out the shopping list, Nora saying she wasn't good enough for Ray.

Laura took the cookbook from Nora's hands. "You can't read, can you?"

Nora shook her head and a tear rolled down her cheek. "I've managed to hide it all my life. Even Sam never knew. I thought I had to stay with him because I never thought I could manage on my own. If only I'd known, everything would have been different . . . for all of us."

Laura understood so much now. The helplessness Nora must have felt. She probably depended on her husband for information, to read the mail, anything and everything. No wonder she'd been afraid to leave him.

But Nora had guts and stamina. "You don't have to hide it. You can get help. There are programs."

"What's the matter, Nora?" Ray asked as he came into the kitchen with Mitch beside him.

"Nothing's wrong." Nora self-consciously wiped a tear from her cheek.

Mitch and Ray were staring at Laura, and she felt as if she was smack-dab in the middle again.

Mitch's voice sliced the air. "What did you say to upset her, Laura?"

What could she say? Nothing that would lessen the tightness in his facial muscles or soften the strict slash of his mouth.

When Laura remained silent, Nora intervened. "She didn't say anything. She asked me to do something for her and I can't. Mitch, Ray, there's something you should know. I'm getting too old to pretend, too old to cover up. I might be too old to get help, but I'm not too old to tell the truth. I can't read."

The shock on Ray's face was quickly replaced by concern. He went to Nora and put his arm around her shoulders. "How difficult life must be for you. But you're never too old to get help. I'll help. I can teach you if you don't want to go somewhere else. We'll get the best program we can find.''

"Ray, you don't want to spend your time teaching me what I was too slow to learn years ago.''

"What better way to spend my time!'' He gave her a gentle squeeze. "I know we can do it—together.''

It had been a long time since Laura had seen this gentleness emanating from her father with anyone but Mandy, and she realized how much he cared about Nora. She knew her eyes were shiny when they met Mitch's. She was unprepared for the animosity there, the doubts that said he wondered if she'd known about this, too.

He joined Ray at Nora's side. "There's nothing to be ashamed of, Mom. If you need my help, too, you have it. I just wish you'd told me years ago.''

Laura heard the regret in Mitch's voice. She remembered what he'd said about her fixing her own life. It was time for her and her father to talk. Before she left. Before it was too late. She wished she could talk to Mitch, too. But from the look in his eyes, she doubted he'd listen. He'd wrapped his anger and sense of betrayal around himself to use as protection against her.

He didn't stay for breakfast but muttered something about getting to the store early. Obviously he couldn't stand being in the same room with her. That hurt even more than his anger.

Laura helped Nora clean up the kitchen, then before she lost her nerve she went in search of her father. He was in the backyard walking along the stream.

She ran to catch up to him. "It's hard to believe it snowed last week.''

"The sun's melted almost all of it. Except along the bank. Nature has a way of protecting itself, of making things last. It's a shame we can't learn how to do that.''

The sun glanced off the silver in her father's hair. "What would you like to last?"

"This time with you and Mandy. Will you really come back to visit?"

"Yes, we will."

"You can write."

"We'll do that, too." She plunged in before she lost her nerve. "Dad, I'm sorry I didn't try to get in touch with you again after I left and at least tell you you had a grand-daughter."

"You have nothing to be sorry about. I made a mess of everything. I'm just so thankful Mitch got in touch with you when I was too afraid to do it."

"Afraid?" She'd never thought of her dad as being afraid of anything.

"That you'd say no," he explained gruffly, looking to-ward the stream. "That you'd want to stay far away."

"Dad, I never wanted to leave. I hoped you'd change your mind and accept Doug. That's why I wrote at first."

He faced her. "I should have answered you. I wanted so much for you. He wasn't it. But if he made you happy, I should have realized that's all you'd care about. It's what *I* should have cared about. Can you forgive a stubborn old man?"

Laura fought the tears valiantly, but it wasn't worth the effort because they leaked out one after the other. She hugged her father as she could never remember hugging him. And she felt his arms come around her to give her the warmth and support she'd missed since she was a child. "I forgive you, Daddy. Can you forgive me for staying away so long?"

"Of course. I'm just glad you're here now." After long moments of them both giving and receiving forgiveness, Ray released her. "Laura, if you'd stay, you'd have free rein with the business. I wouldn't interfere in your personal life, either. I give you my word."

Her fear was gone where that was concerned. With all her heart she wanted to stay. But she couldn't, because of Mitch. "All my life I've wanted to be your partner. And I'd like to now. But I can't." She had to be honest with him. "Mitch doesn't want me here. Before yesterday, I thought we had a chance. But then he found out I knew about Carey..." She bit her lip to keep it from trembling.

"It's more than that, isn't it?"

"Yes. There's your will and the partnership. I can't take away from Mitch what he's worked so hard to earn."

"If you stayed and worked with him—"

"He doesn't trust me, Dad. He doesn't trust his feelings. If he asked me to stay, if he could say he loves me, I'd know he believes in 'us.' But he doesn't. Unless he asks me to stay, I'll know the doubt that I wanted the partnership more than him will always be there. Do you understand?"

Her father's eyes held regrets and sadness. "I've botched it again. If I hadn't said anything about the will..."

"It's not your fault. Mitch has to risk following his heart. If he can't do that, we can't be together."

"You've become a very wise woman." There was pride in Ray's voice.

"Wisdom doesn't make the hurt go away."

"Time will lessen it."

They'd both come to that insight the hard way. "Do you love Nora?"

"How would you feel if I did? She's nothing like your mother." There was a note of concern in his voice.

"Mitch is nothing like Doug." The analogy came easily.

"That's the way it happens, I guess. Nora is sturdy, homey, a woman I can count on."

"You couldn't count on Mom?"

Her dad's smile was bittersweet. "Your mother was like a beautiful butterfly. She never claimed to be a homebody and I didn't demand it of her. I knew she loved me, but she was here, there, everywhere. I think I needed more than that then. I know I need more than that now. It might be selfish, but I want a woman who's devoted to me, not to life in general."

Laura understood because Doug had been like her mother in a way. And she knew what her father meant about devotion. If Mitch could ever make the commitment, he'd be devoted for a lifetime.

She sighed. *Quit thinking about it.* Apparently Mitch could turn off his feelings much easier than she could. And if he could turn them off, he didn't love her.

She hadn't answered her dad's question. "I like Nora, Dad. She's a good woman. And if you can make each other happy, go for it."

He kicked at a stone lying in the grass. "I don't know what will happen. Now that I can drive, maybe I should ask her for a . . . date."

He looked unsure and said the word as if it fit uncomfortably on his tongue.

Laura suppressed a grin. "That would be a good start. Flowers might be nice, too."

A smile tugged at his mouth. "Can I call you for advice?"

"Anytime. I love you, Dad."

"I love you, honey." He cleared his throat. "Do you want me to talk to Mitch? Maybe I can—"

"No. Any decision he makes, he has to make on his own. But thanks for asking."

She'd lost Mitch, but she'd regained her relationship with her father. She'd have to remember that on the flight home.

Chapter Fifteen

He'd wanted more from her than he'd ever wanted from anybody.

Mitch sat in his car and stared at the dingy street with sightless eyes. He'd wanted her joy. He'd wanted her excitement. She'd stirred both in him until he'd known both were possible and good. But he'd also wanted Laura's trust when he couldn't give his. He'd wanted her allegiance without offering commitment. He'd wanted her love before he risked pledging his. Before he'd even realized the extent of his.

Saying goodbye to Mandy had wrung out his heart. Saying goodbye to Laura had made him numb. For a few hours. Then he'd hurt like hell and for self-preservation's sake, he'd started thinking. The thinking had led him here to his roots.

The late afternoon light shimmered from the dented garbage cans sitting at the curb to the rusting wrought iron railings leading down chipped concrete steps. The wooden front door was marred with scrapes and scratches. The transom above the door looked as if more than one pellet had shattered it.

He sat in his car and peered out the window, in his imagination seeing a scene from twenty-odd years before, seeing his father sitting on the porch, beer can in hand. The wind blew a paper cup across the porch. Mitch had escaped from this. So had Carey. But they'd chosen different routes out.

Whether Mitch admitted it or not, the past had always been there, creating discontent. No, he wouldn't become the bastard his father had been, but could he care for a woman and love her for a lifetime? Could he treat her right? Never treat her as his father had treated his mother? The fear that he couldn't, the fear that his father's genes ran stronger in him than he wanted to believe, had been lurking deep inside him since he was a child. It was time to confront that fear. He now realized his father had never loved his mother. He'd used her. If he'd loved her, that love would have changed him.

The poor neighborhood, the drug dealers on the corner, their alcoholic father, had been the basis of the life Mitch wanted to forget. He'd gotten out. He'd gotten his mother out as soon as he could, the only way he knew how—schooling, hard work, perseverance. He'd escaped from it but he hadn't run away. Carey had run...hard...and couldn't keep from looking back.

Mitch crossed his arms over the steering wheel. Was he ashamed of Carey? Had that always been the wedge between them? Mitch needed to forget the past; Carey kept bringing it back. Mitch had never been part of the neighborhood gang, so temptations for pranks and wrongdoing weren't as handy, weren't as necessary. Carey had looked to the gang to give him identity. But he hadn't found it there. Instead he'd turned to gambling.

For the first time in Mitch's life, he was proud of his brother and admired him for the strength to *not* bet, the strength to change his life. He had to tell him that. He had to tell him more. As soon as possible. He'd waited too long already.

Mitch switched on the ignition and took a long last look at the old neighborhood. It no longer repulsed him but showed him how far he'd come.

Mitch got Carey's number from his mother and went to Ray's den to make the call. Carey answered on the second ring.

He was obviously surprised to hear Mitch's voice. "Did I leave something in Ma's apartment? She can send it if I did."

"No. It's not that.... What are you doing for Christmas?"

The silence lasted at least a minute. "I'll probably spend it with friends."

"Wouldn't you rather spend it with your family?"

"I must be hearing things. That sounded strangely like an invitation."

Mitch detected nerves beneath Carey's habitual flippancy. "It is. Mom and I would like you to spend Christmas with us."

"Why? I mean I know Mom wants me there, but why do you care?"

"Because you're my brother and ... I love you." Mitch rushed on. "Changing your life takes a great deal of energy and effort. If I can help you with that, I want to."

Mitch could hear Carey breathing. When he spoke, there were catches in his question. "You really want me there with you and Mom?"

"I really do. I know it's a long drive...."

"I've made long drives before. I'll be there Christmas Eve." He paused. "Mitch ... thanks."

Mitch's throat tightened. "No thanks necessary. I'll see you soon."

Mitch smiled as he put down the receiver, peace and a genuinely good feeling buoying him up. For a few moments. Until he thought about Laura. His "I love you" to Carey had sounded rusty but it hadn't been as difficult to say as he'd thought it would be. But with Laura...

He'd hurt her deeply. The light had gone out of her eyes when he'd told her to stay out of his life. How could he have said that to her? Yes, he'd felt betrayed. But what she'd done for Carey had shown her depth of loyalty, her dedication to a promise. And because of that dedication, Carey had done what was best for a new life.

Then there was his mother. How long would she have kept her secret if it hadn't been for Laura's perceptiveness? Yes, he'd wondered if Laura had known about that, too, and had kept him in the dark. But that didn't matter, either. *He* should have known. *He* should have been perceptive. *He* should have seen it.

His mother had explained to him last night all the tricks she'd used, the coping skills. When they went to a restaurant, she asked for the special or ordered whatever Mitch did. She could remember directions to anywhere in the city—one block up, two blocks over. If she'd been there once, she could get there again even though she couldn't read the street signs. By saying she'd forgotten her glasses, she could get anyone to read her necessary information. He should have seen it, yet he hadn't been looking.

But Laura... He pushed himself up from Ray's desk. He needed fresh air. He needed to clear his head. A few minutes later, he was standing outside, gazing up at the moon. Her lack of trust had hurt. He'd latched onto it because he'd been afraid—afraid of his deepening feelings for her, afraid she didn't feel as deeply about him. When she left, he'd realized he wanted to spend his life with her. It was more than want. It was an excruciating need. Without her, life seemed dull, lacking, meaningless. She'd taught him how to love, but just as important, she'd taught him how to live.

He loved her. He wanted to marry her. He wanted to spend forever with her. At the admission he felt reborn, as if he was seeing the glory of life for the first time. Love, energy, elation swept through him, giving him the courage to risk safety and reach for happiness.

How would Laura react if he showed up in Independence? How would she react if he told her he loved her and wanted to marry her? The elation dimmed and his stomach clenched. Maybe she didn't want to get married again. Maybe once was enough. Living one day at a time was her specialty. Could he do that with her without marriage?

He might as well stop fooling himself; he'd take her however he could get her. Even the store didn't seem important. He hadn't talked to Ray yet, but if he wanted to retire, Mitch could sell out and start over in Independence or Cleveland or wherever Laura wanted to locate.

He was thinking as if her spending her life with him was a foregone conclusion. In his mind's eye, he could see the ring he'd designed. All he had to do was set the stones. From the outset he should've realized he was designing it for Laura. He should've realized a lot of things.

The moon drew his attention and he stared at it as if it held the secrets of the universe. Laura insisted wishing on it worked. Okay. He had nothing to lose.

"I wish for Laura and the chance to love her and Mandy for the rest of their lives." He spoke out loud and he didn't care if the whole world heard him. He said it again louder and hoped beyond hope that wishing on the moon was as magical as Laura thought it was.

Two days later, Mitch stood on Laura's porch. He felt more nervous than he'd ever been. So this was risk-taking.

He couldn't say he liked the feeling. If he was any more tense, his muscles would snap when he walked.

Jabbing the doorbell, he waited. At least there were lights blazing inside so someone was home. The porch lamp went on and the door opened.

George stood there, glaring at Mitch as if he was an intruder. "What are you doing here?"

Mitch stood his ground. "I came to talk to Laura. Can I come in?"

"Are you going to upset her? Never mind. She couldn't be much more upset than she is now."

Mitch entered the living room behind George, his heartbeat heavy in his chest, and met chaos. The furniture zigzagged every which way. An evergreen, bare except for strings of lights dangling from the branches, stood in the tree stand in the corner. Its fresh pine scent flavored the air. The floor was littered with cartons of decorations and tinsel garlands.

Mandy spotted him first and came running. "Mitch! You came for a visit. Can you help decorate our tree?"

Mitch stooped, caught her in his arms and swung her into the air. "I don't know how long I'll be staying. I have to talk to your mom first. Okay?"

She threw her arms around his neck. "I missed you."

He squeezed her. "I missed you, too." He turned his attention to the woman he'd come to see. Laura's red sweatshirt stopped mid-thigh. The elves dancing across it proclaimed a holiday mood. The black spandex pants displayed curving calves he knew well. Her red-and-white striped stockings reminded him of candy canes.

Her hair was tied back with a red ribbon, but her face didn't reflect the same Christmas spirit her outfit did. She looked tired. Her eyes manifested shock that he was standing in her living room. He'd never seen Laura at a loss for words, but she couldn't seem to find any now.

He hoped he could find enough for both of them and convince her he knew what love was because of her. It was more than the earth tilting whenever they touched. It was more than the honest sharing that bared their souls. It was more than risking today to find something better for tomorrow. It was two people joyously in sync, living life the best way they knew how, eager to share their thoughts as well as their bodies. How could he ever get all that out?

George and Anne exchanged knowing looks, then Anne said to Mandy, "Honey, let's go to the attic and see if we can find that other box of ornaments. I know there's one with an angel for the treetop."

"But Mitch just got here and I want him to read me a story."

Mitch rubbed his nose against hers. "I promise I'll read you a story after I talk to your mom for a little while. I would really like to see that angel if you can find it."

She wriggled in his arms so he set her down. "Okay, I'll find it. Maybe you can read two stories?"

Even though his insides were tied in knots, he chuckled and winked. "Maybe."

Laura still hadn't spoken or moved from her position next to the tree after George, Anne and Mandy trekked upstairs. Mitch gazed at her, trying to read any signal, attempting to find a sign she was glad to see him. There were none. The twinkle lights blinking on the tree were shining in her hair. She was a Christmas gift he'd almost lost. He hoped it wasn't too late and she didn't hate him for his stupidity.

Okay, Riley, jump without the parachute. You have no choice unless you want to go back to York alone. He stepped toward her and the movement seemed to wake her up.

Her hands fluttered and she stepped back. "Is it Dad?"

He resisted the urge to yank her into his arms and didn't move closer. "No. This has nothing to do with Ray."

He could see the pulse at her throat beating rapidly. "Then why did you come?"

Honesty was the only way to go. "Because I couldn't stay away."

Her eyes widened. "I don't understand."

His voice was husky with emotion. "I think you do. Do you love me, Laura, the same way I love you? I *do* love you. I was a fool not to admit it sooner. I guess I wasn't ready. But I'm ready now. I want to spend the rest of my life with you. I know I hurt you and I'm sorry. If you give me the chance, I'll spend my life trusting you, loving you, taking care of you—"

She launched herself at him and he almost fell back from the force. But he righted them both and then lifted her until her feet dangled and her mouth was even with his.

She latticed her fingers deep in his hair. "I love you," she whispered.

The skin of her cheek was so, so soft under his thumb. The love and tenderness he felt for her shook him so badly his hands trembled. His head dipped and he rediscovered the wonder of kissing Laura. He took his time and tasted, sipped, reveled. But as always, the passion between them burst. His strength met her strength. His maleness met her femaleness. His need met her need.

No kiss with Laura was ordinary. Each was exceptional, unique, mind-boggling. Her lips caressed his. Her hands stroked his neck until he thought he'd go mad. He couldn't play any longer. His tongue pushed into her mouth. She shuddered and her legs went around his hips. Passion rose in him swift and complete. His hands automatically cupped her bottom as her arms locked tightly around his neck.

Their hunger was naked and wild, ferocious. He kissed her over and over, forgetting they needed to breathe. She returned each kiss, encouraging him, needing him, assuring him this was only the beginning.

The beginning. They couldn't go any further, not here, not now, not with Mandy and Anne and George two floors above.

He tightened his arms before he slowed down the intensity. At first, her yearning increased as he calmed the storm. Then she caught his mood and gently withdrew. His lips separated from hers only after clinging for an eternity.

"We have to wait," he murmured.

She laid her head on his shoulder. "I know. But, Lord, I don't want to."

He chuckled and slowly let her slide down his body so she'd know how much he didn't want to wait either. Only he knew something she didn't know yet which made the wait more bearable.

He led her to the sofa sitting crookedly across the center of the room. There was one more hurdle to cross. She'd said she loved him. But he had to find out about the rest.

Inconspicuously, he took the box out of his jacket pocket, slid off the leather garment and tossed it to a chair. "I am going to stay a while, aren't I?"

She straightened his shirt collar. "You can stay as long as you want. I don't know what you have in mind—"

He produced the velvet box and placed it in her hand. "That depends on you. Open this."

When she did, her eyes glistened and her lower lip quivered. "Mitch, it's beautiful. The midnight sky meeting the sea. Sapphires and a... Oh, my! A blue diamond. This is one of your designs, isn't it?"

"It's yours now. Will you marry me, Laura?"

"Oh yes, Mitch! I'll marry you." She stroked his cheek. "Was there any doubt?"

"Plenty of them. I didn't even know if you'd consider marriage again."

She held out the box to him. "Put it on for me?"

He gently pushed it onto her ring finger. She admired it, then threw her arms around him. "I love you." She backed away and frowned. "What made you come? Did Dad say something . . . ?"

"Your father didn't say anything. Even when I told him I was flying out here, he kept quiet as if he was afraid he'd spoil something."

"He couldn't spoil this. Not in a million years."

Mitch had to straighten out everything between them. "Laura, about Carey. I called him and . . ."

His words were lost as the thumping of feet tripped down the steps. Mandy, with a precarious hold on a white satin angel, ran to the gold-trimmed sofa. "We found it. Are you gonna stay and help decorate the tree?"

He lifted her onto his lap, angel and all. "I sure am. Then I'll read those stories before you go to bed." He leaned over to Laura and whispered into her ear, "And then I have a surprise for you."

Mitch led Laura into the hotel, a secret smile on his lips. She'd never known such happiness. She felt loved, desired, needed. They hadn't had any more time to talk alone as they hung ornaments on the tree and put Mandy to bed. But he'd kissed her freely, touched her often, and with mysterious smiles promised the fulfillment of what their fulminating kiss had begun.

Now, she stood beside him at the entrance to a hotel room almost shaking with anticipation. When he unlocked and opened the door, she gasped. There were flowers everywhere! From roses to daffodils to tiger lilies. At least ten baskets were strategically arranged, filling the room with fragrance.

She turned into his arms and drew his head down for a deep, soul-felt kiss. He swept her into his chest, kicked the door closed and carried her to the bed. They broke the embrace to undress, but they kept coming together again and again to kiss, to caress, to excite, to love. When both their bodies gleamed from anticipation and pulsing heartbeats, when neither could wait a second longer to be one in mind, heart, and body, Mitch thrust into her, driving to her core. Her legs latched around his hips, her fingernails dug into his shoulders, and she cried his name when the crashing of their ultimate union claimed them both.

They floated into their future, their arms tight around one another. Mitch rolled to his side and gathered her as close as he could get her. "I didn't think it could get any better. But I was wrong. Commitment makes loving even more powerful."

"Any more power and we'd blow up the hotel."

"We're going to have to find someplace more permanent to fill with flowers."

Her hair fell across his shoulder as she angled her head to look at him. "Either York or Harrisburg is fine. The commute's not that long—"

"You want to go back?"

She brushed her cheek against his chest. "Dad's there. Nora's there. Dad and I had a long talk before I left. We've forgiven each other. I think we understand each other in a way we never could. In part because of you and your mother."

"You're sure about living there?"

"Your business is there."

"I can move the business anywhere. I want you to be happy."

"I'll be happy. As long as we can visit Anne and George."

"You could keep your investment in the house so they won't be strapped."

"You wouldn't mind?"

"I don't think I'd mind anything you do." He placed a spray of kisses along her throat and hot desire curled in her womb again. Before she could give in to it, she said, "Let's call Dad."

His brows quirked up. "Now?"

She nodded.

He reached for the phone, settled it on his chest and handed her the receiver.

She called her father, gave him the good news, then handed the instrument to Mitch when Ray asked to speak to him. Mitch smiled for the first few minutes, then suddenly looked shocked. His gaze caught Laura's and she felt bowled over by the depth of love there.

When he finally said good-night to Ray and both he and Laura had spoken briefly to Nora, he replaced the receiver. His first words were, "Ray told me about the will. You love me that much? That you were willing to give up your share?"

She took his face between her palms. "I love you more than that."

His fiery lips sought hers and he brought her on top of him. She met his passion with hers, knowing they both knew how to sacrifice, how to compromise, how to love. She had no doubts about their future, only hope and the belief she'd found true happiness with a man she'd love, honor and cherish until time's end.

Epilogue

Laura's ecru satin wedding gown swept behind her as Mitch ushered her away from their reception and onto the patio. They could hear the murmur of friends and relatives inside the dining room's glass doors. Thousands of stars dappled the sky and a full moon fell in swaths of light over the garden before them.

Mitch took off his tux jacket and put it around her shoulders. "I don't want you catching a cold for our honeymoon. We're going to spend a perfect Valentine's Day."

"In Tahiti. I can't believe I'm actually going there. It's fascinated me since I was a child."

"And you began wishing on the moon." His smile was in his voice.

"Yes. I did it last night," she confessed.

"What did you wish for?"

"That today would be perfect." She stroked his cheek. "And it is. Carey looked so proud standing up there as your best man. I think he really likes his new job. Selling medical equipment is an up-and-coming profession."

"He doesn't even seem to mind the suit he has to wear." Mitch curved his arm around her shoulders. "I wished last night, too." He'd told her he'd wished on the moon before he came to Independence to ask her to marry him.

"What did *you* wish?" she asked seriously.

"That I could always make you happy."

"We'll make each other happy."

He produced an envelope and handed it to her.

"What's this? You already gave me earrings to match my ring for a wedding present."

"This is different. Open it."

She undid the flap and pulled out two cards. "These are season's passes for the ice-skating rink. Neither of us knows how to skate!"

"I figured it was about time we learned so we can teach Mandy. What do you think?" His eyes were playful, tempting her to have fun with him.

When she threw her arms around his neck, his coat fell to the ground. But she didn't care. She'd never be cold as long as she was close to him. She remembered the wish she'd made on the moon when she was sixteen. She'd wished for a man who would love her forever. Her wish had been granted.

Silhouette Special Edition

COMING NEXT MONTH

#745 SILENT SAM'S SALVATION—Myrna Temte *Cowboy Country*
Reluctant rancher Sam Dawson hadn't envisioned a housekeeper like Dani
Smith. Fast-talking, stylish, two kids in tow—Dani swept up so well, she
uncovered his secret . . . proving herself Silent Sam's salvation.

#746 DREAMBOAT OF THE WESTERN WORLD—Tracy Sinclair
Struggling single mother Melissa Fairfield wasn't acting. But when movie
star Granger McMasters gazed upon the graceful, capable woman tending
his garden, he saw the makings of a lifelong love scene. . . .

#747 BEYOND THE NIGHT—Christine Flynn
Mitchell Kincaid was drawn to the thrill of dangerous pastimes. He
thought nothing of taking risks, until Jamie Withers made him face the
biggest risk of all—falling in love. . . .

#748 WHEN SOMEBODY LOVES YOU—Trisha Alexander
Only one thing kept Laura Sebastian and Neil Cantrelle apart: Laura's
engagement—to Neil's brother. Brokenhearted, she struggled not to break
her vow, waiting . . . hoping . . . for mending, magical love to prevail.

#749 OUTCAST WOMAN—Lucy Gordon
Mystical beauty Kirsty Trennon was a woman scorned and alone, until
runaway prisoner Mike Stallard appeared. Both outcasts, they shared
earthly passion; could they clear their names and find heavenly love?

#750 ONE PERFECT ROSE—Emilie Richards
Wealthy executive Jase Millington wanted to give homeless Becca Hanks
everything she needed. But to win the strong, independent Becca's love,
Jase needed to take a lesson in receiving. . . .

AVAILABLE THIS MONTH:

Summer romance has never been so hot!

® SILHOUETTE

SUMMER Sizzlers 1992

A collection of hot summer reading by three of Silhouette's hottest authors:

Ann Major
Paula Detmer Riggs
Linda Lael Miller

Put some sizzle into your summer reading. You won't want to miss your ticket to summer fun—with the best summer reading under the sun!
